Maggie Shayne is ...

"... a remarkable talent destined for stardom."
—Teresa Medeiros

PRAISE FOR HER PREVIOUS NOVELS

"Gripping . . . The characters will steal your heart."
—*New York Times* bestselling author Lisa Gardner

"Intricately woven . . . A moving mix of high suspense and romance."
—*Publishers Weekly*

"[A] dark, enthralling brew of love, danger, and perilous fate."
—Jayne Ann Krentz

"Maggie Shayne's gift is that she creates believable characters who react very humanly to unbelievable situations." —*All About Romance*

"A rich, sensual, and bewitching adventure of good vs. evil, with love as the prize."
—*Publishers Weekly*

"A hauntingly beautiful story of love that endures through time itself."
—Kay Hooper

"Maggie Shayne is a reader's joy. Fast-paced, witty, delightful, and shamelessly romantic, her stories will be treasured long after the book is done. A remarkable talent destined for stardom!"
—Teresa Medeiros

"Her characters come to life in a way that makes you feel as if you know every one of them . . . steamy passion, and real emotions with which a reader can identify."
—*Rendezvous*

Sheer Pleasure

MAGGIE SHAYNE

BERKLEY SENSATION, NEW YORK

THE BERKLEY PUBLISHING GROUP
Published by the Penguin Group
Penguin Group (USA) Inc.
375 Hudson Street, New York, New York 10014, USA
Penguin Group (Canada), 90 Eglinton Avenue East, Suite 700, Toronto, Ontario M4P 2Y3, Canada
(a division of Pearson Penguin Canada Inc.)
Penguin Books Ltd., 80 Strand, London WC2R 0RL, England
Penguin Group Ireland, 25 St. Stephen's Green, Dublin 2, Ireland (a division of Penguin Books Ltd.)
Penguin Group (Australia), 250 Camberwell Road, Camberwell, Victoria 3124, Australia
(a division of Pearson Australia Group Pty. Ltd.)
Penguin Books India Pvt. Ltd., 11 Community Centre, Panchsheel Park, New Delhi—110 017, India
Penguin Group (NZ), 67 Apollo Drive, Mairangi Bay, Auckland 1310, New Zealand
(a division of Pearson New Zealand Ltd.)
Penguin Books (South Africa) (Pty.) Ltd., 24 Sturdee Avenue, Rosebank, Johannesburg 2196,
South Africa

Penguin Books Ltd., Registered Offices: 80 Strand, London WC2R 0RL, England

This is a work of fiction. Names, characters, places, and incidents either are the product of the author's imagination or are used fictitiously, and any resemblance to actual persons, living or dead, business establishments, events, or locales is entirely coincidental. The publisher does not have any control over and does not assume any responsibility for author or third-party websites or their content.

SHEER PLEASURE

PRINTING HISTORY
"Leather and Lace" from *Sinful*: Jove mass market paperback edition / January 2000
"Awaiting Moonrise" from *Hot Blooded*: Jove mass market paperback edition / September 2004
"Daydream Believer" from *Man of My Dreams*: Jove mass market paperback edition / November 2004
Berkley Sensation trade paperback omnibus edition / February 2007

Berkley Sensation trade paperback ISBN: 978-0-425-21458-9

PRINTED IN THE UNITED STATES OF AMERICA

10 9 8 7 6 5 4 3 2 1

CONTENTS

Leather and Lace

CHAPTER ONE

GRANTED, Kayla, I *do* need the money. But there is no way I'd
do *that* for it."

"No?"

Hands firmly planted on her hips, Martha Jane Biswell shook
her head. "No."

"It pays one thousand dollars. Cash. In your hand, the second
you finish."

Martha Jane's mouth was already opening to refuse by the time
her roommate's words registered. She snapped it closed so fast she
nearly bit her tongue. "Don't be ridiculous, Kayla. I know you
don't have that kind of money, and I couldn't take it from you even
if you did. I've got almost as much invested in this business as you
do, you know. I want to see it succeed."

"Hey, you're the one who helped me set the budget. One thousand is what we set aside to pay the model. It's already earmarked

for that. And besides, if this doesn't work . . . well, we're finished. It's all or nothing."

Martha Jane shook her head. "*You're* modeling, and you aren't taking any money for it."

Kayla tossed her head. "Okay, what if I do? Say we split it. Five hundred each. Cash."

Biting her lip and battling a desperate need and a heavy-duty guilt trip, Martha Jane waited for a sign to tell her what to do.

"And you could have it in your hands tonight," Kayla went on. "Before you even put your old-maid clothes back on, if you want."

Lowering her head, pacing the apartment they shared, Martha Jane eyed the headless mannequins and the scandalous scraps they wore. Silken teddies. Lacy bustiers. Leather panties. Each piece of lingerie had one thing in common with all the others—a tag that read "Leather and Lace Designs."

Martha Jane's roommate and best friend, Kayla, *was* Leather and Lace. She'd been working her tail off to design this line of lingerie. She was a creative genius. But she'd needed help on the organizational end of things, and that was where Martha Jane had come in. She'd devoted countless hours and long nights and weekends to the cause. In return, Kayla gave her a one-third ownership of this roomful of lingerie. It could become more, someday—maybe—if they could sell the line.

Tonight was their big chance—maybe their *only* chance—to get this company off the ground. To make Kayla's dream come true.

"You know I'd do anything for Leather and Lace, Kayla," Martha Jane began. "But having me parade around in this stuff isn't going to sell it, and I think you know that. Can't we find a *real* model?"

"Are you kidding me? This is the biggest lingerie show of the season, Martha Jane. They're all booked solid. I hired one girl, because you said she was all we could afford, and now she has the flu."

"Everyone in the city has the flu," Martha Jane protested.

"*You* don't," Kayla shot back.

Martha Jane bit her lower lip, opened her mouth, closed it again.

Kayla jumped on the silence like a wolf on a rabbit. "Look, I'll be there with you. We'll parade down the runway wearing next to nothing *together*." She turned Martha Jane around, positioning her in front of the mirror. "Besides," she said, "you've been dying to play dress-up in some of these things."

"I have not."

"Have so. I watch your eyes, girl. I can see what you're thinking."

"Oh, don't be—"

"You're a knockout, you know. You just hide it."

"I'm as plain as a brown paper bag."

"Bull." Kayla pulled the pins out of Martha Jane's hair and shook it loose, letting it spill around her shoulders. "Your hair is incredible. Oh, what I could do with a little mousse and a blow-dryer."

"It's brown. It's plain, straight, and brown, and you couldn't do anything with it even if you had a *whole* moose."

Kayla scowled at the bad pun. "It's not plain *or* brown. It's *mink*," Kayla said. Then, reaching up, she took off Martha Jane's glasses. "And your eyes are so blue they make the sky jealous."

"But pretty much sightless without my glasses," Martha Jane said.

"Lucky for you the runway is straight and free of obstacles."

"I'm too short to be a model."

"You're petite. That's sexy."

"And not nearly skinny enough."

"What, are you kidding me? You got curves, girl!"

"And I'm not exactly . . . perky." Martha Jane looked down at her chest.

"My Dream Bra will take care of that, sweets. That little number is going to be the most talked-about miracle of the twenty-first century! Every woman in the country will want to own a dozen."

Martha Jane sighed. "I just don't know . . ."

"Look, hon, you've been out of work for almost a month, thanks to Mister Wonderful. They're gonna repossess your car if you don't make a payment pretty soon, and the rent's already late. You *have* to do *something.*"

Licking her lips, Martha Jane glanced again at the revealing wardrobe she'd be required to wear. To model. In front of strangers. "And you're sure no one from Gable Brothers will be there?"

"Look, I saw the guest list. I swear, no one from Gable Brothers Department Stores was on it. This thing is exclusive, invitation only."

Martha Jane frowned at her friend. "I can't believe they weren't invited. They're one of the biggest chains in the state."

Kayla shrugged. "Even if someone from Gable Brothers *did* come, it wouldn't be good ol' Clark."

"Richard," Martha Jane said. "My boss's name is Richard, and you know it."

"Hmmph. Couldn't tell it from the way you go on about him." Kayla tipped her head back and fluttered her eyelashes. Then she grinned. "But back to the point. If the Gables did send someone to the show, it would be their lingerie buyer. And she's a female, and besides that, you've never even *met* her." Then Kayla reached out to run her fingertips over the red satin that barely covered a mannequin. "But to tell you the truth, I'd give my right arm to see Richard Gable eating his heart out in the crowd when you took to the runway wearing something like this. The jerk. Firing the best secretary he ever had just so he could hire his latest bimbo of the month."

Martha Jane sighed heavily. She had been devastated when Richard—Mr. Gable—had told her he had to let her go. It had hurt all the more when she'd seen her replacement, a twenty-year-old big-haired blonde with vacant eyes and a D-cup, gravity-resistant chest. The truth was, Martha Jane had been secretly falling head over heels for her boss since her first day on the job. But he would never give a girl like her a second glance. She was smart, efficient, and cool. She didn't bounce or wiggle or giggle, and she supposed it was just as well she was out of there. She'd never had such a foolish, self-destructive urge in her life as when she'd first set eyes on Richard Gable. And she hoped she never would again.

He was something, though. Those dark, smoky eyes, that smile. No wonder women were practically falling at his feet. "He wasn't *completely* heartless about the whole thing," she said softly, automatically defending her former boss, though she knew she shouldn't. "He *did* offer me another position in the company."

"And thank goodness you had enough self-respect to tell him where to stick that offer," Kayla snapped.

It wasn't so much self-respect, Martha Jane thought, as it was wounded pride. Wounded . . . everything. She'd been deeply hurt by Richard's treatment of her. Too hurt to be practical. And now she was suffering for it. She should have taken the offer. Sure, maybe she'd have had to see him fawning over his new secretary every day, but at least she would be able to pay her bills.

Sighing again, she tried not to acknowledge the slight stinging sensation behind her eyes.

"I promise you, no one you know will be at this lingerie show," Kayla was saying. "And the total amount of time you're going to spend on the runway will amount to only minutes when you add it up. It's so simple, Martha Jane. You walk to the end, turn, and walk back. Change your clothes backstage and do it again. You won't even be out there long enough to work up a decent *blush*!"

"If I could be sure of that, then maybe I'd *consider* it," Martha Jane finally said.

"Wait! I have an idea!" Kayla dashed off into the bedroom and emerged a second later with a scrap of black leather that looked like . . . like a mask. Oh, God, it *was* a mask. She quickly wrapped it around Martha Jane's face, the black silk ties going beneath her hair and then knotting in the back. The two almond-shaped eye-holes fit right over her eyes.

"My God," she whispered, squinting into the mirror. "I look like somebody's bondage fetish come to life."

"I've been working on a few different mask designs just to set off the clothes. Come on, now, give it a chance," Kayla cajoled. "When you put these things on, Martha Jane, you're gonna feel like a different woman. Like a . . . like a love goddess. And with the mask . . . well, that just makes the illusion complete." She fluffed Martha Jane's hair. "You can keep the mask on all night— No, no, wait! I have some others, in different colors, one with a feather. We can pair them up, a mask to go with each outfit!"

"I . . . I couldn't . . ."

"Oh, come on, Martha Jane, you have to! Honey, when I get through with you, there'll be no way anyone could *possibly* recognize you! You won't recognize yourself." She tilted her head. "In fact, it'll be good for you. You'll be surprised how freeing it can be to be totally unrecognizable. You might learn a little something you didn't know about yourself." She shrugged. "Either way, to my way of thinking, this means there's not one single reason left why you should turn up your nose at a quick five hundred bucks."

There was a knock on the apartment door and a shout from the hall beyond. "Martha Jane! Come quick!"

Recognizing the voice of Mrs. Crump from upstairs, Martha Jane tugged free of Kayla, pulled off the silly mask, and yanked the door open.

"Someone appears to be stealing your car, dear!" Mrs. Crump said.

"What?" Whirling, Martha Jane raced to the window, grabbing her glasses on the way. She put them on fast and looked at the street below. Sure enough, a white tow truck with BERNIE'S REPO SERVICE painted on the side in fat 1970s-style lettering was backing up to her car.

Something tickled her hand. She looked down to see five crisp hundred-dollar bills sliding into her palm. "Tell you what," Kayla said, closing Martha Jane's hand around the wad of money and her own hand around Martha Jane's. "Take your share of the pay in advance. Go down there and pay Bernie so he'll leave your car alone."

Licking her lips and feeling backed into a corner, Martha Jane closed her eyes, and nodded. "Deal."

RICHARD Gable looked across the desk at his brother and shook his head. "No way in hell, bro. It's Valentine's Day weekend. I have two dates with two gorgeous models. Both at the same time, of course, thanks to the secretarial skills of our niece, Babs the airhead. But frankly, despite the effort it's going to take, I plan to find some way to make the most of each of them."

Michael Gable crooked an eyebrow in the disapproving way that only an older brother could manage. "Since when does your secretary's job include managing your social calendar?"

Richard shrugged. "Martha Jane never had a problem with it. Hell, my life ran like clockwork when she was around. Now I've got Babs and I'm swimming in chaos."

Michael gave him a "serves you right" sort of look. "Luckily, the women you date make our Babs look like a female Einstein, so it shouldn't be too difficult to lie your way out of the situation."

"Exactly," Richard said with a grin, not bothering to defend his women to his brother. He knew what they were and what they were not. He wasn't in denial about any of that.

"But now, you see, you don't *have* to lie your way out of it," Michael said quickly. "You have a *legitimate* excuse to cancel both dates, Richard. You have to haul your big brother's butt out of the fire."

"Being happily married, you may not remember it, Mike, but Valentine's Day sex is usually the best sex of the year."

"Oh, I *remember* it, all right. I'm *living* it, most of the time. When you find the right woman, *every* day is Valentine's Day." Michael grinned and gazed at some distant spot in space. Hell, he'd only been married six months, Richard thought. The guy was practically still on his honeymoon. But Michael's dreamy expression turned serious as he spoke again. "Problem is, I won't be getting anything except divorce papers for Valentine's Day this year if I attend the lingerie show as planned."

Richard sighed, shook his head. "How the hell did Cindy find out you were going, anyway? It's not like you went home and told her about it." His brother averted his eyes. "Is it?" Richard asked.

"What, you thought I was going to *lie* to her?" Michael seemed stunned by the very thought.

"Jesus, Michael, you *didn't* go to your wife and *tell* her that you had to attend a lingerie show on Valentine's Day, did you?"

Michael avoided his brother's gaze. "Of course not. Well . . . not exactly. I, um, I asked her."

"You asked her," Richard repeated, his tone flat.

"I thought she'd understand. I mean, with Hannah Mandrake sick with this damn flu bug, someone has to take her place at the show. Do you realize how important it is? She practically had to jump through hoops to get the ticket. She runs the lingerie department almost single-handedly, and she's doing a fabulous job for us, Richard. So it's fairly obvious that one of us has to stand in for her at this thing. It's important to her, to her department, and to Gable Brothers." He shrugged. "I just thought Cindy would understand. It's business."

"Right," Richard said. "You thought Cindy would agree to let you go watch a gaggle of gorgeous models parade around in their underwear for you on Valentine's Day while she stayed home watching videos, alone."

Michael sighed. "I guess it wasn't the best idea I've ever had. But Richard, one of us has to go. And, hey, come on. These are the kind of women you like best here. Models. *Underwear* models, for heaven's sake. I can't believe you're not wrestling me to the floor to get that ticket away from me."

Richard lowered his head. Oh, yeah, they were his type of women all right. Tall, leggy, lean, gorgeous, vain, and well informed on the latest hot colors, fabrics, vacation spots, and advances in laser surgery, even if they couldn't name the capitals of their own states. Frankly, since he'd been forced to let the best secretary he'd ever had go so he could give his bubbleheaded niece a job, he'd had his fill of that kind of woman. Babs was that kind of woman. *She* ought to be modeling underwear.

He wanted his efficient, myopic, conservative Miss Biswell back.

"Uncle Riiii-charrd," came the singsong voice that could set his teeth on edge in a single note.

Richard reached across his desk and pushed the button on the intercom. "You're supposed to call me 'Mr. Gable' at work, Babs."

A high-pitched titter came back. "Sorry. I thought I'd tell you that you just had a message from Fate."

"I did?"

"Mm-hmm."

Richard looked across the office at his brother, who was biting his lip to keep from grinning. "Babs, um, do you think perhaps it might have been . . . Kate?"

There was a long silence. "Well, I guess it might have been."

"Well, now, let's see. Did she call to tell you my reason for living, Babs, or did she just want to say hello?"

He could almost see his sister's youngest child searching her empty head for the answer. "She wanted to know if you were planning anything special for Valentine's Day."

His throat went dry. It was Kate. Would have been better, though, if it had been Fate, calling to say he was going to hell in a handbasket. "And what did you tell her?" he forced himself to ask.

Her voice came back, brighter than ever. "Same thing I told Heidi and Fawn," she chirped. "That you'd be at the Valentine's Day Ball at the Westcott Room at eight o'clock sharp."

She sounded as if she thought she deserved a raise and a promotion for being so efficient. Ending the intercom connection, Richard gave Michael a desperate look. "Make that three dates."

"And one perfect excuse." Michael held up the ticket. "Or do you want them all showing up at the ball at eight and meeting each other?"

Running a hand through his hair, Richard sighed his surrender and depressed the button again. "Babs?"

"Oh!" she squeaked. "You scared me! What?"

He closed his eyes. It was probably not a good idea to have Babs call Heidi and Fawn and Kate with his regrets. "Never mind, hon. I'll take care of it myself." He walked over to his brother, took the ticket. "This is going to cost me a small fortune in flowers, candy, and apologies," he told Michael.

"Don't bother with the candy, Richard. They're models, remember?"

It was, Richard thought, a good point.

CHAPTER TWO

I CANNOT believe I am doing this."

"Oh, be quiet and suck in!" Kayla slid the zipper up as Martha Jane held her breath. "There!" she said, stepping back. "What do you think?"

Models were running back and forth in various states of undress, all of them at least six inches taller than Martha Jane was, even though she had donned stiletto heels in an effort to appear taller. She felt as insignificant among them as a crow among swans as she lifted her head to the full-length-and-then-some mirror.

Then she widened her eyes. She didn't *look* insignificant or crowlike at all. Her first thought was that she really ought to put on her glasses, but she knew full well she could see up close without them. It was distances that gave her trouble. Kayla had worked wonders on her hair, making it seem fuller and wilder and glossier all at once, simply by her clever use of hairbrush and blow-dryer. It was a big, fluffy, sexy, mink-colored mane now, rather than the straight, lifeless tresses she usually kept captive in a tight bun. "Wow," Martha Jane whispered.

"I told you. You look incredible."

"I look . . . like someone else." Martha Jane eyed herself. Her body was hugged tightly by white leather. The high-cut leg openings and white open-toed spike-heeled shoes made her short legs seem longer, and the white stockings she wore were topped with wide bands of elasticized lace. But the amazing thing was the way the scrap of leather managed to make her waist look so small. And . . . other things look . . . gravity-proof.

"I have *cleavage*," she said, staring at the gentle swells as if they were foreign objects that had suddenly landed on her home planet.

"There's Dream Bra technology built into every piece I create," Kayla announced proudly. She stood beside Martha Jane, wearing a short red baby doll that was almost as transparent as glass. Underneath it were a red-sequinned Dream Bra and matching thong panties. Her stockings were red, as were her shoes, and she wore a little headband with a pair of plastic devil horns.

"Here, get the gloves on." Kayla handed her a pair of long white gloves, then pulled on her own red ones.

Sighing, incredibly uncertain, and feeling a flutter of panic in her chest, Martha Jane put the gloves on and lowered her mask. It was white, like the rest of the outfit, with tipped-up corners accented in white feathers. It was supposed to allude to the wings of an angel. Right now, Martha Jane thought, she felt more like a chicken.

The music Kayla had chosen—Robert Palmer's "Simply

Irresistible"—came crashing over the loudspeaker, and the sultry voice of the female emcee drifted in, announcing the first-ever showing from a new designer. Kayla grabbed Martha Jane by the arm. "Come on! This is it!" She left Martha Jane in the curtained area just off stage left, then raced around to the other side, her heels clicking all the way.

Martha Jane looked across the stage and saw the fuzzy red outline of Kayla waiting on the other side. This meant everything to her friend. Everything. It meant a great deal to Martha Jane as well. It was important. She could do this.

"I give you," the emcee said, "Kayla Hart's brand-new line of fantasy lingerie, Leather and Lace!"

The music boomed louder. Martha Jane held Kayla's gaze—or rather, tried to focus on where that gaze would be—and counted off. On three she took a deep breath and stepped forward. She concentrated on remembering everything Kayla had told her about walking onto that runway. Left foot, right foot, legs crossing in front of each other with every carefully placed step. Back straight, chin up. Eyes wide and not squinting in the bright lights. Lips slightly turned up in a mysterious almost-smile, but not a full-blown one. Keep them slightly parted, and moist. Move the hips with every step.

She made it to the center of the stage, where she and Kayla stopped at the same moment, just the way they'd planned it. A soft swell of applause started, then grew. Kayla caught Martha Jane's eye, and Martha Jane took the signal and began her solitary trek forward along the long, narrow runway, between the lights that lined its sides, heels clicking. Cameras flashed, but the lights were too bright to allow her to see any faces in the crowd—not that she could have seen them anyway without her glasses. She tried to focus on what the emcee read from the card Kayla had provided. Something about the butter-soft leather of the "Angel" ensemble. Something about the built-in Dream Bra.

Martha Jane stopped at the end of the runway, one foot in front of the other, pivoted, pivoted again, turned around fully as the applause suddenly swelled, and made her way back. She kept going, right off the stage as Kayla started down the runway in her "Devil" costume.

Once backstage, Martha Jane felt her knees go weak and her stomach clench up a little bit, but beyond that, there was no paralyzing reaction. No horrible sense of shame. In fact, she felt . . . good. Those people had cheered for her. She lifted her gaze, looked into the mirror. A stranger looked back at her. An utterly feminine, utterly desirable, sexy female looked back at her. The kind of woman who could bring a man like Richard Gable to his knees. The kind of woman she'd always secretly wished she could be.

"Damn!" she whispered. "Kayla was right—I do feel different."

But there was no time to give the feeling the substantial amount of thought and analysis it needed. She had two more outfits to model, the most outrageous one saved for last. She swallowed her shyness, her inhibitions, and found it far easier to do than she had expected. She rapidly yanked off her angel getup and pulled on a black-velvet bodysuit with cat ears and a detachable tail. She had to change her gloves and mask as well, and pull on the tall, shiny, spike-heeled, thigh-high boots. But she did it in time. She was ready to walk out there again by the time Kayla got back.

Oddly, she didn't have to force herself this time. Instinct told her that if this crowd had liked the first getup she'd worn, they were going to like this one even better. She almost smiled when she stepped out onto the stage. And she didn't have to remind herself to move slowly, to take her time, so Kayla would have enough time to get changed. She walked slowly, a little slinkiness in her step to keep to the feline motif. At center stage, just as planned, she paused, turned to one side, then the other. The applause came louder and louder. She really was doing this, and apparently the crowd was believing the lie—that she *was* this she-cat she was pretending to be. Amazing.

She walked slowly along the runway. At the end, she reached behind her, just as she and Kayla had rehearsed. She removed the detachable "tail" and ran it slowly through her fingers, then snapped it hard on the stage to demonstrate how it doubled as a playful velvet whip. It made a satisfying crack and the audience gasped, then burst into wild applause as Martha Jane wound the tail up, turned, and moved slowly back. They were going wild, shouting for more. A wolf whistle pierced the din, and she almost burst out laughing.

A wolf whistle, aimed at plain Martha Jane Biswell. Imagine that!

One more outfit to go, she thought. Just one more. She'd thought it the worst one of them all, at first. Now she thought maybe it was going to be the best. Certainly it was the most shocking. The most taboo. The most . . . *sinful.*

She stepped backstage, passing Kayla on the way.

"Is that a smile?" Kayla whispered as she passed. "I knew it! You're a closet sex kitten, Biswell! I knew it all along!"

Martha Jane stuck out her tongue and picked up the pace, slipping quickly into the final outfit. It was made almost entirely of leather straps with silver buckles. They crisscrossed her entire torso. There was actually no more of her showing than there would have been had she been wearing a bikini—but it seemed like more. A lot more. Still, black leather cupped her breasts and bottom and covered her where she needed covering, held in place by the straps that ran from top to bottom, crisscrossed her middle, encircled her shoulders, and wove their way down her back.

That wasn't the part of the outfit that made it seem so outrageous, though. The mask that went with this one was made to look just like a blindfold, except that, of course, she could see through it. And the little satin-covered bracelets she wore on both wrists had tiny chains hanging from them, which could be linked together. When Kayla came prancing off stage, she paused long enough to hook the chains behind Martha Jane's back.

"You sure you're okay?" she asked.

Kayla's eyes were gleaming and she was smiling ear to ear. Martha Jane swallowed hard and nodded. "How do you think it's going?"

"Oh, they're loving it! And this will be the clincher! Remember, walk tall, head tipped slightly back, chest out, shoulders back. Okay?"

"I remember. I can't walk any other way in this state, anyway."

"Great! Go!"

The music throbbed, and Martha Jane stepped out onto the stage. The crowd went dead silent. Not a sound came. Not a breath, she thought. Swallowing hard, she moved to the center, and the tapping of her spike heels seemed louder than anything she'd ever heard before. She paused at center stage, turned left, and right, then started along the runway. She'd lost them, she thought, wishing she could hurry. But that wasn't an option. She was afraid to walk fast, because if she lost her balance, she would fall on her face. In fact, she was probably walking slower than she had before.

At any rate, she made it to the very end of the runway, and stopped.

Slowly, the clapping began. Bit by bit. Louder, and then louder still. And then it was thunderous, deafening. Martha Jane was startled, but mostly relieved. Then, as the applause went on and on, that other feeling returned to overwhelm everything else. She felt . . . sexual. She felt desirable and physical and feminine. Earthy. Female. Powerful. They were applauding for Kayla's designs, yes— but *she* was the one making them look this good. She'd never believed herself capable of it. Of being . . . sexy.

Smiling, almost giddy with this newfound sense of herself as a woman, she pivoted and headed back. She almost wished Richard Gable *could* see her this way!

Kayla passed her on the way out, wearing regular clothes again—if you could call them regular. She was gorgeous, and as the emcee introduced her as the designer of this bold new line, she paused and gripped Martha Jane's shoulder. "Omigod," she whispered. "Martha Jane . . . *look*."

Martha Jane's back was to the crowd as she'd been leaving the stage, but she turned now and squinted toward the audience. When the stage lights dimmed, she could see them—not clearly, but enough. They were getting up, one by one, rising to their feet. A standing ovation for Kayla's line. They loved it! They loved Kayla and they loved Martha Jane. Kayla's dream was coming true. And she was gripping Martha Jane's arm so tightly that Martha Jane had no choice but to step onto the runway once more, as Kayla received her glory.

Halfway out, Kayla stopped and released her grip on Martha Jane's hand to blow a kiss to the crowd, and Martha Jane pivoted, intending to make a quick escape. But she pivoted too fast, and her damned hands were still hooked together behind her back. She wobbled, teetered, flapped her elbows in a useless effort to regain her balance. In that instant she thanked her stars that the spotlight and all eyes were on Kayla, who had continued on to the end of the runway alone—and then Martha Jane went over the side.

There was a thud as her back hit the floor, fortunately only a few feet below her. It knocked the wind out of her, and she couldn't even speak for a heartbeat. Shaking off the impact, Martha Jane managed to work her arms down the backs of her legs, and push her feet through them so they were linked in front of her, rather than behind her. She sat up, and though clumsy without the use of her hands, she got as far as her knees before she realized there was a man standing in front of her. His hands were on her shoulders, as if he were going to try to help her up, but he had frozen in the middle of it. And no wonder, with her nose about an inch from his zipper. A zipper that seemed to be . . . swelling, she thought, blinking.

She swallowed her embarrassment, ignored the little devil voice inside her that wanted to laugh and shout at this new feminine power, and forced herself to tip her head back and look him in the eye.

Richard Gable stared down at her, too close to be a mistake or a product of her bad eyesight, and he said, "I think I dreamed something like this last night."

She closed her eyes, mortified that he should see her like this.

"Don't be embarrassed," he whispered. "You were the hottest model up there all night. Believe me, I know. What's your name, anyway? I don't think I've seen you before."

She blinked, frowned . . . and realized she was still wearing the mask. He didn't recognize her! The mortification vanished. Something else replaced it. A kind of triumph. He'd said she was the hottest model up there. That was good, right? Her. His efficient little ex-secretary. Miss Biswell, hotter than any of the bimbos he'd preferred over her for so long. Hotter than any of the women he'd fallen all over himself trying to get into bed while ignoring the woman right under his nose who was halfway in love with him.

"My name?"

He nodded, smiling.

"It's, uh, Valentine. Yes—it's Valentine," she lied, trying to keep her voice very soft and slightly deeper than normal so he wouldn't recognize it. The result was a sultry-sounding purr.

"Yeah? Well, you're the nicest Valentine I ever got." His smile deepened. "I'm Richard. Nice to meet you." His hands were still on her shoulders, his crotch still an inch from her face. "I, um, I hate to offer, but can I help you up?"

She looked up, and some demon woman she didn't even recognize said, "If you insist," and sent him a devilish half smile.

He looked as if she'd zapped him with a stun gun. "Damn, woman," he said, sounding a little breathless. "You're deadly, aren't you?" He gripped her outer arms and helped her to her feet, a motion that brought her body very close to his. He remained there, close to her, not speaking.

"Thank you," she said softly.

"No, thank *you*."

A bit of her bravado fled as she felt other eyes on her, but Richard seemed to sense it instantly, because he took off his jacket, and draped it around her shoulders.

Still, people were staring. *Men* were staring. Men who were not Richard, and the looks in their eyes were . . . predatory. She didn't like it. It was fine for him to look at her like that, with that sexual gleam in his eye—God, she'd *dreamed* of him looking at her like that. But not them. Not strangers.

"Anything else I can do for you?" Richard was asking.

"Yes," she said, answering in such a rush that she didn't even think first. "Get me out of here."

He stared at her, his eyes going just a little wider, then gleaming with sexual appreciation. His lips parted in a smile so hot it was indecent, and he said, "Whatever you say, lady." He took her arm, started forward.

Her foot went right out from under her and she almost fell, but he caught her. "Ow . . . oh!"

"What is it?"

"These shoes. I think I broke a heel when I fell," she said.

He smiled again. "Well, I can remedy that easily enough." And before she knew what was happening he scooped her up into his arms and strode through the crowd with her. The next thing she knew, she was being settled into the passenger seat of a low-slung black sports car, and he was climbing into the driver's seat beside her.

He started the engine, turned to face her. "Your place or mine?" he asked, his voice deep and full of innuendo.

She licked her lips, blinked rapidly, told herself to get the hell out of this car and do it *fast*.

The stranger who'd taken over her body whispered, "Yours."

He smiled at her, melting her, and the car lurched forward.

"There's . . . just one thing," she began. He glanced down at her, waiting. "The mask . . . stays on."

Again he smiled. "Now I'm *sure* I dreamed this last night."

She felt herself blush hot and had to avert her eyes.

"I'll tell you what, Valentine. You can keep the mask on, on one condition."

"And what's the condition?" she asked.

He reached down, caught her wrist in his hand, and ran his thumb over the satiny bracelets with their linked chains. "Consider keeping the cuffs on, too?" He grinned, winked at her, and stomped harder on the gas pedal.

CHAPTER THREE

MARTHA Jane didn't know what it was. The two or three drinks she'd had to bolster herself for the show? Her long-time feelings for her boss, combined with the way he'd constantly ignored her as a woman while mooning over brainless twit after brainless twit? The triumph she felt now, that he was finally seeing her the way she'd dreamed of? Or something else?

She only knew that it was Valentine's Day, and she was wearing a mask and taking this chance. She was going to make her most se-cret fantasy come true. She was going to have wild sex with Richard Gable.

He carried her into his house, which was a stunning creation of adobe and knotty pine. Inside, she caught only fleeting, out-of-focus glimpses of a wide foyer with cathedral ceilings, a forest-green and oak living room with a fireplace, and then he was carrying her up an open metalwork staircase and through a door at the top.

His bedroom.

He set her on her feet and stood facing her. He stared down at her for a long moment, and then, finally, he lowered his head and he kissed her. His hands slid the jacket off her shoulders and let it fall to the floor, and then he stood a little straighter, just looking at her.

She'd never felt more exposed. More vulnerable. And yet . . . she felt powerful, too. Because she could see what looking at her was doing to him. He looked as if his dreams were all coming true.

"I . . . I didn't mean what I said before," he told her. "About those, er, bracelet things. You can take them off if you want."

She stared up at him. If she didn't know him so well, she'd be terrified right now. But she did know him. He would never hurt her. She was perfectly safe with him. "I, um, don't have a key."

He closed his eyes. "Then I guess you're . . . at my mercy."

She lifted her head as heat shot through her, met his eyes head on, and knew this was perfect. She didn't have to worry about knowing how—about performing. He'd have to do it all. She didn't even need to feel guilty about it. Or overcome her shyness. Or anything at all. "I guess I am," she whispered.

He smiled a devilish smile and moved her backward, until her back was touching the coolness of a wall. Reaching down, he hooked a finger around the chain between her wrists and slowly lifted it until her hands were above her head. She looked up, saw the little clothes hook on the wall above her, watched him drape the chain over it.

"Oh . . . my . . ."

He paused, waiting, watching her. Giving her time, she knew—

but she said no more. He smiled again. Reaching out with both hands, he touched her breasts, running his fingers over them again and again. Then he shook his head. "This leather is sexy, but, uh, too thick. I think it's going to have to go." He slid his palms around behind her as she tried to control her trembling. His hands lifted her hair, slid along her spine, locating the first of the buckles. Slowly, he unfastened it, and then the next, and the next. She shivered when his fingers trailed over the base of her spine.

"You're shaking," he whispered.

"No, I'm not."

"Yes, you are." He kept his hands where they were, fingers tickling her spine. Leaning in, he kissed her neck and her shoulders and her cheeks. She was breathless and filled with turmoil. He straightened again, and the leather bodice hung loose, about to fall down in front. She wanted to clap her hands to it to hold it in place, but she couldn't. Then it did fall, and he just stood there, staring at her.

She stood there, staring back.

He reached out, gripped the leather, pulled it slowly down. His hands slid over her skin as he did so. Her waist. Her hips. Down her thighs. He let it go, let it fall to the floor around her ankles. Stepping out of the leather, she kicked it aside.

"You're beautiful," he whispered.

God, she'd never felt so exposed. Her hands were itching to cross in front of her body, to cover herself, but she couldn't.

He trailed the backs of his hands over her breasts again, knuckles brushing her nipples. She closed her eyes. Turning his hands, he stroked with his fingers. Then he drew thumb and forefingers together . . . a gentle pinch. A soft sound was wrung from her. His smile widened. He pinched again. "Like that?" he asked.

Breathless, she nodded.

"Good." One more pinch, then without warning his hands fell away, and his head swooped down. He caught a breast in his hungry mouth and suckled her hard, scraping with his teeth, flicking with his tongue, biting and nipping. And now his hand was slipping down her belly, diving between her legs. Fingers spread her, opened her, touched her.

He nipped harder at her breast and drove his fingers inside her. She cried out, moving against his hand, arching against his mouth.

Then suddenly he moved away from her. Stepping back, he stared at her as she opened her eyes. She watched as he slowly unfastened his belt, his zipper. Erotic as some pagan fertility god, he undressed. And she couldn't take her eyes off him as he did. He was big, and dark, and hard. Then he came back to her. Without a word, he slid his hands down her back and cupped her buttocks, squeezed her thighs. Then he lifted her legs, until she wrapped them around his waist, and he plunged himself inside her.

"Richard," she whispered. It was so good. He filled her, stretched her. And when he took his hands away, her weight lowered her farther, so that he sank even more deeply into her. Nothing supported her now but the flimsy chain slung round the hook above her head, and the man inside her. It was the most erotic thing in the world. He bent to nurse at her breasts again as he began to move, driving himself inside her harder and harder until her body was pressed to the wall with every thrust. She panted and moaned as he pushed her closer and closer to climax. She couldn't believe the power of it, couldn't believe the tightening, tensing, coiling sensations going on inside her.

And just as she hovered at the very brink, he lifted his head. "Open your eyes," he whispered. "I want to watch you."

She opened her eyes. He kept driving into her, harder, deeper, faster, and his hands came to her breasts, and his eyes never left hers. "Come for me," he whispered, as he closed his fingers on her nipples. Then he pinched harder. "Now."

She screamed aloud as wave upon wave of feeling washed over her, shaking her to the core. By the time she came to herself again, Richard had slipped her little chain off its hook, fumbled with it until he got it to come apart, and was carrying her with him to the bed.

HOURS later, Richard lay sated and utterly relaxed, with the woman snuggled close in his arms, when it occurred to him that she hadn't said anything for several moments . . . not since she last screamed his name, in fact. He thought she might be sleeping.

He wasn't too certain how he felt about that. His one-night stands didn't usually stay overnight. Then again, this had been . . . different. He couldn't quite put his finger on why, but there was no denying that it had been just that. Different. Intense, yes. Incredible, yes. He thought, though, that the main difference was the woman.

She wasn't putting on a show. She truly had been a bit shy—at first. Trying to hide it behind her mask and her bold lingerie, but still, it had been obvious in those initial tremulous kisses. In her trembling, and the way she would avert her gaze now and then, or the way her cheeks kept coloring hotly when he looked at her. When her hands had been free to touch him, those touches had been almost hesitant. And her responses had been an odd combination of delight and—and surprise. As if every sensation were new to her somehow.

The difference was even more obvious in the way she'd curled up beside him afterward, the way she nestled still in the crook of his arm, so content and relaxed that she might be sleeping. His kind of women were usually in the shower within minutes of lovemaking and on their way home shortly thereafter.

This one was in no hurry. He wasn't even certain she was awake.

"I . . . don't know about you," he said, keeping his voice low, trailing a finger over her cheek. "But I'm starving."

"I could eat an entire side of beef," she murmured.

He felt his face split in a smile. His first thought was that she was no more an ordinary model than she was an ordinary woman. "I thought you might be sleeping."

She sat up a little, staring down at him in the darkness from behind her mysterious mask. "Not sleeping. Just . . . basking." A shy smile tugged at her lips, and she turned her face away a bit. If he could see in the dark, he thought he'd see her blushing. "It was . . . wonderful, Richard."

"It was pretty wonderful for me, too."

"Really?" She seemed surprised, and maybe relieved, too.

"What, it wasn't obvious?"

Again, she looked away. "I guess I just wanted to be sure."

He nodded, once again getting the feeling she wasn't exactly experienced at these sorts of games. "What do you want to eat, Valentine? You name it, I'll get it. Serve it to you in bed." His words surprised him.

"I told you, a side of beef."

He laughed softly. "You're not like any other model I've ever met," he said.

"That's because I'm not a model," she said in her soft, raspy voice.

A little alarm bell went off in Richard's head. "You're not?"

"Well, I was tonight. But for the first and last time." She smiled at him, making his stomach flip over. "Even though I enjoyed it a lot more than I expected to."

Richard cleared his throat. "What . . . do you do? For a living, I mean?"

She quickly looked away. "I've been helping a friend get a new business off the ground. Creatively, she's a genius, but she has no head for books or budgets or organization."

Richard's throat went dry. She was not what he had thought she was—not at all. "You do that full time, then?"

"For the moment, yes."

"And this modeling gig was what, a walk on the wild side?"

She laughed huskily. A deep, rich sound that stroked his nerve endings like brushed velvet. "A favor for a friend. Her model got sick at the last minute."

"I see."

She drew a breath, sighed, looked at him with something soft and intense in her eyes. "I argued hard against the whole thing. But now I'm very glad I let her talk me into it."

"Oh."

She tilted her head then, her eyes narrowing when they saw his expression. No doubt—it was one of impending panic.

"I'm sorry," she said, her voice going a bit harder. "I'm ruining it for you, aren't I? I should have said I was an aspiring actress, and added a breathless little giggle for good measure."

Richard frowned. Her tone had changed, and he hadn't expected to see such sharpness in those eyes. "What are you talking about?"

She shrugged. "That's the kind of woman you usually date, isn't it? They're safe."

"Safe?" He sat up, leaned back against the headboard. This was fascinating. Chilling, too. This woman seemed to know more about him than he'd realized. And from the look in her eyes a moment ago—she might not know a one-night stand when she saw one.

"Convenient," she said. "No demands, no expectations." She shrugged. "Don't worry, Richard. Smart women can have casual sex, too."

He tilted his head to one side. "But it's a first for you, isn't it, Valentine?"

She shrugged and looked away.

"How do you know so much about me?" he asked. He saw her tongue dart out to moisten her lips. She looked around the room as if in search of a change of subject, and her gaze fell on the tripod in the corner.

"I don't know much about you at all," she answered then. "I didn't know you were an artist, for example." She nodded toward the blank canvas on the tripod.

"I'm no artist. I used to draw some, but—"

"Used to?"

He shrugged. "I haven't worked on anything in months." Because he hadn't felt sufficient passion for anything in months to want to capture it in charcoal.

Until tonight.

And that made him even more uncomfortable. So he changed the subject. "Just who are you really, Valentine?"

She sat up quickly, putting her feet on the floor and her back to him, clutching the sheet to her chest. "I really should go . . ."

"No, don't." He said it too quickly, yes. He knew that. He usually couldn't wait for his dates to leave, usually found talking to them as boring as mud. But not this time. This woman was different. Totally different from the others. And in spite of his self-imposed set of rules, he found himself really wanting her to stay. To *talk*, of all things! "Don't go. If it makes you so uncomfortable, I won't ask again."

She wasn't relaxing, though. Not yet.

"Besides, I haven't fixed us that side of beef yet." He ran the backs of his fingers slowly down her spine. She arched in response, and calmed visibly. He saw her lips curve in a slight smile.

"What do you mean, us?" she teased softly. "You don't expect me to share, do you?"

He laughed again, so relieved he was damn near giddy with it. He couldn't remember the last time he'd been out with a woman who'd made him laugh. "Wait here. I'll be back in no time." He got up, reached for a robe, and pulled it on. Then he looked back at her for a long moment. "You intrigue me, Valentine," he heard himself say.

She shook her head. "It's not me," she said, and he thought there was a touch of sadness in her voice. "It's just the mask."

"No. No, it's you."

He turned and headed to the kitchen. As he sliced hunks of left-over roast beef sent home with him by his nurturing sister-in-law, he wondered about his mysterious Valentine. She was disguising her voice, never raising it above that deep whispering tone that told him nothing. She was hiding her face behind that silly mask—and her personality behind the rest of the costume she wore tonight. Even when that costume was nothing more than her delectable skin. She was a shy woman, normally. A woman who must think he would know her if he saw her face or heard her true voice. A woman he must have known at some point in his life—that much was obvious by how well she seemed to know his dating habits. Several times he'd looked at her and caught a glimpse of the truth. But it had been just out of reach, too far away to grab hold of. Nevertheless, there was something very dear, very familiar about this woman.

He heaped a platter with roast beef sandwiches on kaiser rolls, surrounded them with some healthy raw veggies, cheese, pickles, and a bag of potato chips. Then he grabbed a couple of cans of soda and carried the mess of it back into the bedroom.

But when he got there, she was gone. The only thing on his pillow, where her incredible mass of silken hair had been, was a note.

He set the tray down and picked the note up, feeling like Prince Charming picking up a lone glass slipper.

It really was just the mask, Richard. The woman behind it isn't the least bit interesting to you. Believe me, I know this to be true. You've told me yourself . . . without saying a word. Remember this night for what it was: a Valentine from a secret admirer— and a dream come true for a lonely woman. I'll never forget it.

Love,
Valentine

He blinked down at the signature, the handwriting. It was a scrawl he knew, too familiar to be forgotten.

"Oh my God," he whispered, holding the note against his chest as his heart turned over and his blood rushed to his feet. "Miss Biswell!"

CHAPTER FOUR

"WHERE in the name of sin have you *been*?" Kayla had come off the sofa as if she'd been shot out of a cannon the second Martha Jane stepped through the apartment door. "I've been worried sick! I called everywhere. Even the police, but they said you had to be gone for forty-eight hours before they could—" She stopped, her eyes widening as Martha Jane shrugged off the too big jacket she'd *borrowed* from Richard's place. "Omigod, you're still wearing . . . Martha Jane, what *happened* to you last night?"

Martha Jane sighed. She wondered if she looked as shell-shocked as she felt. "I'm not sure. Maybe it was temporary insanity. Or maybe I'm coming down with multiple-personality disorder or something."

"Huh?" Kayla forced the puzzled expression off her face, gripped Martha Jane's shoulders, and dragged her into the nearby bathroom. "Come on, you're a mess. Your makeup is all over your face. Have you been crying? You have, haven't you? God, girl, your hair looks like you just came off a night of wild . . ." She paused there, blinking, leaning closer and peering into Martha Jane's eyes. "No. No way. You didn't . . ."

Martha Jane merely shrugged and looked away.

"You *did*!" Kayla stood there frozen, then shook herself and turned away to start the shower and adjust the water temperature before facing Martha Jane again. "So who was he? You were on-stage with me and then you were gone. I went backstage to wait for you, but you never came." Hands on her hips, she stared at Martha Jane accusingly. "You left with some man, didn't you? You walked out of that place, wearing that getup—with some stranger! Are you out of your freaking—"

"No," Martha Jane denied softly. "No, Kayla, not with a stranger. With Richard Gable." Her voice sounded a little dreamy, and when she looked into the mirror she saw that her eyes were rather vacant.

"Richard Gable?" Kayla was behind her now, unbuckling her, stripping the outfit off her the way a big sister would do. She guided Martha Jane into the shower and slid the door closed, and the entire time she never stopped talking. "*Richard Gable?* As in your ex-boss? The guy who fired you so he could hire some bimbo? The guy you've been secretly in love with for almost a year?"

Martha Jane yanked the sliding door open. "I am *not* secretly in love with him!" She slammed it shut again.

"No, you're not, 'cause it's sure as hell no secret now!"

"Yes, actually, it is." Martha Jane sighed and turned her face up to the warm, soothing spray. "Kayla, it was . . . it was so . . . so *exciting!*"

36

"But . . . but . . . he . . . you . . ."

Martha Jane yanked the sliding door open again. "He never knew it was me! It was the mask. And I don't know, I felt . . . freer somehow. Like I could do anything, be anyone I wanted to be—just like you said."

"Yeah?" Kayla tilted her head to one side. "So who *were* you?"

Martha Jane felt her cheeks heat, and she pressed her hands to them as a trill of laughter escaped her lips.

"My God, you *giggled*. I've never heard you giggle in my life. What did that man do to you?"

"Just about everything, I think." Martha Jane slid the door closed again and ducked her head beneath the rush of water. "It was the most incredible night of my life," she said, water running down her face. She washed her hair and soaped her body, then stood there clean and refreshed, just letting the hot water rush over her.

Suddenly there was an urgent pounding on the apartment door. Martha Jane just continued basking in the afterglow, relaxing in the shower spray. So much to think about. She wondered about this new part of herself—a part she'd never in her wildest dreams expected to find. Kayla sighed and left the bathroom. Martha Jane heard voices, but she didn't let them intrude. She conditioned her hair and rinsed it under the spray. But then the voices got louder and broke into her lovely state of being.

Cranking the water off, she stepped out of the shower and wrapped herself in a big terry robe.

"How did you even find out where I live?" Kayla asked in an overly loud voice, sounding slightly nervous. It was as if she were *deliberately* speaking at high volume. Martha Jane reached for the bathroom doorknob as Kayla went on. "I mean . . . I wasn't expecting company, *Mr. Gable.*"

"Omigod," Martha Jane whispered. She jerked her hand away from the doorknob as if it had burned her. "He's here!"

"Um . . . your address was on your business cards," Richard said, sounding a bit confused at Kayla's behavior. "Everyone who attended the show got one. Surely you knew that?"

"Well . . . well, of course I did. But I thought anyone who wanted to order from me would . . . would call, not drop by unannounced." Then she paused. "Wait a minute—is that why you're here? Do you want to . . . order my line?"

Curious, Martha Jane gripped the doorknob again, turned it, and opened the door just a crack to peer through.

"Well, why else would I be here?" Richard asked.

Martha Jane gasped, pressing a hand to her mouth to cover the sound. In the next room, Kayla looked stunned.

"I expected to find an office, not an apartment," Richard was saying. "I am truly sorry if this is an inconvenience, but if you want to be in business, you really shouldn't greet the customers with open hostility."

Martha Jane closed her eyes. That one had to hurt, even though Richard had said it in his charming, teasing tone. Kayla huffed, gaped, and started over. "We're . . . in the process of . . . relocating our . . . er . . . headquarters," she said.

Martha Jane could almost see Richard's reluctant smile. "Just starting out, huh? Well, you've got nothing to worry about. By the end of the day, you'll have more orders than you can handle. Including a hefty one from Gable Brothers."

"I . . . will?"

"Absolutely."

"Well, I . . ." Kayla clasped her hands together. Probably to keep from high-fiving him, Martha Jane thought. "Thank you. Thank you so much!"

"No need to thank me. It's business. Your clothes are going to make my stores a lot of money. But, uh, that's not the *entire* reason I'm here."

It's not? Martha Jane thought.

"It's not?" Kayla asked.

"No. I, um, I'm trying to track down the, uh, the model you used last night. And I thought—"

"Oh, well, um, you know that's strictly against policy. I mean, no designer in the biz would—well, you know that, Mr. Gable. You've worked in this business long enough to know we absolutely have to protect our models' privacy."

"Well, sure, but she *wasn't* a model. Not really."

Martha Jane gripped the doorknob so hard her knuckles turned white.

"I paid her to walk down a runway wearing my clothes," Kayla said, her voice dry. "Or do you have some other definition of what constitutes professional modeling?"

"Look, I need to speak to her. It's important."

"Well, I'm just not sure I . . ."

Martha Jane opened the door and stepped out. "Mr. Gable?" she asked, feigning surprise. "I *thought* that was your voice I heard. How are you?"

He looked at her in surprise—or she thought it was surprise. But then again, there was something utterly false about it. As if he'd been expecting her to pop in long before she had. But then he smiled broadly. "Martha Jane! I didn't know you lived here! You two are . . . roommates, then?"

Martha Jane nodded.

"How are you?" Richard asked. "I can't tell you how much I've missed you at the office."

Kayla snorted and turned her head.

"Oh, I'm sure Buffy is doing a fine job," Martha Jane managed.

"Uh . . . it's Babbette. And no, she's not half the secretary you were." He shook his head. "If I'd had any choice in the matter, you'd still be there. But, you know that."

"Bimbette has that much control over you, does she?" Kayla drawled.

Richard grinned, shaking his head, either not hearing the not-too-subtle slam in Kayla's tone or pretending not to. "It's Babbette, and she has me wrapped around her little finger, I'm afraid." Martha Jane almost winced. God, he might as well poke her with sharp sticks. "But remember my offer, Martha Jane. I can move you into any department you want, and give you a pay raise to boot. Just say the word."

She opened her mouth.

Kayla spoke first. "Oh, you'll just have to fill those slots with more like Boobette," she said brightly.

"Babbette," Richard corrected.

"Whatever." Kayla waved a hand dismissively. "Martha Jane is working with me now. In fact, she's my second in command. She's way too good to be any man's secretary. Especially a man who'd replace her with some little—"

"Kayla." Martha Jane said it firmly but not loudly. "Richard is our first paying *customer*. I'm sure he's not here to discuss his secretary with us."

Kayla fell silent, and even looked a little apologetic.

Richard looked right into Martha Jane's eyes and said, "I had no idea you were a part of this clothing line." Then he held out a hand. "Well, then, let me be the first to say congratulations, Martha Jane."

"But we haven't even—"

"I imagine your venture—Leather and Lace, isn't it?" Kayla nodded fast when he glanced her way, then he went on, "It's going to be as big as Victoria's Secret. I'd bet money on it, and believe me, I know about these things."

Martha Jane looked past him at Kayla, whose eyes got wider.

"Now, back to the subject at hand. This model . . ."

"I'm sorry," Kayla began.

"I can get a message to her," Martha Jane interrupted quickly.

"You can?"

She nodded.

"You know her, then?"

"Yes. But I can't tell you anything about her. I mean, I'd have to ask her first, and . . . so why don't you just give me the message and I'll pass it along?"

He shook his head slowly. "Is there anything you *can't* do, Martha Jane?"

She shrugged and tried not to blush with pleasure. "I don't suppose I'd be very good at modeling lingerie," she said. Meanwhile, she ignored Kayla, who was staring at her over Richard's shoulder as if she'd grown horns.

Instead of saying anything more, she went to the telephone stand and picked up the pad of paper and pen that lay there. "Here you go, Mr. Gable," she said. "Just jot down what you want to say, and I'll see that she gets it."

He smiled brilliantly and took the pad from her. His fingers brushed hers, and for just a second his eyes, sparkling with some unnamed intensity, met hers and held them. She had to look away. He was probably just thinking of his masked lover. Martha Jane Biswell was the farthest thing from his mind. Finally, he began writing. He wrote for a long time, paused, licked his lips, and wrote some more. Then he tore the sheet off, folded it, and handed it to Martha Jane. "Now, this is for her eyes only. Okay?"

"You can trust me, Mr. Gable."

"I know I can," he murmured. "Martha Jane, in all the time you worked for me, didn't I ever once tell you to call me Richard?"

Lifting her head, she met his gaze. Still intense, still probing. His eyes this morning seemed to be examining her, over and over again, as if he'd never seen her before. "No," she answered him honestly. "You never did."

"I was an idiot, then." He closed his hand over hers, around the note. "Thank you, Martha Jane. This means a lot to me." Then he leaned closer and pressed his lips to her cheek. It was, she thought, the most intimate cheek kiss she'd ever had. Long, and tender. Then he turned to Kayla. "And again, congratulations on your success. The buyers from Gable Brothers will be calling you later on today to officially place that order."

"Thank you, Mr. Gable."

He nodded, smiling, then turned and left the apartment, but as they pushed the door closed, he put a hand out, holding it open.

"Your morning paper is here," he said, bending to pick it up and hand it in to them. "I've already seen mine. You might want to check out the fashion section."

Then he nodded good-bye and pulled the door closed behind him.

Kayla's wide eyes met Martha Jane's. "Fashion section?" Kayla whispered. Her hands were shaking as she pushed the newspaper at Martha. "You do it! I can't!" Martha Jane took the newspaper, knelt on the floor, and began flipping through it.

She didn't have to look far. A full-color photo of Kayla and Martha Jane, wearing their angel and devil numbers, side by side, center stage, covered the front page. Above it was the banner headline: NEWCOMER KAYLA HART, LINGERIE'S HOTTEST NEW STAR!

The two women, squealing with laughter, hugged each other and danced in circles.

JUST outside the door, Richard went still as he heard the sound of his mystery lady's laughter. He waited, listening, unable to move away.

"But why did you go and tell him I was working with you?" he heard Martha Jane ask.

"Because you were about to take him up on the job offer! I could see it in your eyes, Martha Jane. And you're too good for a man who'd fire you just to give one of his floozies a job. Way too good."

Martha Jane lowered her voice. "He's not as bad as all that."

"Oh, no? He's bad enough that he doesn't even look at you as a woman. My God, he stood right here and didn't even know you were the same one he spent the night with. The same one he's driving himself crazy trying to find now. He's shallow, Martha Jane. He's a Neanderthal who's convinced himself that a decent, intelligent woman can't be sexy and that a sexy woman can't be decent or intelligent. Besides, you don't need to take his job offer now. If what this fashion editor says turns out to be even close to the truth, we're both gonna end up millionaires, honey. Men like Richard Gable will be looking at you in a whole new way—and you won't have to fall at their feet in your underwear to get them to do it, either."

Martha Jane sighed loudly. "I don't really *want* any other man looking at me that way. But the rest sounds great."

Richard stepped away from the door slowly, feeling more confused than he ever had in his life. More rotten and selfish and shallow, too. Kayla had him nailed. "She's right," he whispered. "I've been the world's biggest, blindest fool. But damned if I know how to make it up to her. Or if I should even try." He shrugged, pushing his hands into his pockets, and walked back down the hall. If he let Martha Jane know how special he thought she was, she might get the wrong idea. She might think he was serious about this thing, that he wanted—he swallowed hard—a *relationship*.

Hell, maybe it was better to pretend he didn't know her identity. But one thing was certain. He *had* to see her again. He had to.

CHAPTER FIVE

WHILE Kayla took her turn in the shower, Martha Jane slipped into her bedroom, closed the door, put on her glasses, and took Richard's note from her pocket.

> *Valentine,*
> *I have to see you again. I've never met anyone like you before, and I want to know you. I'm not talking about sharing secrets here, or even unmasking you. But . . . you fascinate me. And I want to see you again. No more than that. Meet me tonight, at midnight, at the fountain in the park. I'll be there. I'll wait for you.*
>
> *Richard*

Martha Jane stared at the note, striving to read more into it than what was there. What did it mean? Why would he want to meet her outdoors, in the middle of February? She couldn't very well show up in a negligee there. What did he want from her? She swallowed hard, trying with everything in her not to believe she meant any more to him than any of his other one-night stands. She knew her ex-boss. She'd seen him go through women like selections on a dessert tray. A different flavor every time. She was no more to him than a new flavor. If she let herself think she was, she'd be in for a broken heart.

Besides, the note made it pretty clear. It was one more round of sex he wanted. Nothing more. At least he hadn't written "bring the handcuffs."

Kayla was right. He really was a bastard. Martha Jane swallowed hard. She loved the bastard. Had for months now.

The telephone shrilled, breaking into her thoughts. Absently, she reached for it. "Hello?"

"Um, yes, I was trying to reach Leather and Lace?"

Oh, hell! That didn't sound very professional, did it? What was she thinking? "I'm sorry, you must have dialed the wrong number," she lied.

"Oh. Sorry to bother you." Click.

Two seconds later the telephone rang again. She took a deep breath, let it ring twice more, then picked it up and put on her best secretary voice. Crisp and efficient. "Leather and Lace, please hold."

She covered the mouthpiece with her hand, counted slowly to ten, then came back. "I'm sorry for the delay," she said. "How may I direct your call?"

"This is Boudoir Boutique," the female voice replied. "And I'm calling to order your line of lingerie."

"One moment, please."

She reached for something to write on, smiling ear to ear. But as she was in the middle of jotting down the boutique's list, the Call Waiting beeped and she had to put the first caller on hold. It was another chain, placing another order. And Gable Brothers hadn't even called yet.

Martha Jane bit her lip, kept her cool, and took down the information.

Kayla came out of the bathroom wrapped in a big robe, and Martha Jane put down the phone. "The newspaper and Richard were right," she exclaimed. "We've got to get in gear, Kayla. We need office space, and a secretary, and another computer, just for starters. Then we need to go through the offers from manufacturers, find the best bid, and get this line into mass production."

Kayla was frowning, shaking her head. Not getting it.

"Kayla, hon, we just got orders from two chains, for almost a thousand items, and Gable's hasn't even called yet, and—"

The phone shrilled again.

"Leather and Lace, may I help you?" Martha Jane said. "I'm sorry, can you say that again? Twenty-five sets of the entire collection? Oh, for each store? And how many stores would that be, Mr.—" She bit her lip. "A hundred and one, you say?"

Kayla smacked her palm on her forehead. "I'm not ready for this!" she exclaimed as Martha Jane jotted the order on the back of an overdue electric bill.

"Well, you'd better *get* ready, kid. 'Cause we're in business. Listen, can you man the phones?"

"I guess so, but I—"

"Good. I'm going to get us some help. See you in an hour."

Martha Jane ran back into her room, shaking off the remnants of that other woman she'd briefly become. It wasn't difficult. She tossed on a sensible suit, pinned up her hair, and looked in the mirror to see the logical, dependable Miss Biswell looking back at her. Even if she *did* seem to have a new sparkle in her eyes. Sending herself a secret smile, Martha Jane headed out of the apartment at a brisk pace.

RICHARD sat in his office, a cup of coffee in his still-shaking hand, and told his brother about his date—minus the more personal details—with the mystery lady who turned out to be his own efficient, prim, and proper Miss Biswell.

Michael sat in a chair across from him, and all he did was shrug. "So what part of this surprises you, Richard? That Martha Jane is a knockout? That she is an actual woman? You're telling me you never noticed it before?"

"Oh, come on, Michael! She wears blazers and—and *tweed*. And those big glasses. And her hair is always—"

"So she doesn't go around the office in a thong and a bustier," Michael said. "It might surprise you to learn this, little brother, but most women don't."

"I just never . . ."

"Bothered to give her a second glance," Michael said, shaking his head. "I just wish I'd realized she was nursing a crush on you, Richard."

"Why?"

"*Why?* Why do you think? Must have been like a slap in the face when you told her you were letting her go so we could hire our niece."

Richard sighed. "She doesn't even realize Babs *is* our niece. I think she believes she's one of my . . . you know."

"Oh, hell. No wonder she threw your job offer back in your face."

Richard lowered his head. "All this time, she was a few yards away from me, day in and day out. And I never got to know her at all. I mean, there's so much more to the woman than meets the eye."

"What, just because she's fun in bed?"

Richard's head came up sharply, and he fixed his brother with a stern glare. "Don't even— That wasn't what I meant, and you know it. She's . . . she's funny. And sexy. And smart. She's an entrepreneur, for crying out loud. And all this time I thought she was just . . ."

"Just a secretary," Michael finished for him. "So does this mean you're considering . . . an actual relationship?"

Richard frowned at him. "A second date," he said. "Just a second date. I haven't *entirely* lost my mind."

The buzzer on Richard's desk sounded and he heard a familiar titter that set his teeth on edge. "Oh, Riiiicharrd . . ." Babs sang out over the intercom.

He sighed heavily. "What is it, Babs?"

"There's a lady here to see you," she said. Then she whispered, "And she's kinda cute, but not very friendly."

"Does she have a name?"

"Well, of course she does, silly!" Babs giggled again.

Richard clenched his teeth. But then another voice came, one so familiar his heart ached with missing its soothing sound on the other end of an intercom. "Richard, it's Martha Jane, and it's important."

He looked up and met his brother's eyes, his own widening. "You know nothing, you understand? She still thinks I don't know it was her last night, and I want to keep it that way."

"Why, for the love of God?"

He opened his mouth, closed it, shook his head. "Damned if I know. Because I can't think of anything else to do at the moment."

Michael rolled his eyes, and Richard went to the office door, opened it, and saw Martha Jane standing there, looking at Babs with blatant disapproval. He felt lower than pond slime. "Martha Jane," he said. "I didn't expect to see you again so soon. I see you've met Babs."

"Yes."

"She's, uh . . . our niece."

Martha Jane looked at him with one eyebrow raised. "Of course she is."

"Hi, Martha Jane," Michael said, coming out of the office. Then he looked at his brother, and Richard tried to send him a plea for help without saying anything out loud.

Michael sighed and glanced at his niece. "Babs, are you and your mom still coming to our place for dinner on Sunday? Cindy's been planning all week."

Babs smiled from ear to ear. "Sure are, Uncle Mike. We still having that special roasted chicken Aunt Cindy makes?"

"Absolutely." He sent a wink at Martha Jane. "My sister's been trying to get that secret recipe out of my wife for months. Maybe she'll succeed this time." Then he sauntered away, and Richard sent a silent thank-you after him.

Martha Jane was blinking, looking from Babs to Richard again and again. "You mean . . . she *really* is your niece?"

Richard bit his lip to keep from saying anything rude in front of Babs. Instead, he took Martha Jane's elbow and led her into his office, closing the door before he spoke. "Martha Jane, I had no choice but to give her the job. No one else in the company would have put up with her. And with Michael's secretary six months from retirement, we couldn't very well—"

She held up a hand. "It's okay. I . . . understand."

"It's not okay. It wasn't fair, and believe me I've been suffering for it every minute of every day since you've been gone."

He watched her battle a smile. The smile finally won. "I know. I heard her on the intercom." The smile grew into the soft, sultry laugh he'd become enchanted with last night. "I was thinking it served you right."

He nodded, studying her. Those eyes, deep and mysterious. The makeup had only enhanced what was already there. And the mask had just made her eyes even more noticeable. But when he looked into them now, he saw that she was the same woman . . . the same beautiful, sexy woman he'd spent the night with. It was all there. He'd just never looked deeply enough to see it.

He wanted her so much it hurt!

"I came here to ask for your help, Richard. Kayla's getting swamped with orders already this morning, and we just—well, we weren't ready for it."

He nodded at a chair, and she sat down. He didn't. He hovered close by, not wanting to move too far from her. Why hadn't he noticed before how gracefully she moved? She crossed her legs, nylons whispering as her thighs brushed each other. Richard's blood was running hot, and he had to clear his throat before he could speak again. "So what can I do?"

"Well, we need to get some office space set up, put in a computer, get some phone lines turned on . . . not to mention see the bank, get our line of credit raised, and write a big fat check to a manufacturer so they can start sewing. The problem is, we need someone at the apartment manning the phones while we do all that."

"And?"

"And we don't have time to interview secretaries. I was hoping we could borrow one of yours."

He looked at her and smiled.

She looked right back, her head tilting up to do it, and he could see that she read him loud and clear. "No. Not Babbette."

"Well, it was worth a try," he said, grinning back at her.

And then her smile died and she was frowning at him. "What's going on with you today, Richard?"

He blinked down at her. "What?"

"You're . . . different. Almost . . . playful."

He drew a breath, then took the time to walk back to his desk while formulating a response to that. She was right, he realized. At work, he was usually brusque and businesslike. Not relaxed and teasing, as he was with her today. But then again, she was usually stiff and tense with him. She was different today, too.

He took his seat, folded his hands on his desk. "You seem a bit more relaxed today yourself," he told her.

She smiled, and her cheeks got pinker as she averted her eyes. "Well, I'm no longer your employee. I suppose that makes a difference."

"Was I that tough to work for?"

She shrugged. "Obviously your new secretary agrees with you. She's certainly improved your mood."

"She's driving me insane," he blurted. "The only thing improving my mood is what happened to me last night." He clamped his mouth closed.

Too late. Martha Jane had popped out of her chair so fast you'd have thought he'd electrocuted her. "That's really none of my—"

"This one was . . . different." He wasn't sure why he said it. Maybe just to see how she'd react. But then, it didn't matter, because he couldn't tell how she was reacting. She just went very still, her face frozen and expressionless.

"How was she . . . different?"

He watched her standing there in front of her chair, looking ready to run. "She had a brain, for starters. She . . . made me laugh. I talked to her, you know what I mean? I don't usually talk to the women I date. But this one, this one made me want to talk to her."

"Really?"

He nodded.

"What did she look like, this . . . this woman?" She had turned now, paced softly over to the windows and pretended great interest in the traffic below.

"She was beautiful. But not in the way the others have been. She wasn't tall or reed-thin. In fact, she must have been similar to you, physically speaking."

She didn't reply to that.

"I never saw her face fully, you know. She . . . she wore a mask."

"How mysterious," Martha Jane whispered. "I suppose that's why you're really so intrigued, Richard. Not because of the woman, but because of the mystery she presents."

"Funny, she suggested the same thing. But no. No, I don't think that's it at all." He walked over to where Martha Jane stood in her tweed skirt and white blouse and color-coordinated blazer. Her hair was in a neat bun, and her eyes hid behind big tortoiseshell glasses. He stood very close behind her, and felt her body stiffen, and heat.

"Suppose she wore that mask because she has some horrible scar on her face? Or is missing an eye or something?" Her voice trembled as she spoke.

"I thought of that. And you know what? It didn't matter. In fact, this morning when I woke up and thought back on the night, it hit me that for the first time in my life, what a woman looked like didn't matter in the least to me."

"I don't believe that for a minute, Richard. And I don't think you do either."

"Don't I?"

She turned to face him. "Oh, no. Tell me, what was this mystery woman wearing besides a mask? Something revealing? Something that told you she was the sex-kitten, one-night-stand type of girl you always go for? Would you have noticed her at all if she'd been wearing something else? Something like . . . oh, say, like this?" She spread her hands, palms up, down the front of her, indicating her outfit.

"If I hadn't, it would have been my mistake. My loss."

She held his gaze, her eyes probing. "So how special is she?" she asked flat out. "Special enough to make you want to give up all the others and take her home to the family? Hmm? Or just special enough that you'd like a replay of last night?"

He swallowed hard, feeling as if she'd driven a dagger through his heart to the hilt. "I just want to see her again," he muttered.

"And what makes you think *she* wants to see *you* again?"

He looked up fast, meeting her eyes. "Doesn't she?" he asked, startled at the very thought.

Martha Jane looked away quickly. "I don't know. I

haven't . . . spoken to her yet. And I . . . I think we got a bit off the subject here."

"I guess we did." He took a step away from her, just to put some distance between them. She had him off balance. Confused. Uncertain. And that wasn't good. He didn't like it one bit. He could see that it wasn't going to be easy to convince his prim Miss Biswell to see him again. No. Not when she seemed to think there was something wrong with a casual relationship like the one he had in mind. Sex wasn't going to be the answer to this, either—never mind how unbelievably great it was. He gave his head a shake, having no clue what to do. Best to get back to the subject at hand, give himself time to think, to regroup.

"You wanted to borrow a secretary—but not Babs," he said. "Who did you have in mind?"

"Mrs. Nye," she said, seeming relieved to be back on safer ground.

"Done." He said it without giving it a second thought.

Her brows went up. "Just like that?"

"Just like that." He racked his brain for something to say, because she looked toward the door, and he knew she was thinking about leaving, and he really didn't want her to do that. Not unless he went with her.

What the hell was wrong with him?

"I'll need a few minutes," he heard himself saying. "Then I'll bring her over to your place myself."

Martha Jane blinked, licked her lips. And Richard wondered why he'd never noticed how full and sensual those lips were, until last night. Hell, they were even just the tiniest bit swollen this morning. He could still taste them.

55

"You don't need to do all that," she said.

"But I want to. In fact, I'm taking the rest of the day off and spending it with you and Kayla. I'm an old hand at business matters. I can be a lot of help to you two."

"But, um, I mean—that's just not . . . What will your brother do without his partner *or* his secretary?"

"Oh, never fear. He can have my secretary for the day." Richard wiggled his eyebrows, relaxing again now that *she* seemed to be the one off balance. "Babs to the rescue."

Martha Jane's smile appeared like sunshine on a cloudy day, and her eyes sparkled up at him. Damn, so much for his ability to relax a little. Surely she was more beautiful this morning than she'd ever been before. She couldn't *possibly* have been this incredible before.

But she had been. She always had been. He'd been stepping over a diamond to pick up bits of glass, and he hadn't even noticed.

CHAPTER SIX

MARTHA Jane was feeling as if she'd stepped out of the ordinary world into some parallel dimension, where nothing was as it should be. By the time she got back to the apartment, Kayla had promoted herself from bathrobe and towel to a sexy red suit and from scribbling on the backs of old bills to keying them in on her laptop computer. She was typing in orders slowly, still not up to speed on the software she'd bought for "someday."

Martha Jane had barely had time to explain what was going on, when Richard arrived with Mrs. Nye in tow. The older woman knew the program backward and forward, she assured Kayla, and she sent the three of them on their way.

The first stop they made was the bank. And that was where Martha Jane finally realized that her life was never going to be the same again. Because they didn't get stuck in a hard chair in the lobby, only to be led later to one of the cubicles out there. No. They were taken straight through the doors in the back and into a real office, where a fat man who smelled like cigars smiled at them as if they were his best friends.

He listened to their plans but didn't make any notes. And when they left his office, they had an unlimited line of credit.

Unlimited.

Kayla was smiling all over, and Martha Jane couldn't quite absorb it. She blinked in the sunlight outside the bank, and still couldn't digest it all.

"I have a suggestion, if you want to hear it," Richard said.

"Shoot! You suggest to your heart's content," Kayla said. "I'm too excited even to think straight."

"Well, the top floor of my building is vacant. We've been planning to lease it to local businesses, but the remodeling just wrapped up last week, so no one's even seen it yet. I'll tell you, there are some great suites up there."

Martha Jane shook her head and said automatically, "Richard, we can't afford . . ." But she let the words die as she met Kayla's eyes. "*Can* we?"

Richard smiled at her in a very un-ex-boss-like manner. "Yeah, you can," he said. "Ladies, the orders you've taken this morning alone are . . . well, here. Just off the top of my head"—he yanked a calculator out of his jacket pocket and began punching in numbers, muttering as he went—"let's see, you've got orders for about, what, four thousand pieces?" Click, click, click. "I can make an educated guess what it will cost to produce them, and I know what you're charging for them—it was on the program from the show." Click, click, click. Then he turned the little screen to face them. "Here's your profit for this morning's orders. Roughly."

Kayla looked at it, then looked again.

"So—do you think you can afford office space?"

Kayla looked at Martha Jane. Martha Jane looked at Kayla. They both smiled.

For the rest of the morning, Richard helped them get their offices set up on the top floor of the Gable Brothers Building. Martha Jane, despite her lengthy list of things to do, found herself pausing often just to watch him. He was like a different man. Or maybe she was just seeing him as he really was for the first time. Before, he'd been her boss, her dream, a fantasy beyond her reach. Now, he was just . . . a man.

He'd taken off his jacket and his tie. His shirtsleeves were rolled up to the elbows, and she couldn't help staring at his forearms at every opportunity. Strong. Tanned. Dusted with hair. Flexing when he lugged office furniture right along with the deliverymen. She watched him when he crouched behind desks, hooking up computer cables, too. Because she knew the shape and feel of his backside, his thighs, and she couldn't help remembering.

He was amazing.

It wasn't fair, Martha Jane thought, that he should turn out to be even more wonderful than she'd thought. She was eating her heart out. Oh, sure, he'd said all those sweet things about his mystery date. But he hadn't known she was plain old Martha Jane.

"So, this desk is for your office, right?"

Richard's voice was soft and close to her ear, and it startled her so much that she jumped. He just smiled and laid a calming hand on her shoulder. "Sorry. You must have been a million miles away."

"I—yes, I was thinking."

"About what?"

His eyes . . . they were so dark and deep, so knowing as they probed hers. Oh, but that was ridiculous. He couldn't know. She'd die if she thought he knew!

"Why did you stop drawing?" she asked.

He tilted his head to one side, those dark eyes on hers like a touch. "Now, how did you know I ever *did* any drawing?"

"I . . . I guess . . . I must have heard someone mention it around the office. Your brother, maybe." She spoke fast, wishing she could grab the words from the air and shove them back into her mouth. Stupid, stupid, stupid!

But he only shrugged. "I don't know why I stopped. But it's funny you should ask me now that I've started again."

She blinked twice. "You have?"

"Maybe I just hadn't come across anything worth drawing in a while."

They stood in what would be the reception area of the office suite. The door behind them led to the hall and the rest of the building. The one on the left wall led to what would be Kayla's office, and the one on the back wall to her studio, where Kayla was already ensconced and having the time of her life. The double doorway on the right led to the office that would be Martha Jane's. That was the one Richard had been referring to, and the one he was heading into even now.

"Oh, this is going to be great," he said. He stood beside the open door until she came in, and then he closed it. "Look at the view."

The entire outer wall was windows, floor to ceiling. "Oh!" she breathed. "My goodness. It's like sitting on a mountaintop throne, with the whole city at my feet," she said. "I'm never going to want curtains in here, or blinds, or anything like that."

Richard smiled at her. "In that case, you're going to want your desk—" He pointed. "Over here, I think, is best." As he spoke he walked to the spot. "You can't really have your back to the door, and if you have the windows behind you, then the glare on the computer screen will make it invisible most of the day. So, here."

"It's perfect."

He smiled, walked back into the reception area, and easily pushed the padding-wrapped desk through the double doors and across the carpet into the proper spot. Then he sat on the floor and began snipping the packing tape and padding away from the sides. With a sigh, Martha Jane began to do the same with the foam and tape covering her chair.

"So what else are you going to put in here?" he asked her.

"I can't believe you'd really want to know," she said.

"Well, believe it. The way you decorate your office says a lot about who you are."

"You think so?"

"Sure."

Martha Jane looked at him quizzically. "Then what does your choice of office decor say about you?" she asked. "You've got all these extreme-type photographs blown up and framed on every wall. The hang glider, the rock climber, the windsurfer . . ."

"All the things I wanted to do before I got too old," he explained.

She lifted her brows in surprise. "And did you?"

"What is that, some crack about my age?" He grinned at her, and she shook her head. "Yes, I've done them all. Often enough that they bored me. Everything's seemed to bore me for a while now." Then he looked at her. "Well, until lately."

She cleared her throat and changed the subject. "What about

that birdcage you have hanging in the corner with the stuffed parrot inside?"

"That? Oh, that's there to remind me never to let myself be caged."

"Like your brother?"

Richard nodded slowly. "That was the idea I had when I put the bird up, yes."

She averted her gaze. She was right—he would never change.

"So, you didn't tell me—what are you going to put in your office?"

She looked around the room, thought about her life. "I want a print behind the desk, there. I saw one last week that I haven't been able to get out of my mind. A woman with three faces, each one representing some different part of her personality."

"I've seen that piece," he said. "So you'll put it here to remind people that there's more to you than what they see?"

She shook her head slowly. "To remind myself. I've been living a one-dimensional life for a long time. I didn't even know there was more to me, until— Anyway, I don't want to forget again."

He muttered something that sounded like, "I don't plan to let you."

She turned quickly, frowning at him. "What?"

"I said, uh, what would you like me to get you? As an office-warming present."

She shrugged. "You don't have to get me anything at all."

"Well, of course I do," he said, as if it bore no argument. "What else do you have in mind?"

"Oh, I don't know. Lots of plants, I suppose. Maybe an aquarium. And by the windows I want a giant rock."

"A rock?"

"Mm-hmm. A pretty one. I saw one in a shop once, amethyst spikes all over one side of it. All pointy and sparkly purple. It would catch the sun in these windows and shine like a diamond."

"And why would you want a rock in your office? Does that have some significance, too?"

She nodded. "To remind me that what I want in life is security and stability. Permanence. The occasional walk on the wild side is one thing, but I wouldn't want to lose sight of what I really want."

"Walk on the wild side?" he asked. He looked surprised . . . but the expression seemed contrived somehow. As if he were teasing her. "I never would have guessed."

She shrugged. "Maybe I should borrow some of your extreme prints," she said with a smile. "There are a lot of things I've never done that I intend to try. Rock climbing, hang gliding . . ." She could have sworn he shuddered.

"Those things are dangerous, Martha Jane. Besides, I thought you said you wanted stability and permanence."

"But I don't have them yet," she said, smiling a little bit, thinking again about the night they'd shared. "So why shouldn't I go for the thrills in the meantime?" Then she frowned. "Besides, who's to say a person can't have both?"

Richard stood there looking at her as if she'd just confessed to selling government secrets to China. Finally, he shook his head. "Tell you what. If you really want to try any extreme sports, you just say so. I'll take you myself. At least that way I can make sure you don't break your pretty neck."

She looked at him and tilted her head to one side. One hand flew to her neck automatically, fingers trailing over her pulse point.

"What's wrong?" he asked, an almost-smile tugging at his lips, his eyes, once again, holding that gleam that could give her chills. "Haven't I ever told you that you have a pretty neck before, Martha Jane?"

She swallowed the lump in her throat.

"You do, you know."

Was he . . . flirting with her? With plain Martha Jane Biswell? No. This was all in her head. He'd awakened some primal, sex-craving part of her last night, and that was where all these false impressions were coming from. She was being ridiculous. She had known what last night was before it even began. An adventure, like one of his extreme sports. Dangerous, and thrilling, and very, very brief. A one-night stand. Over and done. It meant nothing to him. *She* meant nothing to him, not as Valentine and certainly not as Martha Jane Biswell. He wouldn't give his former secretary a second glance.

And it would really, *really* be a huge mistake to see him again tonight. A huge mistake.

Oh, but dammit, how she wanted to. Stability and permanence were fine. But she didn't have them yet. She'd only been teasing him, but now she wondered—what would be so wrong about taking just one more thrill ride?

CHAPTER SEVEN

*H*E didn't think she was going to show up. He almost hoped
she wouldn't. Because she'd scared him today with all her
talk of stability and permanence. He knew what she meant. One
man, one woman, and one whopper of a commitment. He knew
himself too well to think he could be happy with that kind of an
arrangement. So it was probably just as well that she wasn't coming
tonight. Better not get too used to her.

Then again—when he'd offered to escort her on those . . . thrill
rides, as she called them . . . he'd meant it. The things that had become boring to him had taken on a new allure when he thought of
doing them with her. And maybe that was what she'd meant about
stability *and* excitement. About being able to have both.

No. No, he knew what he wanted and what he didn't want, and
it would be best for both of them if he made that clear to her before
she got any crazy ideas in her head.

He paced away from the park bench. The fountain was behind him, making so much noise with its incessant splashing that he wouldn't be able to hear her coming if she wore bells on her ankles. Not that she was going to show up, anyway.

"Hello, Richard."

He spun around so fast he almost tipped over.

She kept her voice low, all rough and soft at once, like velvet on tender skin. He knew she did that just so he wouldn't recognize her. But it turned him on nevertheless. Now that he knew her *intimately*, Martha Jane Biswell *always* turned him on. Even in her tweed business suits. Even in the full-length houndstooth-check coat and woolen hat she was bundled in now. Even with her shoulders hunched against the cold and her hands stuffed into her pockets.

He narrowed his eyes on her. It was dark, but . . . oh, God, she was wearing a mask again. A different one this time. Kind of a horn-rimmed number, in black something—velvet, maybe. Another of Kayla's kinky creations, he thought, aching. So she still wasn't ready to let him know who she was. Well, fine. Maybe it was better if he kept up the pretense, just a little longer.

"I didn't think you were coming," he whispered.

"I didn't want to come," she told him. "But I couldn't seem to help myself."

He nodded. "We should talk." He put a hand on her shoulder, walked her back toward the bench, nodded at her to sit down, and she did. He sat down next to her. He could see her breath, and his own. It was damn cold out here tonight.

She just sat there, waiting.

"I like you," he finally blurted.

She took one hand out of her pocket. A black glove covered

it. Her fingertip touched his lapel, trailed slowly down it. "I like you, too."

"Last night was . . . it was incredible. I never . . ."

"Me neither," she whispered.

He closed his hand over hers. Then he stared hard into her eyes. "You aren't . . . all that experienced at this sort of thing."

"So? I thought men liked a bit of innocence in a woman."

"I just want to make sure you know where we stand. I feel bad that we didn't talk about any of this the first time."

She shrugged. "I don't. In fact, I was hoping the second time could be . . . similar."

He looked at her, stared at her, and couldn't believe this was the same woman who'd been discussing office decor with him earlier today. But she was the same. "No," he said. "Look, we're not going to go any further with this until we talk it through. Now I know you probably want different things in life than I do, and so it's only fair that you know up front—"

"I do want different things in life," she said. "But I don't want them from you, Richard. You don't need to worry about that." She smiled at him slowly.

"What the hell is that supposed to mean?"

"Well, you're not exactly the kind of boy a girl would bring home to her mother."

"I'm *not*?"

"Oh, no. But don't take it too hard, Richard. You have your . . . talents."

He sat there, staring, not getting it. What the hell was she doing? Using his own words against him like that?

"I— Look, maybe tonight wasn't such a good idea," he said

suddenly. Why not? his mind wanted to know. This was the way he liked it. Wasn't it? One-nighters. No commitment. No expectations.

"Really?" she asked in that sexy whisper. "Well, I can go home, then. If . . . you're sure that's what you want." She got to her feet, and as she did, she let her coat fall open.

He almost fell off the bench onto the ground. She was wearing another of those sinful creations—a tiny scrap of black. He didn't see detail. Just those legs, encased in dark stockings. Those breasts, swelling over the top of the thing.

She smiled softly at him, pulled the coat around her, and tied the sash. "Good-bye, Richard," she said, and she turned and started to walk away.

He lunged after her, caught her shoulders in his hands, and spun her around. "Don't go." His own voice was hoarse, choked.

"Why not?"

He stared down at her, but no words came. He just couldn't think of a damned thing to say—or to do—except . . .

He tugged her against him and covered her mouth with his. And she parted for him, opened to him, arched against him. Hot. The inside of her mouth, her breath, her cheeks. All of her. He scooped her right up off her feet just the way he had before and carried her to the car with his mouth still clamped to hers. And then somehow he managed to open a door and tumble into the vehicle with her. Backseat. Door still open. He didn't give a damn. He landed on top of her, her back across the seat, her legs sticking out the open door, spread, and cradling him in between.

He pushed hard against her, arching his hips. She pushed back, and then she said, "No."

She said it softly, firmly. It hit his brain like ice water. "What?"

"I said no. Not here. Not like this."

He frowned, not quite understanding the woman. What was she trying to do, drive him insane? She pressed against his chest until he sat up, getting slowly off her. "Drive, Richard. Take me to your house."

"Jesus, it's too damn far."

She shrugged. "Then pick someplace closer."

He smiled down at her, liking this bossy new mood. Okay, so maybe she thought he needed a lesson. Whatever. He was going to have her, tonight, soon, wrapped around him hot and tight, and that was really the only thing he could think about right now. He got up and clambered over the front seat, got the car started. He adjusted the mirror so he could see her. Watch her. She sat up and closed the door as he pulled away. She stared back at him in that mirror, never looking away.

He had to look away, of course. He had to watch the traffic or kill them both. But he watched her, too. She'd let the coat fall open again . . . just for his viewing pleasure, he was sure.

God, she was hot.

He pulled into the parking garage of the Gable Brothers Building, got out of the car, and yanked open her door. He took her wrist and tugged her out.

"Your office?" she said, sounding scandalized.

He almost quipped, "Or yours," but stopped himself just in time. She still didn't know he knew her. And he had a feeling that was the only reason she felt free enough to play these sexy little games with him. "Yes, baby. My office." He held her hand and ran for the nearest elevator, took it straight up to the ninth floor, and ran almost all the way to his office. He could barely hold his hand still enough to get the key in the lock.

Then he flung the door open, jerked her through it, slammed it closed, and reached for her.

She took a step backward, smiling slowly. "Sit down," she told him.

He was shaking all over, burning and sweating and shivering. He went to the nearest chair, and he sat.

Sweet, innocent little Martha Jane opened the coat and let it fall to the floor. Hell, it was the cat suit. That's what she had on tonight. She reached behind her, snapped off the whiplike tail, and came toward him, sliding it around his neck. She straddled his lap and used the tail to pull his head to her for a kiss. She opened her mouth. She used her tongue.

He damn near exploded.

When she sat back again, she reached down to undo the snaps that held the little suit together between her legs. Then she unfastened his jeans, and freed him, and then she sat down again. And this time, when she did, she took him inside her. Fully, deeply.

Holding him close, she moved over him. She took her time, moving slow, and he was content to hold on and enjoy the ride. She was the best he'd ever had. The best he ever would have.

He kissed her mouth when he exploded inside her.

She screamed his name, tightened around him, convulsed and shuddered and gripped, and finally, slowly, she relaxed. Then she lifted her head lazily, looked him in the eye, and said, "I'm sorry, Richard, but I can't see you anymore."

"What?" He searched her face, panic bubbling up in his chest.

"It's like you said—we want different things out of life. And if I spend all this time with a . . . well, a casual fling, then I'll never find what I *do* want."

"How . . . how do you know *I'm* not what you want?" he asked, amazed he'd even said the words.

She smiled. "I know I'm not what you want. That's enough."

"But what if you are?"

She pressed her lips together, swallowed hard. "You don't even know me."

"No? Well let me take a stab at it, hmm?"

She shrugged as if she could care less.

"I know you were fairly inexperienced until the other night with me. I know you've never done anything like this before in your life. And I know you wouldn't have the guts to let go like this now, if you couldn't hide behind that mask." He studied her. "Am I close?"

She lowered her eyes. "Without the mask, you wouldn't even know me. And if you did, you wouldn't give me a second glance."

She got to her feet, reached for her coat, pulled it on. "This was the last time. I'm the furthest thing from what you want or need. So—"

"So you're saying good-bye."

"I'm afraid so."

He opened his mouth, then closed it, and told himself not to do anything rash. He needed to think. He needed to approach this thing just right. He didn't want to let her go—but she wouldn't be gone. Not really. "I'll find you, you know," he said.

She shook her head.

"I will. Don't be surprised if you find out that . . . that I'm not the man you think I am."

"Of course you are."

"Maybe, maybe not," he told her. "Maybe I'm not even the man I think I am."

CHAPTER EIGHT

*T*HIS is—I don't—I'm stunned."

Martha Jane stood in the reception area, staring through the open door into her office. She and Kayla had come in early Monday morning, eager to get things up and running. Martha Jane had been secretly glad, thinking there would be less chance of running into Richard this way.

He'd said he wanted to see her again. But it wasn't *her* he wanted. It was his sex kitten. His fantasy lover. And part of what he liked about her was that she expected nothing from him.

Well, she had let him know that nothing wasn't quite enough. And she imagined he probably thought he'd had a narrow escape once he'd had time to give it any thought at all.

It had been a mistake to see him again Saturday night, just as she had known it would be. She might have convinced herself that one more night of passion with Richard would be anything less than shattering to her, but she knew better. Had known better all along. It only made her ache more for him than she already had. And as for that mean streak that had driven her to strike back just a little bit—to show him two could play the "let's-not-get-serious" game—well, that had blown up in her face, hadn't it? Because she still wanted him. She'd barely slept all weekend, and she'd done some crying, too, which was totally unlike her.

Even more unlike her, she'd been thinking maybe she could stand to keep seeing him, knowing he would never commit to more than a sexual relationship. Maybe it would be worth it.

She'd been kidding herself, though. It would kill her, and she knew it. She was in love with the man.

At any rate, there had been a surprise waiting for her in her office this morning. She stood in the open doorway, blinking at the huge hunk of amethyst sitting near the bank of windows on the far side of the room. The early-morning sun slanted in on the concave stone, and its crystals glittered as if they were artificially lit from within. Or filled with captive fireflies.

"I can't believe this."

Martha Jane walked closer to the stone. It was waist-high, shaped like half an egg split lengthwise and standing on end. The inside of it was a crystal cave of sparkling amethyst. The outside was rough and gray.

"That thing is big enough to crawl inside," Kayla observed from the doorway. "But where did it come from?"

She didn't need to, but Martha Jane bent to pick up the folded sheet of notepaper that lay within the amethyst cluster. "It's beautiful, and it's exciting—*and* it's solid. No wonder you liked it so much. It's just like you." The note was signed with an elaborate "R."

"Well?" Kayla asked.

Licking her lips, Martha Jane said, "It's from Richard." Then, seeing the gleam in her best friend's eyes, she rushed on. "But it doesn't mean anything."

"If it doesn't mean anything, then there will be one just like it in my office. But I'm guessing there isn't." Kayla bounded across the room, snatched the note from Martha Jane's hand, and read it. "Well, well, well! Isn't *that* interesting?"

"He's just repeating something I said to him yesterday."

"Sure, and I'm a natural blonde. Honey, are you *sure* he doesn't know it was you behind that mask?"

Martha Jane's head came up. "Of course I'm sure. God, I couldn't look him in the eye if I wasn't!"

"Sure you could! You've obviously got the man tied up in knots, hon. You don't have a thing to feel self-conscious about."

Martha Jane shrugged. "Anyway, it's over. I told him Saturday night—"

"Told who what, Saturday night?" Richard called from behind a huge box in the doorway. Only the bottoms of his legs and the top of his head were visible.

"What in the world? Here, let me help you with that." Martha Jane rushed forward, grabbed the other end of the box, and together she and Richard lowered it to the floor. Then, straightening, she looked at him, the big box between them. "What are you doing here, Richard?"

"Errands." He smiled at her, looking less like himself than he ever had. He had circles under his eyes and whiskers shadowing his cheeks. His shirt was wrinkled and looked as if he'd been wearing it all night. "A ton of errands, actually. This was just the most recent one." He patted the box. "I was hoping to get it all set up before you arrived, but . . . well, it's been a busy weekend."

"It looks it." She wanted to go to him, smooth his tousled hair, and run her palm over his stubbly cheeks. "Are you all right, Richard?"

His grin was lopsided. "Better than I've ever been. You know, I haven't slept in . . ." He glanced at his watch. "Shoot, I don't even remember anymore."

"Why not?" She was growing more concerned by the minute. What was wrong with him?

"Did you like the rock?" he asked, smiling.

She looked at Kayla, who shrugged and shook her head.

"I love it, Richard. It's incredible and stunning and so generous, but I . . . Richard?"

He was bent over now, opening the flaps of the cardboard box and pulling stuff out of it. Long, slender tubing, and a plastic scuba diver, a miniature oyster shell, some plastic seaweed.

"What *is* all that?" Kayla squeaked.

"It's an aquarium," Richard said. "A big one, with all the trimmings. Top of the line. And I've got a whole boxful of filters and pumps and various other paraphernalia. It's still in the trunk of my car, but—"

"Richard, you're not making any sense here. What is this all about?"

He looked up, met Martha Jane's eyes, and his narrowed as they slid down her, making her feel as if he could see right through her sensible suit. "Kayla," he said, without looking away. "Would you excuse us for a second?"

"Whooo-boy," Kayla said, "I'm outta here. In fact, um, I'm going out to breakfast. I'll be back in . . . an hour?"

"Make it two," Richard said, and his eyes were dark, intense.

Martha Jane shivered when Kayla left and closed the door. He looked dangerous this way. Tired, running on no sleep. Unshaven. His shirt wrinkled. "Richard, what is this all about?"

He shrugged. "You're so good, you know that?"

"What do you mean?" She took a step backward.

He took a step forward. "I mean, you've had me jumping through hoops, you've driven me insane, and you stand here pretending to be . . . innocent. But the jig is up, Valentine. No more games. No more masks."

Blinking rapidly, she whispered, "I don't know what you're talking about."

"Don't you?"

She shook her head.

"Prove it, then."

Her throat went dry. "H-how?"

"Take off the suit, Miss Biswell."

"*What?*"

Smiling, he came closer. She backed away until she hit the desk, and still he came on, until his chest was an inch from hers. "Take it off, Martha Jane. I'm curious to know what you're wearing underneath."

He lifted a hand to her jacket, undid the button, and slid it down her shoulders. She would have resisted had she been capable of it. Instead, she froze, because he bent so close that his warm breath fanned her mouth and made her go limp.

Her hands braced on the desk behind her, her blazer pooled

around her wrists, she could only stand there as Richard unbuttoned her blouse, one button at a time. "A prim, proper woman like the one you pretend to be would have something boring under here," he murmured. "But you're not all that prim and proper, are you, Miss Biswell?"

"I—"

The blouse unbuttoned, he smiled and pushed it open, staring at the lacy black camisole. "See that?"

"Richard, I—"

"Shhh. I know, you see? I know you didn't mean what you said. You still want me. Don't you?"

Holding his gaze, helpless, she nodded.

"So, let's see what you have on for me today, hmm? What about underneath the skirt? What delicious little fantasy do you have for me down there, Valentine? Hmm?"

She couldn't speak. Without her mask, her boldness was gone.

It didn't matter. He closed his hands on her waist, lifted her until she perched on the edge of the desk, and then dropped to his knees. Before she knew what he was doing, he was lifting her skirt, poking his head right up inside it. "Oh, yeah," he whispered. "No panties at all. You read my mind." His hands shoved her thighs apart, and then he kissed her. She shivered, and threw her head back. He just shoved the skirt up higher and licked at her until she was biting her lip to keep from screaming out loud.

When he finally got to his feet again, it was only to ease her back onto the desk and climb on top of her. He pressed himself inside her, slid his hands underneath to grasp her buttocks and hold her to him as he rode her hard. She clung to him, too swept up in passion to worry about not having her mask anymore. And when her nails dug into his shoulders, and they both climaxed at once, she whispered, "I love you, Richard," in a voice gone hoarse with ecstasy.

He held her for a long time. Then slowly, he got off her and gently righted her clothes. "I haven't slept all weekend. I—you made me crazy, Martha Jane."

Maybe, she thought, he hadn't heard that final stupid declaration. If he had, he would be running for the hills by now. "How long have you known?"

He smiled at her, a lopsided, boyish grin. God, he was too damned good-looking to be going around unshaven and sleepy-eyed. It was killing her! "Did I ever tell you?" he asked. "That I always wanted an aquarium?" He finished buttoning her blouse, but left it untucked. The jacket, he tossed aside. Then he took her hand, drew her to her feet, and knelt down to smooth her skirt, sliding both his palms down over her hips, her thighs, until it was just so.

Breathless, she said, "No, I guess you never did."

"I even bought all the stuff, but I never took the time to set it up or actually start collecting fish." He shrugged, got to his feet, looked into her eyes again. "I think maybe I liked the *idea* of having one, but I was a little bit shy of all the work involved. Major commitment, keeping fish, you know." He shook his head slowly. "You know how funny that is? It's like some kind of microcosmic mirror of what's wrong with me."

"*What?*"

"Never mind. Suffice it to say, I figured since you wanted an aquarium, too, we could make it a . . . joint project."

"You did, did you?"

"Yeah. Oh, don't worry. I promise to do my share of the work. I mean, that's sort of the point."

"It is?"

He nodded. Then, studying her face, he sighed. "Look, I haven't lost my mind or had a breakdown, I swear. I'm running on adrenaline and caffeine here. And I'm a little bit worked up." He slipped his arms around her waist, bent closer to press his lips to the line of her jaw. She wanted to touch him. Hold him. Tell him that whatever had him so worked up, it was going to be okay.

Instead she just nodded slowly. "I don't think you're insane or having a breakdown," she told him.

He nodded at the boxful of fish stuff. "Once we get it set up, maybe we can go shopping for some fish. You know . . . together."

She raised her eyebrows. "You want to take me fish shopping?"

He nodded, his eyes serious. "Among other things."

She was starting to feel a hint of panic in her chest. He mustn't go saying things to make her believe he might want her for more than just sex. He mustn't. She couldn't stand the disappointment if he did.

"What . . . other things?"

Richard seemed genuinely . . . nervous. Rubbing his chin, he walked away from her as if thinking very deeply about his answer. She looked around the office, at the rock, the fish stuff. "Why are you doing all this, Richard?"

He whirled and came back to her, gripped her shoulders gently. "Because I'm a changed man. Saturday night I learned how it felt to be treated like a piece of meat. How it felt to be told that I was only good for a one-night stand, to be left longing for more from a relationship than I was allowed to want. I didn't like it. I didn't like it a bit, Martha Jane."

"I'm . . . sorry. I didn't realize it would upset you this much. I was only trying to show you—"

"How I'd been making you feel. Right, Martha Jane?"

She turned away from him and walked toward the windows. As she did, she saw something she hadn't noticed before. On the far left wall was a charcoal drawing, framed and hanging in the perfect spot. Only—it was different from the one she'd admired. Same idea, but a whole different style. A different artist. Then it hit her, and her eyes widened.

"Do you like it?" Richard asked, coming up behind her. His hands slid upward, over her shoulders, closing on them, warm and strong.

She stared at the drawing. It was a woman with three faces. And she looked like—she looked like—like *her*. Like Martha Jane. The face shown in right profile wore a mask and her hair was big and fluffy. The one shown in left profile had her hair in a tight bun and wore large glasses. But the one facing front was the most striking, because she was so simply drawn. Hair loose, yes, but hanging gently, not "done." She stood there, looking out from the wall, her eyes soft but large, and deep, and filled with love. She held out one hand, as if reaching for someone.

"It's been a long time since I made an attempt at anything artistic," he said. "But I couldn't resist."

"You . . . *you* did this?"

"Do you hate it?"

"My God, Richard, you made me . . . beautiful."

"You are beautiful," he said. "You're beautiful—even when you cover your face with a mask."

She closed her eyes.

"I knew it was you that first night," he said softly, his lips near her ear.

"You didn't!"

"Oh, yes, I did. And now, I think it's time for you to face me without any masks to hide behind. You said you loved me, Martha Jane. Did you mean it?"

"I—" She turned away, knowing that it had been the worst possible thing to say to a man like Richard. The surest way to make him bolt.

He gently turned her around to face him. "You didn't think I was going to let you turn my world upside down and then just walk away, did you?"

"Richard—Richard, I didn't mean—"

He smiled at her. "I hope you did. Because I am in love with you, Martha Jane. Valentine." He slid his arms around her waist and held her close, so her body was pressed to his. "My brother told me once that every day is Valentine's Day when you find the right woman. I didn't believe him then. But I do now."

"You do?"

"It's been running through my mind all weekend. I couldn't stop it, not by trying to forget you, not by drawing you. I didn't think I wanted . . . this. But it's the only thing I want. I just don't know why it took me so long to realize that I've been head over heels for my prim little Miss Biswell for months but was too damned dense to admit it. That's why I've been so depressed and moody and bored since you left, Martha Jane. I was missing you."

"You were?" She blinked up at him, then shook her head, terrified that this was all a mistake. An infatuation. He would change his mind in a week or a month and leave her devastated. "Richard, you're tired and confused and—"

"You going to make me beg? Fine, I'll beg." He dropped to his knees. She closed her eyes, and he took her hand, sat back a little, looked up at her. "I can be what you want," he said softly. "Solid, stable . . . I swear to God I can."

"I don't know if I can be what *you* want," she whispered.

"Martha Jane, you already are. You have been all along. You're what I was looking for in all those other women and not finding."

"I am?"

He nodded, then smiled slightly. "It's not entirely my fault, you know. You were hiding yourself from me awfully well."

She lowered her eyelids. "I didn't think I stood a chance beside the bombshells waiting in line for you."

"There won't be any more bombshells, sweetie. You nuked me for all the rest. I only want you."

Finally, she met his eyes, held them. "Do you mean that, Richard? Because I couldn't take being just one of your flings."

"Then don't be," he said. "Be . . . be my wife instead."

She smiled very slowly. "Richard . . . ?"

But he was already pulling the ring from his pocket, slipping it on her finger, pressing his lips there to seal his promise. "I mean it," he told her. "I want you to marry me. I want to love you every night, whether you're wearing a negligee or flannel pajamas. I mean it. I honestly mean it, Martha Jane."

Blinking back her tears, Martha Jane sank to her knees and into Richard's waiting arms. "I love you," she whispered. "I've loved you all along."

"Is that a yes?"

"Yes, Richard," she said. "Yes."

He sighed as if he'd been holding his breath, clasped her tight to him, and rose to his feet, picking her right up off hers. "I love you, Martha Jane!" he shouted. "You really are the best Valentine I ever got."

Awaiting Moonrise

CHAPTER ONE

MIST rose from the rain-soaked pavement and wound its way upward, tangling in the endless veils of Spanish moss. A Hollywood director couldn't have come up with a more likely setting, although Jenny supposed she should be wearing heels that would *tap-tap-tap* over the macadam and turn her ankle when she ran, instead of her royal and teal Nike cross trainers. And a flowing white dress would be more atmospheric than the jeans and loose, gauzy top. The blouse *was* white, though, and floaty enough to create the right effect. It was important to wear white. She wanted to be seen.

The plantation house was a solid half-mile back along the narrow road that meandered through the dark bayou. There wasn't a streetlight or a vehicle in sight, and the moon was full, though tough to see through the low-level fog. The air was so heavy that her skin and hair had been wet as soon as she'd left the house. Not with sweat, though that followed soon enough. Midsummer in Louisiana had the same feeling she imagined swimming in a bowl of hot soup would have.

Something rustled in the trees.

She stopped, turned to look toward the trees along the roadside, where the sound seemed to have come from, as she slowly unzipped the waist-pack that was concealed by the loose material of her blouse. She couldn't see a damned thing, though the mists seemed to move differently there.

Her hand closed around the cool metal of her flashlight, but she didn't take it out. Shining a light in the creature's eyes would only frighten it away. She let the flashlight go and dug deeper, finding the rough diamond-patterned grip of the gun instead. She tugged it out of the bag, but not out from under the soft white gauze of the blouse. If the beast saw it, would it know it for what it was? She couldn't be sure.

So she stood there, with deer scent wafting from her shoes, and she waited. Human bait.

The wind, as heavy and hot as a lover's breath, picked up, causing the mists around her feet to swirl and rise. Her heart beat faster. The grasses and brush moved—or something moved them. She strained her eyes to see. And then, in one burst of motion, the animal exploded out of the trees and raced toward her. She jerked the gun up fast, and damn near darted the wild boar before she realized what it was and stopped herself. The barrel-shaped animal, grunting and snuffling, scuttled past her and crossed the road, vanishing into the swamp on the other side.

She stood there, the tranquilizer gun still in her hands, arms outstretched as if about to fire, and felt the nervous laughter bubble up in her chest. Slowly, she lowered her head, her arms. God, she'd almost bagged herself a pig.

The low, deep growl came from behind her, and her laughter froze in her throat. It was close. Dammit, why had she let her guard down? She lifted the gun again, turning at the same time.

Too late. The thing hit her like a linebacker, bringing a set of razor-sharp claws across her chest even as her back slammed onto the hot pavement. The gun went skidding across the road. She lay there, staring up at the thing, as amazed and awestruck as she was afraid. Maybe more.

It half crouched over her, panting quickly, a soft growl emerging with every exhalation. The face was misshapen, the jaw elongated while the nose seemed abbreviated. Its face wasn't as hair-covered as she'd expected. The eyebrows were full and thick, the eyes deep set and dark. The hairline seemed to extend farther down onto the face than it would on a human, and its chin was covered in hair, like a beard. It was dark, coarse hair. Not fur, not exactly.

It had, she realized as she lay there waiting for death, beautiful eyes.

But was it human?

She forced her own eyes away from its dark brown ones, and examined the rest of its body. Hands, very humanlike, except for the thick layer of hair coating the backs of them. The palms were smooth, hairless. Claws curled from the ends of the fingers. Claws that cut, she thought, momentarily acknowledging the pain in her chest. Its torso was unclothed, muscular, hairy, with bits of tattered white material clinging here and there. Its lower extremities—wore jeans.

She blinked and looked again, but they remained. Denim jeans, torn and dirty, but there. So much for her theory that the sightings were of some previously undiscovered species. The jeans told her otherwise. Animals didn't routinely wear human clothing.

But just how human was it?

"Can you understand me?" she asked, forcing her voice to come out clearly, if not quite calmly.

The beast leaned closer, its dark eyes moving over her body. It seemed, she thought, to be looking her over as thoroughly as she'd been doing to it. But its gaze stopped on the front of her, and she glanced down and saw three bloody tears in her blouse, and in the flesh beneath.

She lifted her head, found those eyes waiting there. It bent still closer. She thought it might be catching the scent of her blood. Of her. And it was changing, even as she watched, the body altering in the darkness, the snout elongating.

"I mean you no harm," she said.

It growled loudly and leapt at her, would have landed fully upon her if she hadn't reacted instantly. She lifted both her legs and thrust her feet against its chest with all her might. Its forward momentum halted, the creature shot backward so fast that its feet—paws—left the pavement a second before its entire body landed there. It didn't look like it had before. It was a wolf now, and she wondered vaguely if it had been all along. But she knew better than to question her own senses.

She jumped to her feet, scrambled for her tranq gun and spun around with it aimed and ready.

The creature was gone. She caught a glimpse of the wolf leaping a ditch with a graceful power that took her breath away. It landed easily, never breaking its stride. The bayou and the mists soon swallowed it up.

"My God," she whispered. "It's real."

She touched the wounds on her chest, wincing in pain as she did. Damn, those cuts were painful. They were also fabulous. Physical evidence!

Looking around the road, seeing no sign of danger, she replaced the gun in her pack as she dug for the more important items. The flashlight, a mini-camera, sterile bags to collect samples. Maybe the creature had left a few hairs behind. She photographed the area, marked it with a discreet orange chalk X, noted the time. She was disappointed when she found no samples. She had been so close, too. Why the hell hadn't she reached out and plucked a few hairs when it had been leaning over her?

As she packed her stuff back up, she went still as an unearthly howl came floating on the night from somewhere far away. It was, she thought, the most heartbreaking sound she had ever heard.

At 8 a.m., when the doctor arrived at the small town's only clinic, carrying a half-full cup of coffee and looking a bit bleary-eyed, she was there waiting. He glanced at her when he walked through the reception area. She wasn't sitting, but instead pacing the waiting room. He stopped short, eying her from head to toe, and making her so self-conscious she ran a hand through her short red curls and wondered if they were standing on end.

"I hope you're the doctor," she said. *And damn,* she thought, *I really mean that.* He was the best-looking man she'd seen in six months.

He held her eyes as if he'd heard her thoughts, then turned away to glance toward the receptionist behind her desk.

"She was waiting outside when I got in, and that was a half-hour ago," the woman, whose nameplate read SALLY HAYNES, told him, shaking her head.

He looked back at Jenny again, and she shivered just a little. "If it was an emergency you should have gone to the—"

"The ER, I know. It isn't that kind of an emergency."

"What kind? Medical?"

"Could we talk in an exam room?"

He lowered his head. "Sure. Follow me."

Sally held out a fresh white lab coat, and he took it as he passed, pulling it on as he led the way to the first exam room. He tugged a stethoscope from his shirt pocket and draped it around his neck on the way. Once in the room, he nodded at the paper-covered table. "Have a seat while I wash my hands." Then he glanced at her. "I do have time to wash my hands, don't I?"

She nodded once, so he went ahead and scrubbed, dried with paper towels, tossed them, and finally turned to face her again. Then he went still, seeming surprised that she had taken off her blouse. The way he looked at her, you'd have thought she was wearing a black lace negligee instead of a serviceable white bra and a pair of blue jeans.

"What, you've never seen a half-dressed female before, Doc?"

He didn't even pretend not to look his fill. "It's just that patients usually wait until I tell them to undress before doing it. Not that I'm complaining."

She should have been offended. She really should. "I'm in a little bit of a hurry."

"Shame," he muttered. Then, frowning, he moved closer, and she thought he was finally seeing the angry red scratches across her chest. "That looks nasty. What happened?" He moved still closer, leaning in. She felt his breath across her breasts and told herself it was not turning her on.

She knew what the scratches looked like. There were three of them, deep enough in places to qualify as cuts, raked across her skin from just above the left clavicle to the upper part of the right breast.

"Something with big claws took a swipe at me."

"That much I could have guessed." He turned away from her to open a cabinet, and began setting items on the stainless steel tray beside her. Gauze pads, sterile water and alcohol, antibiotic ointment. "What was it, a dog?"

"Not exactly."

He pulled on latex gloves and began carefully cleaning the cuts. She winced as he worked, but was secretly glad of the sting. Without it, she'd have been enjoying his touch way more than she should. "So what, exactly, was it?"

"I don't know yet. But if pressed, Doc, I'd say it was a lycanthrope."

He grinned suddenly, tried not to let the chuckle escape. "You're another werewolf hunter, hmm? Come down here looking for the loup-garou?"

"I'm a professor at Dunkirk University. I'm here doing research."

"A professor of what?"

She cleared her throat. "Cryptozoology."

This time he couldn't contain the laugh. It escaped, and she flinched and shot him an angry look. He stopped in midchuckle.

"I'm sorry. It's just—you didn't really come down here to research werewolves, did you?"

"I came down to determine whether there might be a previously unknown species of mammal hiding out in the Louisiana bayou."

"Sounds so much more rational your way," he told her.

She shrugged. "Well, rational or not, something attacked me on the road last night. And I can tell you, Doc, whatever it was, it was no *known* species."

"And the moon *was* full."

"Are you making fun?"

"Just stating a fact." He frowned, more serious now. "Whatever it was, it did a number on you. This is no laughing matter. It could have been rabid."

"It wasn't."

"You can't know that for sure."

"Doesn't matter. I've been immunized."

"Against rabies?"

"Of course. I have a masters in zoology and a Ph.D. in veterinary medicine. I have been immunized against just about anything you can think of that can be transmitted from animal to human."

He took a step back, seemingly satisfied that the wound was thoroughly clean. "You're a vet, huh?"

"Mmm-hmm."

Pursing his lips, nodding slowly, he reached for the ointment. "So it's safe to say you could have patched this up yourself."

"Could have. Didn't want to."

"Why don't you stop playing games and tell me why you're really here?"

She was surprised. She felt her eyes widen as they shot to his.

He'd startled her by being so direct. "I wasn't playing games, Doctor. I had planned to come and see you anyway, and I simply thought as long as I was here, I'd get myself patched up. Okay?"

"Okay." He began smearing ointment over the cuts. She began wishing the latex gloves were not between his fingertips and her flesh. "Why were you coming to see me anyway?"

"To ask you how often you see patients with marks like the ones on my chest."

He shrugged. "I haven't seen a chest quite like yours in a long time," he said, without cracking a smile. Totally inappropriate— the way he was looking at her breasts where they swelled over the top of the bra. And yet it made her warm all over.

"You know that's not what I was asking."

He didn't look away from his work. She thought his hands were moving way more slowly than necessary, smoothing that ointment on her cuts, rubbing it in, his touch soft and erotic. "How often, Doctor?" she managed to ask. Did her voice sound slightly hoarse to him?

"Not more often than would be considered normal."

"These kinds of attacks are what you call normal?"

"Scratches are normal. People get them in numerous ways. Tangling with thorny bushes, angry cats or rambunctious dogs, falling on a lawn rake. Getting a little carried away during sex." He pushed a bra strap down over her shoulder, then pulled the cup away and downward, exposing her breast completely.

It wasn't exactly unnecessary, she told herself. The scratches did continue an inch or so beyond the fabric. What was unnecessary was the way her body reacted to his intense scrutiny, and the way her nipple tightened in the chilled air of the examining room.

When he licked his lips, she almost moaned.

"Did any of those other patients with scratches ever claim they were attacked by a werewolf?" she asked, but her voice was barely more than a whisper.

His eyes still on her breast, he put a little more ointment on his gloved hand. "Not a one. Until now."

She blinked slowly. "You wouldn't lie to me about that, now, would you?"

"Not on your life." He met her eyes, held them as his hand moved to massage the ointment over her breast. He had, she thought, beautiful eyes. Dark and intense and full of sexual promises that didn't need to be spoken aloud. His fingers brushed her nipple and she bit her bottom lip.

"So do you suppose you'll turn into a werewolf now, too?"

His voice, too, had lowered, turned rough.

He was teasing her now, with his words as well as his fingers, and she wasn't objecting. Shivers tiptoed up her spine. "I don't know. The mythology says it has to be a bite for that to happen, but—"

"He didn't bite you, then?"

"N-no."

"Damn stupid werewolf, if you ask me." Again his fingers flicked across her nipple.

She sucked in a breath and drew back, just a little. With more regret than she could even believe, she tugged the bra's cup back into place.

He sighed as if he regretted it, too. "So just what does a hundred-pound redhead do with a werewolf, once she finds it?"

"Study it. Talk to it, if that's possible. Try to learn what it is, how much of the folklore is true and how much isn't."

He smirked a little, lowering his eyes.

"I take it you don't approve of those goals?"

He shrugged. "Lie back and I'll bind you up." He caught her quick look. She knew damn well he'd intended the double entendre. "Bandage your cuts," he corrected.

She lay down on the table, and he unrolled soft gauze over the ointment-daubed scratches. "What would *you* do?"

He smoothed tape over the gauze to hold it in place. "I'm a doctor," he said. "I suppose I'd try to help it, if that were possible. Cure it, if that was what it wanted. And I'd keep its secrets, either way. Not write them up for some scientific journal and my own fame and glory."

"Is that what you think I'm after? Fame and glory?"

"Isn't it?"

"No," she said. He finished with the bandages, never baring her breast again. She sat up, and he handed her the blouse.

"Well, that's good to know." He didn't sound as if he believed her. And he watched her while she pulled her blouse on, watched her while she buttoned it.

"Thank you for patching me up," she said.

"It was my pleasure." He put extra emphasis on the word "pleasure."

"Don't be too sure about that."

He met her eyes, silently acknowledging that he got the message, loud and clear.

CHAPTER TWO

J ENNY walked back to the sprawling white plantation house and went inside to find the crew—three grad students who thought they were smarter than her and one department head who knew he was—gathered in the dining room, munching on pastries and slugging down coffee.

"Where have you been all morning?" Professor Hinkle asked in his usual tone—the one that always seemed to insinuate something, never quite letting on what.

"Interviewing some of the locals in town. No hits, so far." She wasn't about to tell him about her lycanthropic encounter and subsequent visit to the hotter-than-hell doctor. He wouldn't believe her about the werewolf anyway. No, not until she had *proof*.

"Did you see anything last night?" Carrie asked. She was the most gullible. Believed everything until it was proven false, when the ideal cryptozoologist practiced the opposite. She had a long way to go.

"Wild boar," she replied. "Ran out of the woods at me so suddenly, I almost darted it."

Carrie grinned. Mike and Toby exchanged smirks that said only a woman would be so jumpy. Right, she'd like to see one of the "twins" come face-to-face with that thing from last night. They'd have jumped right out of their matching chinos and Ralph Lauren polo shirts. They were unrelated, but wore nearly identical ultrashort, slightly gelled hairstyles, one a little blonder than the other. The two were practically clones as far as she was concerned. Not only in style choices, but in attitude and arrogance. She was well aware they'd only signed up for this program because they thought it would give them four easy credits. Or maybe they were both planning a masters thesis that would attempt to debunk her profession.

They wouldn't succeed.

"So, how's the research coming?" she asked, turning her attention to the eager pupil.

"I found tons of stuff!" Carrie said, reaching with one hand for the notebook that was never far from her side and flipping her expertly cut hair with the other.

"Yeah. Fairy tales and folklore," Toby sneered. "Nothing legitimate."

"Folklore is what led us to the giant gorillas, Toby."

"Here we go with the giant gorillas again."

"Until scientists began taking the local legends seriously, no one believed they existed, but they do. They'd been living in the jungles for centuries, and only those natives who lived among them knew the truth. No one believed them, just as no one believes people today when they see something strange and have the nerve to tell someone about it."

"Right."

Carrie shot the boys a killing look and opened her notebook to a page of neatly typed text. "I've got reams of stuff here. Most of the sources include legends about how to kill them with a silver bullet, but some take that a lot further. They have to be decapitated and burned afterward."

Jenny shot her a look. "Carrie, if we find a specimen we certainly won't be looking for ways to kill it."

"I figured—you know, just in case."

Jenny moved closer, taking Carrie's notebook from her and carrying it to the table. She grabbed a beignet from the tray of pastries on the table, filled an empty china cup with fragrant, steaming coffee, and flipped through pages.

"To become a werewolf," she read.

"Oh, great," Toby said. "Recipes."

Jenny smiled a little, because it was close. " 'On the night of the dark moon, or the third night of the full, betake thyself to a place far from the haunts of man—deep in the forest. There, draw a circle no less than seven feet in diameter, and within it draw another of three feet. Within the smaller circle, erect a tripod of iron, and from it suspend a cauldron of iron, and fill the cauldron with water taken from a stream in which three wolves have been seen to drink. Build a fire beneath, and when the water boils, add to it any three of the following herbs: blind bluff, devil's eye, bittersweet, devil's dung, beaver poison or opium.' "

"I daresay," Professor Hinkle remarked, "a few whiffs of the steam from that brew might convince any of us we'd become a werewolf."

Jenny almost gasped. Had the old sourpuss actually made a joke?

"The only real ingredient in there is the opium," Toby said. "That other stuff is made up."

"Oh, you're dead wrong there," Jenny corrected. "These are folk names. Blind bluff is poppy. Devil's eye is henbane. Bittersweet is solanum. Devil's dung is aesophetida, named quite aptly for its smell."

"And beaver poison is hemlock," Carrie put in. "Keep reading, Professor Rose. It's fascinating."

She shrugged. "After that it says to strip naked and rub your body all over with an ointment made from," she glanced at the page to find her place, "the fat of a freshly killed feline, mixed with opium, camphor, and anise seed."

"Clever," the professor said. "The camphor would open the pores, allowing one to absorb the opium more quickly."

"Then 'wrap thy loins in the hide of a wolf, speak the charm, and await the advent of the unknown.'" She nodded. "How many of you have taken anthropology classes?"

All hands went up, including the professor's, though his came with a sarcastic look.

"Good. Now, think back and tell me what this recipe reminds you of."

"Oh, oh, I know!" Carrie said. "It's just like what some shamans of various cultures do. They ingest a hallucinogenic and go on a journey into the other realms. Shape-shifting is often a part of the experience."

Jenny nodded. "Good. Any other similar examples?"

Mike raised a reluctant hand, then looked at it sheepishly and spoke up. "The so-called flying ointments used by witches?"

"Bingo. Animal-fat base, fly agaric being the most commonly used active ingredient. So what does this tell us about this particular account of turning oneself into a werewolf? Where did this author get his information?"

They looked at each other blankly.

"He got it from someone who was into magic. A shaman or sage or village witch. What he's talking about is magic, not reality. We are scientists. Is the creature we're looking for something that was created by cat fat and opium? No. The only things created by that blend were hallucinations. What is our werewolf, then?"

She held out her hands, palms up.

All together, the three students intoned, "A previously undiscovered species."

"Precisely. So what can we get out of this?"

"Not a hell of a lot?" Toby suggested.

"Not a lot, but some. We can learn that the creature in question dwells in very deep forests, avoids humans when possible, and is somewhat manlike in appearance. See, that's the key. Take the folklore, sift out the impossible, and take a look at what's left. The solid stuff that can lead you to the truth."

"But, Professor Rose," Carrie asked, "what if the werewolf really was created by some kind of curse, some kind of magic?"

"Carrie, you're a science student. There is no such thing as magic. The sooner you get that through your head, the better you'll do." She shut the notebook. "Now, I want you to go through these notes, pick out all the fantasy and magic, and compile what's left for me."

"I'd like copies of those notes as well, Carrie," Dr. Hinkle added. "Before you do any deleting."

"What about us?" Mike asked.

"You and Toby do some more canvassing of the locals. Ask them what they've heard about the loup-garou. Tape-record their answers so you don't inadvertently leave out something I can use," Jenny told him.

"And what do you plan to spend *your* morning doing, Professor Rose?" Hinkle asked.

"I'm going out into the woods to see if I can find any sign of an unknown species. You're welcome to come along, Professor, but you'll need good hiking shoes and a backpack for supplies. I plan to go deep into the forest, and the terrain won't be gentle."

" 'Far from the haunts of man?' " he asked, smirking.

"Exactly."

It was, of course, an outright lie. She was going into the woods along the roadside, where she'd encountered that beast last night. She might be able to see clues in daylight that she hadn't seen in the darkness. She didn't want or need Hinkle looking over her shoulder, second-guessing her every move and constantly looking for something to use against her.

It would suit him just fine if her proposal of a cryptozoology department at Dunkirk University—a department she proposed to head up herself—be annihilated as soon as possible. He hated the idea.

He hated her.

"You coming?" she asked, glancing at him.

"Of course not. You know better. I'll just stay here and read through your notes."

She smiled as if that thought didn't make her nervous. It shouldn't. Like Al Capone's accountant, she kept two sets of books. No one saw her private thoughts.

"I'll see you later then," she said, turning to go.

"Don't forget the feline fat," he called after her, then he chuckled at his own lame joke, while Toby and Mike laughed obediently.

Puppies, Jenny thought. She would have called them were-pups, but that would imply they were half-man, and she didn't think they qualified.

She jogged up the stairs to her rooms to change clothes before heading back to the place where she'd seen—what she'd seen last night.

Mamma Louisa was in the bedroom, busily making the bed, her head wrapped in a pure white turban, her blouse and skirt just as white. Spotless, bleached and in stark contrast to her dark skin.

Women of her size didn't wear a lot of white up north. Jenny thought it was a shame. Mamma Louisa looked good. Big and beautiful and proud. She carried herself like royalty.

She looked up when Jenny walked in and sent her a smile. "I can come back later," she said, the bayou thick in her voice.

"No, no, don't stop. I'm just grabbing a few things and heading back out."

"All right, then. How is de research goin'?"

"Fine. Better than fine, actually." Jenny turned to the dresser, tugged open a drawer, and found a T-shirt. Then she peeled her blouse over her head, facing the mirror.

"*Osé, osé, osé,*" Mamma Louisa whispered urgently, and when

Jenny met her eyes in the mirror, she saw that the other woman's gaze was on her own bandaged chest. "What happened to you last night, *chère?*"

Dammit, how could she be so careless? She pulled the T-shirt over her head quickly. "Nothing—it's just a scratch. I brushed up against a thorn tree."

"Did you, now?" The woman eyed the blouse that was lying on the floor beside the bed—white fabric with a few tears and some dried blood. She took a single step toward it, and Jenny rushed forward, getting there first and snatching it off the floor and wadding it up.

"Somethin' there you don't want me to see, child?"

"I'm not used to being waited on, Mamma Louisa. It makes me uncomfortable to have someone picking up after me."

"You prefer to tend your own bedroom from now on, then?"

"Yes. Yes, actually, I do."

Mamma shrugged. "Well, I be paid good money to keep the house and do the cookin' for the guests here, Miss Jenny. But if it makes you uneasy, I stay clear of your room . . . and your secrets."

"I have no secrets."

She nodded. "I'll let Eva Lynn know, so she'll stay out of your rooms as well." She started for the door, leaving the bed half-made, but when she reached the door, she paused.

"There be things out there, *chère*. Things you would never believe. Things that ought to be left alone."

Blinking out of the shock those words caused, Jenny raced forward after Mamma Louisa left the room and closed the door behind her.

She yanked the door open and lunged into the long corridor. "Wait. What do you know about this?"

But Mamma Louisa was nowhere in sight.

CHAPTER THREE

J ENNY knelt on the spongelike ground and forcibly resisted the urge to release a shriek of joy. In front of her, clear as day, was a footprint sunken into the moist earth. It was too large and too oblong to belong to an animal, she thought. The creature hadn't been a wolf when it had left this track, but it hadn't been a man, either. She supposed the print might belong to a bear, though that would be more rounded. Perhaps a gorilla, but there were no gorillas running wild in the bayou. None she knew of, at least. She would run it through the computer to make sure, and she was trying hard not to jump to conclusions in the meantime. It was tough, though, to maintain her scientific skepticism in the face of such a discovery.

This could be major.

She shrugged off her backpack, unzipped it, and removed supplies. She mixed the powdered plaster with bottled water until it was just the right consistency, then carefully she brushed loose bits of grass and dirt from the print. Finally, she poured the plaster into it and stood back to wait for it to harden.

As she waited, she looked around. She stood in a wooded area several yards from the road. She'd started off in the direction she thought the creature had come from last night, then moved in a half-circle around the spot where she'd first seen it, increasing the size of her search area, inspecting the ground and trees for any sign at all of wildlife. And she'd found it, too. A raven feather. The tracks of a wild pig, probably the one she'd encountered last night. A few bristly hairs stuck in the bark of a tree, probably where that same pig had scratched a pesky itch. And near the place where the swamp met the dry land, a long, smooth patch of mud that was probably a gator slide.

And then, the footprint.

Kneeling, she checked the plaster. Still wet.

The sound of a vehicle's motor brought her head up again, and as she searched for the source, she frowned. It wasn't coming from the road, which was behind her, but from somewhere ahead. Was there another road skirting this patch of swamp and woods?

As she strained to listen, the motor cut off, then a door slammed.

Someone was out there. She gathered a few large, leafy plants and laid them over her plaster cast to keep it out of sight, then shouldered her pack and started forward, deeper into the woods. Fifty yards, then sixty, and just when she thought she was going to find nothing, she saw it. A square shape within the trees, almost perfectly camouflaged—a log cabin.

Frowning, she moved closer, peering through the trees until she had a clear view of the little house. It was charming, with a cobblestone chimney and green painted window shutters, with moon-shaped cutouts in each of them. The door was green, too, a deep, piney color that blended well with the surrounding foliage.

The car in the driveway was a familiar one—the same dark-brown jeep she'd seen when she'd left the doctor's office this morning. Frowning, she double-checked the plates, saw the MD tag on the corner.

"Did you come for me?" a deep voice asked.

The voice came from right behind her and startled her so much she nearly jumped out of her skin as she spun around. He stood there, looking at her, not even cracking a smile.

"What are you doing here, Professor Rose?"

She released the breath she'd sucked in before it could burst her lungs. "Sheesh, you scared the daylights out of me."

"That's what happens, I suppose, when you are caught sneaking around on private property."

"I wasn't sneaking around! I was working. And what are you doing out here, anyway, making a house call?"

He shook his head slowly, holding her eyes. "I came home for lunch. I do that sometimes."

Jenny licked her lips and tried to calm her racing heart. "You . . . live here?"

"And you don't. So again, I have to ask, what are you doing here?"

He seemed awfully irritated for someone who'd seemed as into her as he had earlier. She couldn't hide her disappointment. "Look, I didn't know it was private property. There are no signs—"

He pointed, and she turned her head to see a POSTED: NO TRES-PASSING sign tacked to a nearby tree.

"Okay, so I wasn't looking for signs, or maybe I would have seen them."

"Then what were you looking for?"

She didn't answer.

"The loup-garou?" She didn't miss the sarcasm loaded onto the word. "They only come out at night, Professor Rose. But I would have thought a woman of your expertise would know that."

"That's what the folklore says. I don't take anything as fact until I've found proof of it, though."

He nodded slowly. "So is that what you're out here looking for? Proof?" He narrowed his eyes. "Or is this where you had your . . . encounter last night?"

"Not far from here," she said. "Out on the road."

"I see."

She drew a deep breath, then sighed. "I've really pissed you off, haven't I? I'm really sorry about the trespassing, Doctor . . ." She searched her memory for his last name. She was sure she'd seen or heard it this morning, but—

"La Roque," he said.

"Right. La Roque. It's not my habit to traipse around on private property. It really isn't. I always ask permission before walking on private land. I insist my students do the same. I just—I was overzealous and forgot my protocol." She held his eyes, hoping he could see the sincerity in hers.

He studied her face as if weighing her words. When he spoke again, he said the last thing she expected to hear. "You want to come in? Join me for lunch?"

For some reason she thought of Little Red Riding Hood and the

Big Bad Wolf. At least he didn't say he wanted to have her for
lunch, she thought grimly. She wanted to get back to her plaster
cast, which should be hard enough by now, but he lived here. He
could have seen or heard something, especially if the creature fre-
quented this area. She couldn't pass up the opportunity to pick his
brain, and she thought he knew it.

Besides, now that he'd decided to accept her apology, that look
was creeping back into his eyes. The one that heated her blood.

"Sure," she said at last. "I'm kind of surprised you would ask."

"You shouldn't be. Or didn't you get the message back there in
my office that I would like to see you again while you're in town?"

She licked her lips. "I . . . yeah, I did."

With a nod, he moved past her, leading the way out of the trees
and into the clearing that surrounded his cabin. She noticed that the
long driveway angled back out, probably to the road. She scanned
the ground as they walked, straining her eyes in search of any other
odd tracks, but the ground was hard and dry. Not a good medium
for footprints.

He opened the door, then stood aside to let her enter first. She
did, and stopped just inside, looking around at the cozy cabin. The
living and dining rooms were combined in one large, open space,
with a cobblestone fireplace at one end. The room was open to the
peak, log rafters at intervals. A loft took up half of the upper part,
its floor forming the ceiling of the small kitchen.

"This is a great cabin."

"It suits me."

"Very private, out of the way."

"That's what I like best about it." He walked into the kitchen, opened the fridge, and began taking items out of it. "I'm having a ham sandwich. That okay with you?"

"Fine, if you hold the ham."

"What?" He looked at her, puzzled.

"I'm a vegetarian."

He blinked slowly. Then, finally, he smiled. It was like a light dawning on his face, and it reached his eyes. "That's almost funny. A vegetarian werewolf hunter."

"I'm no hunter, Dr. La—"

"Call me Samuel. We don't stand much on formality in these parts." He yanked tomatoes and lettuce out of the fridge, a brick of cheese, a jar of locally produced gourmet mayonnaise, and a package of deli-sliced ham.

"Samuel. Is that what your patients call you?"

"Only the ones I all but seduce during an exam," he said softly.

She shot him a look. His eyes were smoky. "And are there a lot of those?"

"You were the first. Should I apologize for being so far out of line?"

Holding his gaze, she shook her head slowly.

"That's good, because I wouldn't mean it if I did."

She had to avert her eyes, it was getting so hot, and the way his hard, strong hand was cupping the tomato was making her shake. "So what do your patients call you?" she asked, just to break the tension.

"Mostly they call me Doc Rock. They think it's funny."

"But you don't?"

He shrugged. "Call me Samuel."

"Okay. So Samuel, were you home last night?"

He put her sandwich together first, slicing hunks from a huge loaf of bread, and laying them on a paper plate before adding the mayo, veggies, and cheese. "What time?" he asked, not even glancing at her as he worked.

"Must have been around nine or a little after."

He nodded, putting the top slice of bread on the sandwich, slicing it diagonally, setting the plate aside, and beginning work on his own. "Is that what time you bumped into the werewolf?"

"That's what time I encountered an unknown species of mammal. What it is remains to be determined."

He nodded slowly, finishing his sandwich and then bringing both plates to the table and setting them down. "I was sound asleep. No witnesses of course."

"You live alone, then?" she asked.

He met her eyes, a little spark appearing in their dark-brown depths. "Yeah. You?"

"Yeah. I mean, I do when I'm home. Right now I'm sharing a house with three grad students and a doctor of zoology with an attitude."

"The Branson Estate, right?"

She nodded.

"Have you seen anything . . . interesting there yet?"

Frowning, she searched his face. "Like what?"

He turned away, returning the veggies and meat to the fridge and removing two cold beers while he was there, opening them both. He didn't answer, only shrugged.

"Come on, Sam, spill it."

"Samuel." He sat down, handed her a bottle of beer, took a swig of his own. "I'd rather show you than tell you."

"Now you're just teasing me. Not to mention changing the subject."

"I didn't see or hear anything out of the ordinary last night, Jenny."

She warmed a little at his use of her first name. "Oh." She took a bite of her sandwich.

"Aren't you going to ask me the rest?"

She chewed, swallowed, washed the food down with a swig of beer. "What do you mean?"

"You know exactly what I mean. You want to know if I changed under the light of the full moon, went out on the hunt. You want to know if I chased a wild boar out of the woods, then changed my mind about my prey when I caught a glimpse of you out there, all alone."

She swallowed hard, her blood having gone cold. "That's silly."

"Is it?"

She shrugged, lowering her gaze. "D-did you?"

He licked his lips. "What makes you think I'd remember it if I had?"

She shrugged and looked away, but when she looked back again he was probing her eyes with his.

"You really shouldn't walk that road alone at night, Jenny," he said. "It's not playing fair."

"What . . . what do you mean?"

He reached across the table, stroked a little path over her cheek with the tip of one finger. "You're beautiful, young, tender . . . I don't know a wolf who could resist just a little taste."

Blinking fast, shivering from the power of that touch—just one finger trailing over her skin shouldn't make her shiver like that!— she lowered her eyes. "Are you coming on to me, Samuel?"

He drew a deep breath, lowered his hand. "As hard as I can, Jenny. Do you mind?"

Lifting her eyes again, she met his. He was smiling now, that intense, almost predatory look gone. "You're handsome, and single, and a doctor. Why would I mind?"

His smile grew. "This is unusual for me. I don't usually get to see a woman naked before asking her out."

"I was only half naked."

"Well, there's always the follow-up appointment."

She laughed softly, warming to his teasing tone. "Tell me again that you really don't behave this way with all your patients."

"If I did, I wouldn't have a license for long. No, Jenny, I'm not nearly this unprofessional. I swear it. I guess there's just something about you." He smiled again, slowly this time. "You bring out the beast in me."

She tried to laugh it off, but a chill raced right up her spine. She returned to eating her sandwich, and he watched her. Watched every bite she took, watched her chew, watched her swallow and lick her lips. He watched her like no one had ever watched her before. When she put the beer bottle to her lips and tipped it up to drink, his eyes were glued to her mouth, and she felt almost stripped naked the way they looked at her.

He made every single part of her body tingle with awareness, all without even touching her. Those eyes—they were powerful.

She set the bottle down. "I should go."

"You haven't agreed to go out with me yet."

She thought maybe she'd rather stay in with him, but she couldn't very well say so. "How about tonight?"

He nodded. "I'll be at your place at six. We'll have dinner. And maybe I'll show you some of the secrets of the Branson Estate."

"There's a full moon tonight," she whispered. "I really should be out patrolling, keeping an eye out for the werewolf."

"The moon rises at nine twenty-two tonight. I promise I'll kiss you goodnight long before then."

Her stomach knotted. "What makes you think I'm going to let you kiss me?"

"Oh, I'm going to kiss you. Consider yourself forewarned."

His eyes were on her mouth, and she was fighting the urge to lean across the table and press it to his. She pushed her chair away from the table, got to her feet. "I really have to go." Because if she stayed here much longer, she was going to start tearing off her clothes.

"Have a good afternoon, Jenny. I'll see you at six."

She started for the door, then paused. "Samuel, the others—the grad students and Dr. Hinkle—they don't know about what happened last night. I'd just as soon keep it that way."

"You didn't tell them?" he asked, getting to his feet, coming with her to the door. "Why not?"

She shrugged. "I wanted to have proof first."

"You think they won't believe you."

"I don't know if they would or not. Just—don't say anything about it if you see any of them tonight, okay?"

"Your secret's safe with me," he murmured. Then he opened the door and was distracted by something beyond her. When she turned and saw the giant dog loping toward them, she almost jumped. Then she looked again and realized it wasn't a dog at all. It was a large black wolf.

"Mojo! There you are. You're late for lunch," Samuel called.

She stepped out of the way as the wolf raced past her into the house and leapt on Samuel, standing on its hind legs, paws to his chest. Samuel ran his hands through the animal's lush, deep fur.

"My pet, Mojo."

"He's a wolf."

"Just garden variety, I swear."

She nodded, patting the dog on the head with a hesitant hand before turning to go.

"See you later, Jenny."

"Thanks for lunch." She left the cabin in a rush, hurried back into the woods, and, as soon as she was out of sight, stopped to lean back against a tree, hug her arms, close her eyes, and ask herself just when in her life she had ever been as turned on as she had been just now. He had barely touched her. My God, she was trembling.

She took a few breaths, tried to steady her frayed, tingling nerves, and finally got moving again, heading back to the site where she'd left her plaster to dry.

When she got there, the leaves she'd placed over the footprint were gone. The plaster was missing as well, and the footprint itself had been smeared beyond recognition.

CHAPTER FOUR

WHEN she returned to the plantation house, she crept in quietly, using a side door and hoping not to encounter anyone on the way to her rooms. She was upset, shaken, and still trying to remember the events of the day exactly as they'd happened. First, she'd created the plaster cast. Second, she'd heard the vehicle. Third, she'd moved away from her precious footprint, leaving it unguarded, in order to find the source of the noise, and she'd crept up on the little cabin in the woods, and the by-then-silent Jeep. And fourth, Samuel La Roque had come up behind her.

Behind her.

Why hadn't he just gotten out of his Jeep and gone into his house? It wasn't as if she'd made any noise that would have alerted him to her presence. What had possessed him to creep into the woods, past her, and then come up behind her? And most important of all, had he been the one who'd sabotaged what might have been the most important discovery of her career?

She moved through the kitchen, where Eva Lynn was mixing some thick, fragrant batter in a big metal bowl. She smiled hello, her face a younger version of her mother's flawless complexion, her body more slender and willowy. Like her mother, she dressed all in white, right to the turban on her head. She didn't say a word, sensing, perhaps, that Jenny wished to slip in unseen. She just nodded knowingly and returned her attention to her batter.

Jenny pushed open the swinging door to the back stairs and took them up to the second floor. The stairs continued on to the third floor, where Eva Lynn and Mamma Louisa lived. But Jenny stopped at the second-floor landing, pushed open the door, and stepped into the massive hall, with its black and red velvet runner, its gold-painted stands, mirrors, and vases, and its mini-chandeliers dangling every few yards from the high ceilings. She crept along the hallway to her room, wiping sweat from her brow. No AC in the hallways. Just the rooms themselves. The hallways were like saunas, almost as thick with wet heat as the outdoors.

She stopped outside the door to her room. It was standing slightly open, and she was certain she had closed it when she'd left.

Frowning, Jenny pushed the door gently, opening it a little farther. Dr. Hinkle sat at the small table in the sitting room portion of her suite, squinting at the screen of her laptop, which hadn't been left on.

She stepped inside and cleared her throat.

He looked up fast, clearly startled. For just an instant, guilt clouded his pinched face, but it vanished just as quickly. "Have a pleasant expedition?" he asked, as if he hadn't been doing anything so much as out of the ordinary, much less dead wrong.

"What the hell are you doing in my room?"

He lifted his brows. "Going over your notes, supervising your handling of this project, which is exactly what I was sent here to do, Professor Rose."

"You could do that without invading my privacy and going through my personal things."

"How?" he asked with an innocent shrug that was patently false. "The files are on the computer, and the computer was in here."

"I would be happy to provide you with a copy of all my files on diskette or CD, whichever you prefer. All you have to do is ask. But my room, Dr. Hinkle, is off-limits."

"I am the ranking scientist on this mission," he reminded her. "Not to mention the head of the department."

"But how long would you be if I were to call the dean right now and tell him I caught you sneaking around in my bedroom?" She smiled slowly. "Sexual harassment is such an ugly term. I'd hate to use it if I didn't have to."

He lowered the lid on the laptop while rising to his feet. "You win, this round at least. I'll stay out of your rooms."

"I think I'll keep them locked from now on, just to make sure."

"One would almost think you had something to hide, Professor Rose."

She stepped aside, opening her door wider so he could leave.

"Why are there password-protected files on your hard drive?"

She shrugged. "Those are my diaries. I fill those files with romantic daydreams and other girlish things that wouldn't interest you in the least."

"Why am I certain you're lying?"

"Maybe you just have a suspicious mind. At any rate, it's no concern of mine. I'd like to shower and change clothes now, if you don't mind. . . ."

"What did you find on your expedition this morning?"

She met his eyes and kept her gaze steady and strong. "Not a thing."

He smirked, then turned and left her bedroom. She closed the door, intending to do exactly what she'd told him she would do, take a shower and rinse away the sticky heat of the bayou. But as she started across the room, something crunched under her shoes, making her look down. Mud, dried mud. Cussing silently, she heeled off her shoes and wished she had taken them off when she'd first come into the house. Shame on her for tracking up the place like that. She left her shoes near the door and started across the room again, but more dried mud crumbled under her socks, and she realized it was scattered in places where her muddy shoes had never been.

Narrowing her eyes, she scanned the sitting room, and then the bedroom floor, seeing bits of it everywhere. That nosy old buzzard had been all through her rooms. What the hell was he looking for?

And where had he been that he'd managed to get swamp mud on his boots?

Maybe it hadn't been Samuel La Roque who'd sabotaged and stolen her evidence today, after all.

On Saturdays, Mamma Louisa and Eva Lynn went off duty at noon and didn't have to work again until Monday morning. When there were guests in residence, the two spent all Saturday morning cooking and baking and shopping to be sure there was plenty of food in the house while they were off duty. After all, this was Louisiana: there wasn't much that was more important to a host than keeping the guests well fed.

So they were already gone when Jenny came down the stairs at 5:50 p.m. She'd spent the afternoon making notes of everything that had happened that day and storing them in one of the password-protected files on her laptop. She'd located the key to her suite of rooms, hanging from a hook just inside the bedroom door, and she'd locked the rooms up when she'd left.

She thought her privacy would be safe tonight. It had better be.

"Wow," Carrie said when she reached the bottom of the stairs. "You look great. What's the occasion?" She wiggled her eyebrows. "Hot date?"

"What are you talking about?" She glanced down at her clothes, a simple tank-style dress in white cotton: a belt made of turquoise beads hung loosely around her waist and dipped downward at one side; a matching strand of the big turquoise stones around her throat, and one at each ear; flat, brown sandals that didn't go with anything, and no nylons at all. It was too hot for nylons.

"You put your hair up," Carrie said, nodding toward the normally wild red curls that Jenny had scooped into a comb. They tumbled from it like a waterfall, but were at least out of her eyes. "And . . . you're wearing makeup."

"I am not wearing makeup. What would be the point? It would only melt off in ten minutes."

She was lying. She'd applied a very light touch of shadow, slightly darker than flesh tone, and a coat of mascara. She'd darkened her lips with tinted lip gloss that tasted like cherries, and told herself it was because *she* liked the taste.

"So who's the lucky guy?"

She shrugged and was saved from having to answer when the twins walked in from the kitchen, each carrying a plate of leftovers. They stopped when they saw her, and Mike said, "Holy shit," and Toby said, "Are you wearing anything under that?"

"Keep it up, you two, and I'll toss you out on your asses without a credit to show for it."

They grinned, exchanged glances, shrugged, and continued on their way.

"This is strictly business," she told Carrie, who was now eying the dress as if she too wondered what was underneath. "This guy lives near . . . one of the areas where our creature has allegedly been sighted. I am having dinner with him so I can pick his brain, and that's all."

"Sure it is. Is he gorgeous?"

Jenny pursed her lips. "Where is Dr. Hinkle, anyway?"

"Took his dinner up to his room. Said he needed quiet time tonight. And I'm not gonna say a word to him about this, because it's none of his business. But I wouldn't count on the same from those two morons. So *is* he gorgeous?"

The doorbell chimed. Carrie spun around and ran for it so fast her hair flew like a comet's tail behind her. She jerked the heavy door open without even asking who was there, and stood there blinking up at Samuel. "Yep. He is," she said.

"Pardon me?" he asked.

"Nothing," she said quickly, and stepped aside. "Come on in."

He did, then he saw Jenny coming across the room toward him, and he stopped moving, maybe even stopped breathing. He just stared at her, and when his eyes slid down the soft, clingy dress, she got the feeling he didn't have to wonder what she wore underneath. She got the feeling he knew what was under there. Or more accurately, what wasn't.

"Hello, Jenny," he said. But the tone of his voice and the look in his eyes said more.

"Hi." Since when did she speak in a throaty whisper?

"You look—" He shook his head, licked his lips.

"Thanks."

He slid a hand around her bare upper arm and led her out the door. As soon as they were out of earshot, he leaned close to her. "Hungry?"

"Yeah, I am."

"For food?"

She looked at him quickly, and he gave her an evil smile. " 'Cause the way you look tonight, Jenny, I'm thinking I'd be happy with you as the main course."

"Let's just start with dinner, Sam."

"Samuel."

"Right." He opened the passenger door of his Jeep and she slid inside. He watched her move, stared at her legs, then leaned in so close she thought he might kiss her right there, only to buckle the seat belt around her.

The breath stuttered out of her.

"You smell like cherries," he whispered. "I love cherries." Then he closed her door and went to his own, got behind the wheel, and drove.

CHAPTER FIVE

⦿⦿

*T*HE restaurant was quiet and dark, even though the sun hadn't yet set outside. The dinner rush hadn't begun, but for the doctor, a table was ready and waiting in a dim corner where not another table was occupied. Candles glowed on the table, and soft music wafted from unseen speakers.

She noticed when Samuel met the waiter's eyes, nodded, and mouthed the word "perfect."

The waiter held out her chair for her, and Samuel stood until she was seated. Then he took his own seat and ordered wine. The way the candlelight lit his eyes was almost eerie. They glowed.

"This is a beautiful restaurant," she said, trying to break the tension that seemed to hover in the air between them. The car had been filled with it.

"For a beautiful woman."

She smiled a little. "You don't waste any time, do you?"

"I don't believe in wasting time. I used to. Used to wait for things to happen at their own pace and try to be patient, and calm. Keep things . . . toned down."

"And that changed?"

He nodded.

"Why?"

With a little shrug, he said, "Because I changed, I guess. I learned the thrill of going after what I wanted, no holds barred. And of living life in a way that lends itself to relishing every single moment. There's a lot to be said for instant gratification."

"That might be true. But what happens when you can't get what you want?"

He smiled slowly. "I always get what I want."

The waiter returned with the wine, showed Samuel the bottle, then poured a bit into his glass. Samuel sniffed it, swirled it, tasted it, and then gave a nod. The waiter filled both glasses and left the bottle, in its ice-filled silver bucket, on the table.

"Try the wine."

She took a sip. "It's good."

"No. Not like that. Experience the wine, Jenny. Smell it, taste it. Feel it sliding over your tongue and down your throat—relish the moment."

She lifted her glass again.

"Close your eyes, think of nothing but the wine. Open your senses."

She did as he said, trying to focus everything on the wine, though it was difficult with the man sitting across from her, absorbing her attention in a way no wine would ever do. She smelled the wine, let its scent fill her, then took a slow sip and held it in her mouth to taste it thoroughly before swallowing. The wine's taste remained on her tongue even as its warmth spread through her belly.

"Mmm." She opened her eyes to see his fixed on her face.

A throat cleared nearby, and Jenny looked up to see the waiter standing ready with two menus in his hands. "May I tell you about our specials?" he asked.

Samuel let his eyes tell her to answer for them both. She said, "No, I know what I want. I've been dying for some authentic gumbo. Do you make a vegetarian version?"

"Of course. A wonderful choice," he said, then turned to Samuel.

"Steak. Rare."

"And which of our sides do you want with that?"

"None. Just bring the steak."

The waiter turned and hurried away.

Jenny watched the doctor closely throughout the meal, and she found that his words were more than just talk. He really *did* seem to relish every taste, every smell, every sound. He seemed to relish *her*. Looking at her. Watching her.

"Dessert?" he asked when he'd finished the entire steak and pushed the plate aside.

"No, I couldn't even finish this vat of gumbo they brought me." She glanced down at the food remaining and felt a little guilty. "It was delicious, though."

He smiled. "I'm glad you enjoyed it." He lifted a hand without turning his head, catching the attention of the waiter, who was facing in their direction, across the room. Whether he somehow knew the man was looking at them, or just got lucky, she couldn't guess.

"Yes, is everything all right?"

Samuel nodded. "We're ready to leave now." He slipped a bill into the man's hand. Jenny couldn't see what it was. "We're taking the bottle with us. Tally it up and keep the change."

"Yes, sir," the waiter said. From the look on his face as he tucked the money away, it must have been plenty. "It's been a pleasure serving you, Dr. La Roque." He nodded at Jenny. "And you, Professor Rose."

She was surprised he knew her name, but she only smiled back at him and slid out of her chair. Samuel came around the table, slid a hand around her waist, and let it rest on her hip as he walked close beside her, out to the Jeep.

"You don't believe in lingering over dinner, do you, Samuel?"

He looked down at her. "I hope you didn't feel rushed. It's just—I'm eager to show you around the plantation, and we don't have all that much time."

"It's fine. I'm eager to see it. I've been staying there several days, and I really haven't had a free second to explore the grounds. What I have seen is breathtaking, though." Somehow, she thought it would be even more so in this man's company. "How is it you're so familiar with the place?"

"I've lived here all my life," he told her matter-of-factly. "And . . . it once belonged to my family."

She turned toward him, surprised. "I didn't know that."

He nodded. "A hundred years ago. My great-grandfather lost it. It had been in the family since the eighteenth century."

"How? What happened?"

He shrugged, sending her a sidelong glance. "Gossip, rumors. He was driven out of town for his alleged crimes. Had he returned he'd have faced a hangman's noose. The place was deemed abandoned and confiscated by the state, then sold at auction."

"That's terrible." She tipped her head to one side. "What was he accused of doing?"

He paused, not answering right away.

"I'm sorry. Was that a rude question?"

"No. Not at all. I just . . . prefer not to sully our time together with talk of past tragedies."

She nodded slowly. "I doubt anything could spoil this evening for me, Samuel." She could hardly believe the words came from her mouth, almost bit her tongue. But then again, why be coy about it? She enjoyed being with him.

He reached across the car to stroke a slow path down her cheek with the backs of his fingers. "Don't be so sure," he whispered. And before she could ask what he meant by that, he said, "Here we are."

She looked out her window, but saw only rolling fields lined by woods. "This isn't the plantation."

"It's the southernmost border. And the most interesting spot." He got out, came around to open her door, and took her hand. She hesitated. "What's wrong, Jenny? You think I've brought you out here to hurt you?"

"Of course I don't think that." She got out of the car, rubbed her arms. "It's just . . . kind of creepy out here."

"Alone, with a man you barely know, a man who has been wanting to take you since the moment he laid eyes on you."

She met his eyes. "I'm not the kind of woman who has sex with strangers."

"I never thought you were." He moved a step closer. "But I'm no stranger, am I Jenny? Something inside you knows something inside me. Something inside you craves me, just the way I crave you."

She lowered her head. He moved closer, lifted her chin, stared into her eyes. "You do, don't you?"

She nodded mutely.

"Good," he said. "That's good." And then he pulled her hard against him and kissed her. His mouth covered hers, pushed hers open. He closed his hands on her backside and held her tight to his groin, so she could feel how hard he was, how badly he wanted her.

She couldn't resist the heat flooding her—God, he set her on fire. She twined her arms around his neck and wriggled her hips against him. She opened her mouth, and let his tongue probe and taste and lick all it wanted. This was madness—sweet, hot, delicious madness.

Finally, with a deep growl, he lifted his mouth from hers, dragged his gaze from her eyes to look past her, at the sky. "It's dark. The stars will be coming out soon."

"I've changed my mind. I don't have to work tonight. I—"

"Ssshh." He stroked her hair, her face. "Of course you do. You have a commitment to keep, and so do I. And that leaves us no time to do what we both want to do. But there will be another time. I promise you that."

She wasn't sure she would live that long.

"Besides, I haven't shown you what I promised. One of the secrets of this place. Come."

He turned, taking her by the hand and leading her across the field, through a patch of woods.

"Listen," he said.

She stopped walking, listened. At first, she thought she was hearing a heartbeat, a deep, pulsing heartbeat as if of the earth itself. But then it came more clearly, and she frowned up at him. "Is that . . . a drum?"

He nodded, tugging her forward. Soon they were walking along the bank of a river, wide and deep, and there were voices floating on the night air in addition to the beat of the drums. She saw light in the distance, the light of a fire.

"What is this?" she whispered.

"Shhh. You must be quiet now. Come."

He led her closer, until they were both crouching in the trees just beyond the glowing circle of firelight. She saw men beating huge, painted drums in a rhythm so compelling she felt her body tugged to move. She saw women, wearing white skirts and turbans, dancing. And then she caught her breath, because one of those women was Mamma Louisa.

She leaned closer, only to feel a strong hand on her shoulder, tugging her back into a hidden position.

"Is that . . . Voodoo?"

He nodded. "Mamma Louisa is a Voudon priestess." He nodded. "See how the others give her plenty of space? Watch, they won't stop the dancing until she does."

She watched Mamma Louisa, glorious and beautiful, round and lush, moving as if she'd become one with the driving beat of the drums. She was incredible. Her dance, beautiful and erotic.

"She's the housekeeper at the plantation."

"I know. Her family has always worked there."

She swallowed hard. "Should I be worried?"

He frowned at her. "I thought you were an educated woman, Jenny. It's only a religion. Don't you know that?"

"Knowing it and living under the same roof with it are slightly different things, Samuel." She looked longingly at the firelight, the dancers moving around it, the glow it cast on their faces. "Can we let them know we're here? Talk to them?"

He shook his head. "It would be an invasion. We're uninvited."

"It isn't an invasion to be out here watching them like this?"

"It is. But it's the kind of thing I figured you'd have to see to believe. Besides," he said, tracing a slow path along her forearm with his fingertips. "It made a great excuse to get you out in the middle of nowhere alone."

The drummers pounded faster, harder.

"It worked," she whispered, and she felt the reverberations of the drums echoing in her chest. The drums and the firelight, the sight of the wild dancing, were heady. It made her want to join in the movement. Her body rocked a little in time, hips twitching irresistibly as she crouched in the bushes beside Samuel.

"There's something compelling about it, isn't there?" he asked her, leaning so close she could feel his breath on her neck.

"It's enticing. Almost . . . irresistible."

"Yes."

Again his breath was warm—hot—on her neck. She turned her head just a little, to look into his eyes, and she found him so close her lips brushed his with the movement.

He made a sound deep in his throat, and kissed her.

CHAPTER SIX

*H*E drew her up until she was standing, all the while exploring her mouth with his tongue. He moved her backward until her back was pressed to a tree, and he crushed his body to hers, pinning her there.

His breathing was harsh and heavy. Hers was rapid and shallow. She threaded her fingers into his hair as his mouth moved, hot and hungry, from her lips to her jaw, to her neck, where he sucked at her skin, bit it gently.

He'd said there was no time for this tonight. But, God, she was going to go up in flames if she didn't make love to him soon.

He seemed to have forgotten his earlier words anyway, as his hands moved between them to cup her breasts through the dress she wore. Then he shoved the straps from her shoulders and pushed the dress downward, baring her breasts to his rough hands. He covered them, squeezed them, lifted them as he slid his mouth lower over her skin, sliding from her neck, to her chest, to her breast. He took it into his mouth, sucking until she moaned softly. When her fingers tangled in his hair, pulling his head harder to her, he bit down, teeth closing sharply on her nipple. Then he did it again, and matched the sweet pain with his fingers on the other breast, pinching, tugging until she was shaking all over and wriggling her hips shamelessly against his erection.

One hand slid up under her dress, found her center, and didn't even hesitate to invade. Shocking, the sudden feeling of his callused fingers on her, opening her, entering her. She rocked with the invasion, taking as much as he gave her. Three fingers, four, she didn't know. She only knew his thumb was ruthlessly working her while his fingers drove in and out, and his mouth and teeth tormented her breast. His teeth bit down hard, then his tongue licked away the hurt, and then he bit down again, harder than before. She rocked her hips, taking his fingers in and out, riding his hand.

His mouth left her breast, but his free hand took its place there, pinching and twisting and pulling. He leaned close to her, whispered in her ear, saying things that made her even hotter. And when she exploded with the force of the orgasm, he kept working her, making it go on and on and on.

He was still holding her, still kissing her, when the blood stopped pounding in her ears, and it occurred to her that the drumbeat no longer echoed in her chest. It was just her heart pounding now. She was standing with her back braced against a tree, and his body was pressed tight to hers. Her dress was hiked up higher than her hips, and she was breathless and burning. He'd returned his hands to her hips, and his mouth to her mouth.

She didn't remember pushing his shirt off his shoulders, but it was. Her hands ran over his hard shoulders and chest, and then her lips followed suit. He moaned, his fingers dragging through her hair.

She lifted her head away. "The Voudons have gone home."

His eyes opened slowly, revealing a predatory gleam.

"My heart's pounding so hard, I thought the drums were still beating."

His gaze seemed to clear, his brows drawing together. Passion faded slightly, and some kind of worry replaced it. He withdrew his arms from around her, and she shivered in the sudden chill while he squinted down at his wristwatch in the darkness. Jenny righted her dress. "What's wrong, Samuel?"

"The time . . . I—"

"Look," she whispered. "The moon's rising."

His head came up fast, eyes spearing her, then he turned to follow her gaze. "No . . ."

Jenny put her hand on his shoulder, longing for his touch, his arms around her. "It's all right."

"I . . . lost track of the time."

"I did, too. It's my fault as much as yours." She moved in front of him, sliding her hands up his chest.

He turned away again, this time pushing his hands through his hair as he lowered his head. "Go back to the car, Jenny."

She frowned. "But—I don't understand."

"Go!" His hands clenched in his hair, his face pulling into a tight grimace.

"God, Samuel, what's wrong? Are you all right?"

He dropped to his knees, right there in the forest. He seemed, suddenly, to be in excruciating pain. Jenny hovered nearby, unsure what to do. Every time she touched him he jerked away as if her touch burned. "Samuel?"

He fell forward, hands pressing to the soil, head hanging down between his arms.

"Samuel, what can I do to help you? Please." Tears choked her. She got in front of him, crouching low, running a hand over his hair. "Please, let me help you. What can I do, Samuel?"

He lifted his head, and his eyes gleamed with yellow light. He uttered a single word that drew out into a growl. "Run."

His face—God, his face was . . . changing.

Jenny backed away, one step, then two. She couldn't take her eyes from him. His hair twisted and lengthened. His face contorted, deep wrinkles appearing where none had been before. His lips pulled away from his teeth, and incisors, no—canines—gleamed in the moonlight.

She turned, and she ran. Roots sprang up to trip her. Limbs swiped at her face from every tree. She crashed through the woods headlong, unsure which way to go, thinking only of escape. She couldn't tell if he—or it—was pursuing her, but she felt as if it was. Chills raced up her spine, the back of her neck tingling as the fine hairs there stood on end.

Which way is the road? God, where the hell is the car? Did he leave the keys?

Her foot caught on a root and she smashed face-first into the ground. Scrambling to get to her feet again, she heard a low growl at her back.

"Oh, God!" She rolled onto her back, and saw it. A huge black wolf, front paws splayed widely, back legs bent, ready to spring. Its teeth were bared, its eyes on her.

Never taking her eyes from the wolf, she clawed the ground, her hand closing around a limb. She brought it upward, knowing by its lack of weight that it would make a poor weapon against such a powerful animal.

And then, suddenly, the wolf's stance changed. It shifted its gaze upward, looking at something beyond Jenny.

"Go, now!" a woman's voice said. "Oya commands it! Go!"

The wolf's ears perked forward, and then suddenly, it turned and loped gracefully into the dark woods.

Only then did Jenny dare to turn and look at the woman who stood behind her. Mamma Louisa stood there, looking like a tribal angel. She held something in her hand, a red pouch of some kind that bulged with its contents and had feathers and stones dangling from its drawstrings.

"Come, child. Get up on your feet. We're not safe, even now."

She hurried to obey, while Mamma Louisa stood there, eyes scanning the trees around them, the pouch held up like a weapon. When Jenny was beside her, she turned. "This way."

She followed the woman in white over a path that meandered through the woods, along the river's edge, wondering where on earth they were going, right until she saw the welcoming lights gleaming from the windows of the plantation house up ahead. Mamma Louisa led her right to the back of the house, through the kitchen entrance door, and up the back stairs to the third floor. As they moved through the door at the top, she found herself in a cozy living room. Rattan furnishings, stained a deep brown color and stacked with jewel-toned cushions, littered the room. One wall sported a hardwood stand, draped in a brightly colored cloth, its entire surface filled with fascinating objects, statues, stones, crosses. In its very center was a shrine with a dark-skinned Madonna enthroned within it.

"Sit, child," Mamma Louisa said, nodding toward one of the comfy-looking chairs. She locked the door behind them and then turned and came to her, eyes concerned. "Are you hurt?" she asked.

"No. I don't think so."

All the same, the woman was examining her. She ran her hands over Jenny's arm, eyes sharp and probing. She repeated the process with her other arm, then lifted her hair and examined her neck and ears. Kneeling, she inspected Jenny's legs, even her ankles. Every bit of exposed skin was subjected to her scrutiny.

"What are you looking for?"

"The mark of the wolf." She nodded as if satisfied. "Your dress is torn here. Better let me see the skin underneath."

Jenny didn't know why she complied so easily, but she did. She lowered the strap of the dress, exposing her shoulder to Mamma Louisa's steady gaze.

Finally, the woman nodded. "Nothing, it's good, you escaped without injury." She met Jenny's eyes. "The wolf didn't harm you, then."

"But it was no ordinary wolf, was it, Mamma Louisa?"

The woman's gaze shifted so quickly Jenny knew she was going to lie. "What else could it have been?"

"A werewolf. The loup-garou."

"Every child knows there's no such thing."

"But you know different."

She moved to her altar, then opened a cupboard underneath. Jenny saw mason jars, filled with herbs and roots and other things she couldn't identify.

"You've seen the wolf before, haven't you? You know about it."

The other woman shrugged, removing several jars and setting them upon the altar. "I know some things."

"Will you tell me? The things you know?"

She straightened, closing the cupboard, a small red pouch in her hands. It was empty. "Some things are better left alone, *chère*." She opened her jars, taking a pinch of this and a bit of that and dropping it into the red pouch. She added a gleaming black stone and then knotted the drawstrings while chanting something in a language Jenny didn't know. She held her hands over the bag and whispered what sounded like "Ah-say, ah-say, ah-say." Then she brought the pouch to Jenny, pressed it into her hands. "Keep this with you. Don't be without it. It will keep the wolf away."

Jenny looked down at the pouch. "What if I don't want to keep it away?" She lifted her eyes to Mamma Louisa's. "I came here to find the werewolf, to prove it exists. I can't do that unless I see it again."

"You saw the wolf with your own eyes, *chère*. What more proof do you need?"

She shrugged. "Photographs. A sample of its fur, or its blood. A footprint." She shook her head. "If I could get hold of the carcass from one of its kills, something it's fed on, I might be able to extract a DNA sample from the saliva."

"Mmm," Mamma Louisa said slowly. "If it kills you, maybe it leaves some spit on your remains, eh?"

"It's not going to kill me."

"It's a wolf. Its nature is to hunt, to kill."

"It's also a man."

She blinked, but didn't look away this time. "Your science tells you that?"

"No. My science tells me that would be impossible. But I saw it. I saw it change. . . ."

"Then you know who he is? The loup-garou?"

It was Jenny's turn to avert her eyes. "You mean you don't?"

"I'm a powerful woman. What I know puts me in no danger. What you know—might. He's a killer, a predator."

"How do you know he's preyed on anyone?"

Mamma Louisa shrugged. "It's as I said. It's the nature of the wolf to hunt, to kill."

"But that's not the nature of the man."

The older woman arched her brow. "You wish to think of this thing as harmless, then?"

"I only want to know the truth before I judge a man a killer."

"That kind of thinking will only make you his next victim, *chère*. Take the 'gree-gree.' "

"The what?"

"The gris-gris bag, take it. Keep it tucked inside a pocket and take it out only if your life is in danger."

She nodded, getting to her feet and taking the bag. "I have to get to work," she said. "I've got a lot to do tonight." She rose and started for the door.

"Take the other door, *chère*. It leads down to the main house." Mamma Louisa pointed at a second door, on the opposite side of the room.

Turning, Jenny paused. "I don't quite know how to thank you. If you hadn't shown up when you had—I don't know what might have happened."

"You do," she said. "You just wish you didn't."

CHAPTER SEVEN

SHE entered every detail of her encounter—except for the name of the shape-shifting doctor—in her computer's password-protected files, watching the clock the entire time. Maybe, she thought, she ought to take the precaution of telling someone what her passwords were, just in case anything happened to her. Just in case Mamma Louisa was right, and Samuel was a killer.

She closed her eyes, battling the shiver that chilled her marrow. In her mind's eye she saw him, Samuel, the man, his eyes burning with passion, hunger, longing—for her. And then she saw the wolf, with its teeth bared, and its eyes gleaming with a far different sort of hunger.

Which was real? Which was true? Could both of them truly live within one being? One man? Was it a constant struggle—the animal against the human? Would one eventually win out over the other? And if so, which would win?

She had to know. Not only because it was her job, her life's work, but because—because she cared about Samuel. And maybe that made no sense, and maybe she'd only just met him and all of this was based on nothing more than the most intense chemistry she'd ever felt with any man in her life. Or maybe it was something more. Samuel told her that there was something inside her that recognized something inside him. It felt—it felt very much as if that were true.

When she finished entering all the data, describing all she'd seen in as much detail as she could, she changed her clothes, donning a comfy pair of jeans and a ribbed baby-blue tank top. She pulled thick cushy socks and running shoes onto her feet.

Then she took out her trusty backpack and double-checked its contents. The good camera, with high-speed, low-light film. The bottles of water, compass, flashlight. The plaster-cast kit, plastic bags and test tubes for collecting samples, tweezers, sticky-tape. And most important of all—the guns. One, the tranquilizer gun, was already near at hand, but the other was locked away in her briefcase, protected by a combination dial lock.

She spun the lock open and retrieved the revolver. She flipped open the cylinder and checked the six rounds she'd had specially made. While the bullet casings looked perfectly ordinary, with their coppery hue, the tips of the bullets—the parts that actually flew toward a target when the trigger was pulled—were pure silver.

Clapping the cylinder closed again, she tucked the gun into the most easily accessible side pocket of her pack and yanked it up over her shoulders, but then she paused. Almost as an afterthought, she picked up the red gris-gris bag, and added that to the backpack as well. Finally, she headed out of the house.

Long before dawn, Jenny had gained entry to Samuel La Roque's cabin. The door had been locked, but she had no compunction about breaking in, especially after knocking and making enough racket that he would have surely come to the door had he been home. She entered through a side window, breaking the glass from a single pane, and reaching through to free the latch to open it. Before climbing inside, she whistled, called for Mojo, the doc's oversized wolf-dog, but there was no sign of the animal around. Then and only then did she clamber through the window, closing it behind her. She took a look around, just to assure herself that she was alone, and even took the time to sweep up the broken glass, before tossing a log on the fire, and finding a comfy spot to wait out the remainder of the night with her backpack right at her side.

Unfortunately, it was a little too comfy in Samuel's overstuffed easy chair. Especially with the fire's warmth reaching out and wrapping around her like a warm blanket. She only realized she'd fallen asleep when the dull thump at the front door startled her right out of her chair. She was on her feet before she even came fully awake. When she did, all was silent. She hugged herself, eyes glued to the door, every sense on alert.

The knob jiggled just a little. Then there was a low moan, and a soft sound, as if something slid over the door.

Swallowing her fear, Jenny yanked the gun from the backpack at her side, then moved forward very slowly. She reached for the doorknob.

A soft snuffling sound, then a low bark almost made her hit the ceiling. She jerked backward three steps, then hurried to a side window to peer out.

She could see the wagging tail of Samuel's pet. It was standing on the door-stoop, head down, but she could only see the back of it.

Dare she open that door to see what was going on outside? It was still dark, but not fully. The distant sky was beginning to pale to gray, and the moon was nowhere in sight. Not that she'd ever once believed the moon had to be visible in order for a man to assume wolf form. Nor even that a man *could* assume wolf form under any circumstances. Still . . .

Mojo had been friendly before. It might be different now, however.

The wolf barked again. A friendly, if urgent-sounding yip, aimed at the door, from the sounds of it.

"He's a wolf," she told herself aloud. "It's not as if he doesn't already know I'm in here."

Tucking the gun into the back of her jeans, she moved to the door, gripped the knob, and opened it just a crack.

Then she flung it open the rest of the way, because Samuel was lying at her feet, completely naked, his pet nuzzling and licking at his face, pushing him as if to get him up.

For just an instant she could only stand there, staring at him. He looked like a fallen, battered God—Lucifer after the fall. The lines of him, the planes and angles—he was stunning; he was perfect.

She dropped to her knees, hands gripping Samuel's warm, hard shoulders, rolling him carefully onto his back. His chest was sculpted, powerful, his belly lean. "Samuel? Are you all right?"

His eyes were closed, but she wasn't sure if that was because he was unconscious, or because they were cut and bruised and swollen. "My God, what happened to you?"

"Why are . . . you here?" he asked, his words broken, hoarse.

"Waiting for you."

He tried to get into a sitting position, and she gripped his forearms and helped him as he struggled to his feet and limped into the house with his dog dancing around his feet. She winced in sympathy with his pain and closed the door. He said, "It's nothing. I'll be fine in a few hours."

"Some doctor you are. It'll be more like a few weeks."

"I need . . . my bed."

"You need a hospital bed. Yours will have to do for now." She kept hold of him as they made their way to his bedroom. "Hold on." She peeled back the covers on the huge bed, a rustic four-poster made of knotty pine logs.

As soon as the blankets were out of the way, he fell facedown onto the bed, his head turned away from her.

Jenny tugged the covers over him again. "Is anything broken, do you think? Is there anything more serious than cuts and bruises?"

He said nothing. Not a word.

"Samuel?"

Nothing.

She rounded the bed so she could see his face, and watched the slow, steady rise and fall of his powerful back as he breathed. Gently, she reached out, brushed a wisp of dark hair away from his forehead.

"Samuel."

She didn't know what had happened to him, but she could guess. She imagined that the same kind of behavior that would constitute hunting, or even frolicking for a wild wolf, would mean physical exhaustion for a human being. The branches and twigs that snapped against the fur-covered hide of a wolf would leave welts on a human.

But it looked as if more than that had happened. It looked as if he'd run a gauntlet of sadists armed with whips and clubs. It looked as if he'd been beaten to within an inch of his life.

Sighing, she got to her feet, only to feel the brush of Mojo's head on her leg. She looked down at the animal, and it whined plaintively. Jenny stroked the dog's head. "It's okay, Mojo. I'm not going to leave him, if that's what you're asking."

The animal seemed relieved, its jaw falling open and tongue lolling between sharp teeth, almost like a doggie smile.

Jenny went into the bathroom just off the bedroom, found a washcloth, towels, soap, and some antiseptic ointments. There was even a tube of old-fashioned liniment. Carrying them all back into the bedroom, she dumped them on the bedside stand. Then she hurried out to the kitchen, rummaged in the cupboards until she located a large basin, and filled it with the hottest water she could bear on her skin.

She took the water with her back to the bedroom, set it on a chair, and poured antiseptic into it until it turned a mustard-tinted brown. She settled herself on the edge of his mattress, shaking her head at the scratches and cuts on his back as she pulled the covers away. Then she dipped the washcloth into the hot water, squeezed it out, and began the slow, gentle work of washing him.

The cuts, scratches, and scrapes on his back were numerous. There were a couple of punctures, tiny ones, and she even found a thorn poking from one of them. That put a delay on her work as she paused to locate tweezers, then removed the offending thorn, and made sure plenty of the antiseptic got into the tiny wound it left behind.

After washing one section of his body, she applied ointment to every scrape and scratch, ointment and bandages to the larger cuts. She paused over each bruise to gently rub liniment into it.

When she finished with his back, shoulders, and arms, she moved lower. His buttocks were covered in injuries as well, mostly bruises, and she worked there just as diligently, even if not quite as calmly. He had a perfectly shaped butt and rock-solid thighs. She couldn't resist touching him as she worked, running her hands over him, knowing he would never know the difference, and wouldn't mind if he did.

He felt good. She liked the smooth feel of his toned skin and hard muscle beneath her palms.

Finally, she moved on to his feet, the soles of which were not a pretty sight. Nothing more sensitive than the sole of a man's foot. Well, almost nothing.

She worked on him for a long, long time, losing herself to an almost hypnotic state induced by the act of rubbing, caressing, healing him.

She rolled him onto his back as carefully as she could and started all over again. And ministering to the front of him was even more interesting, even more arousing and exciting. She ran her washcloth, and then her hands, over his chest, exploring and touching every inch of it. Touching him this way, this freely, this boldly, made every part of her body come alive. Every nerve ending tingled. She savored him, the way he had taught her to savor her meal last night. The feel of him, the sight of him, the smell of him. The sound of her palms brushing over his skin. The sound of her heart pounding in her chest. The sound of him sighing in contentment in his sleep.

Carefully, she leaned closer, pressing her lips to his chest, daring to part them, to taste him, just a little flick of her tongue. He would want her to do it. She knew he would.

He groaned deep in his throat, and his arms came around her, pulling her into the bed. He was hard and far stronger than she'd have given him credit for, as he rolled her over and covered her body with his. He took her mouth, and even while she began to protest that he shouldn't, that he was hurt, and should wait, he began working her clothing free.

His strong hands slid over her waist, to the bottom of her tank top, then slid upward again, lifting the fabric with them higher, baring her belly, and then her breasts. He pressed her arms upward, so he could strip the blouse away, and then he paused, staring down at her.

"You're hurt," he whispered.

"It's nothing—branches and briars when I ran through the woods."

"I frightened you."

"Not you," she told him, pressing her hand to his cheek. "The wolf."

"But I *am* the wolf." He closed his eyes and lowered his head until his lips brushed gently over the scratch on her collarbone. He kissed the length of it, then kept moving, finding her breast and kissing it as well. When he tended the nipple with soft, teasing kisses, her blood heated beyond endurance.

"Samuel," she whispered.

He took that as encouragement, changed tactics, taking her nipple into his mouth, suckling now, tugging and nibbling.

She threaded her hands in his hair to urge him onward. And he obliged her, even while he slid his hand over her belly and undid her jeans. Then he kept going, down the front of them, inside her panties. His fingers found their target, and parted and probed.

She moved against his hand, even as her own hands traced the contours of his skin, his back and shoulders, so broad and firm, smooth beneath her palms.

He slid her jeans lower, and she kicked free of them, as eager as he was to be rid of any barrier between his flesh and hers. Then he lowered himself between her thighs, and she wrapped her legs around him. His hardness pressed to her center, but he paused, waited there, and he kissed her mouth and then opened his eyes. "Don't be afraid of me, Jenny. I'd never hurt you."

"I'm not afraid of you."

He sighed as if in relief, and then gently slid inside her. Jenny felt the very breath driven from her lungs as he filled her, and she held him tighter, tipping her hips to receive him.

After that, she lost her ability to think or reason. There was only pleasure, the delicious friction and stroking rhythm of the two of them, moving within and around each other. He moved faster, held her to him more tightly. His kisses grew more feverish and the words he whispered into her ear hotter as her body twisted into a tight little knot of need. And finally, he pushed her over the edge of release. Every part of her quivered and trembled. She cried his name out loud and clung to him while the waves of pleasure washed through her. And she felt the same intense sensations rippling through him as he held her beneath him.

Finally, her body uncoiled, the muscles relaxing as warmth and a sense of perfection suffused her.

"My God," Samuel whispered, carefully rolling to one side and then gathering her into his arms as if she were something too fragile to be real. "My God, it's never been like that before."

She snuggled in his embrace, nodding her agreement, and knowing that it would never be like this again, either. Not with any other man but him.

CHAPTER EIGHT

*J*ENNY lay cradled in Samuel's arms as the sun rose higher, slanting its beams through the windows to paint her skin in heat and light. Sex with Samuel had been the most intense experience of her life. Desperate, even rough at times, and then so tender it brought tears to her eyes at others.

"How do you do it?" she asked him softly.

He'd opened the bedroom window. As the sun heated the room, a warm bayou breeze played with the sheer white curtains. "Do what?"

She shrugged. "You were exhausted, hurt."

"Not anymore."

She averted her eyes, fighting a blush.

"I'm not kidding, Jenny. Look at me. Look." He sat up, letting the sheets fall away from his powerful chest, lifting her with him. When she was upright, she let her gaze travel over his chest, and then she frowned. Lifting her hands, she touched the spots where, only a few hours earlier, cuts, scrapes and bruises had made her wince in sympathy. But there was nothing there. The places where she'd rubbed ointment and liniment looked as perfect, as flawless, as the rest of him.

Frowning even more deeply, she put a hand on his shoulder, turning him so she could see his back. But it was the same there. Even the worst of the bruises, a huge purple blotch on his hip, had faded until it was barely visible.

Blinking in confusion, she let him return to his former position. He was staring at her face, but she couldn't hold his gaze.

"We haven't talked about . . . about what you saw happening to me last night. I never . . . I never meant for you to see that."

"What, exactly, *did* I see, Samuel?"

He looked away. "You know what you saw. You saw me changing forms. Becoming . . . the wolf. I'm the one you've been looking for."

She closed her eyes. "Then it's true. It's . . . you're a . . . God, I can't even say it. It's too outlandish to be real."

"I'm the werewolf, the loup-garou, the shape-shifter. It's me. I'm the one you've been looking for, Jenny. The only question is, now that you've found me, what do you plan to do about it?"

She lifted her eyes slowly, met his and was amazed at the amount of courage it took to do so, and not look away. "Will you cooperate with me? Help me with my research?"

"By answering your questions? Yes, if you'll keep my name out of it."

She swallowed hard. "What about videotape?"

He held her gaze steadily. "You think I'm insane? Or just suicidal?"

"Samuel, I'd protect you. I'd never let anyone—"

"No. What I go through, what I become—no, it's personal. I can't think of a moment more private than those three nights a month, when . . . when it happens. I can hardly stand the idea that you watched it happen. I couldn't bear to let you tape it."

"Samuel, you don't understand. This is my life's work."

"Jenny, *you* don't understand." He cupped her cheek in one hand, gently, lovingly. His eyes beamed his feelings into hers. "This is my *life*."

She lowered her head, drew her knees up to her chest, sitting up in the bed. "If you don't cooperate with my research, how can you ever hope to find a cure?"

"Who says I *want* a cure?"

She looked at him, wide-eyed. "Don't you?"

He was quiet for a moment, his gaze turning inward.

"Samuel?"

"I don't know. I don't . . . I just don't know, all right?"

"My God, Samuel, how on earth could you even consider wanting to stay like this if you don't have to?"

He shook his head slowly. "How could I not? Look at me, Jenny. My senses are sharper than they've ever been. Sharper than they ever could have been, if the family curse hadn't found its way to me. Before the changes began, I was . . . I was barely alive. Going through life in a kind of complacent daze. Now, I experience everything. I *feel* everything."

His eyes sparkled when he talked about this thing. She couldn't believe it, hadn't even considered that he might see this affliction as having a positive side. "Are you in control of what you do, when you . . . change?"

He lowered his gaze. "I don't know. Afterward, it's . . . it's difficult to remember what I've done. But don't think I'm not watching for signs. There have been no unexplained injuries, no violent deaths, no one reporting that they were attacked. I have to believe that, even as the wolf, I'm incapable of causing harm to another human being."

"But you don't know that for sure."

With a heavy sigh, he conceded the point. Then he lifted his eyes to hers. "I could have hurt you, that night on the road. But I didn't."

"I guess the scratches across my chest don't count, then."

"I can't believe I intended to harm you. Not you, Jenny." He made a halfhearted attempt at a smile. "Maybe I was just trying to get your blouse off."

The joke fell flat for her. "I'm sorry, Samuel, but I can't laugh about this. You came after me in the woods last night. If Mamma Louisa hadn't come along when she did—I don't know. I don't know what might have happened."

"Mamma Louisa?" She heard the change in his tone when he repeated the woman's name. He sounded . . . angry. "Tell me what happened," he said.

"I fell. You—the wolf was crouching, poised as if to spring. Its teeth were bared, hair on its neck bristling up, and it was growling. It did not appear to be friendly, Samuel. Not like . . ." She glanced at the floor, where Mojo lay napping on a braided throw rug. "Not like Mojo. I was sure I was done for."

"But it didn't hurt you. I didn't hurt you."

She nodded, admitting that much was true.

"What happened next?"

"Mamma Louisa said something—an incantation or something. She waved her little red gris-gris bag around, and the wolf just ran away."

He sighed, shaking his head. "Ironic that she should be the one to step in."

Jenny frowned. "Why?"

He didn't answer, and she touched his face, turned it toward hers. "What has she got to do with this, Samuel?"

"Everything. It was her family who put this curse on mine. Her great-grandmother started it all, taking out her vengeance against my great-grandfather with Voodoo magic."

"Vengeance?"

He nodded. "God knows he had it coming if he did what . . . what her family claimed he did. My great-grandfather, Beckett Branson La Roque owned the plantation back then. He inherited it from his mother's family, the Bransons. Mamma Louisa's family, the DuVal's, worked for him just as they'd worked for his mother's family. Her great-grandmother, Celeste, was the matriarch of the clan then, and she was also a Voudon priestess."

She nodded, listening, rapt.

"They said my great-grandfather raped a girl, Alana DuVal, Celeste's daughter. Mamma Louisa's grandmother. She was only sixteen."

"Do you believe it?"

He shrugged. "I don't know why she would have made it up. My grandfather never admitted it, but more importantly, he never denied it." There was a long pause. "Yeah, I believe it. But it doesn't really matter what I believe. Celeste believed it, and she avenged her daughter's innocence by cursing my ancestor and my line. In each generation, a La Roque male will be possessed by the spirit of the loup-garou, until there are no more males born."

"The curse dies with the line."

He nodded.

"Do you think Mamma Louisa knows how to remove it?"

"Of course she knows how—but she won't. I've asked her, believe me."

"Then you *do* want to be rid of it." He shot her a look. "You said you'd asked her," she rushed on. "You wouldn't have asked if you didn't want it gone."

"Early on, I thought the curse was the end of my life. I hated it. I fought it. I raged against it. But over time, I learned to live with it. And over a little more time, I began to realize that it wasn't all bad. I even learned to . . . to embrace it."

"But you may not have to."

"It's a part of who I am now, Jenny." He climbed out of the bed, paced away from her, then turned suddenly. "It's made me a better doctor."

Jenny frowned. "How?"

"I don't know. The heightened senses, maybe. The sharper instincts. I can tell what a patient's problem is even before I've run tests to confirm it. I spot potentially fatal complications before they happen, and I'm able to avert them." He shook his head. "I don't want to give that up."

"And you don't want anyone to know. But they will, Samuel. Eventually, the people around you are going to catch on. How are you going to deal with that?"

He shrugged. "I'll cross that bridge when I come to it."

She closed her eyes.

He came back to the bed. "I know you're disappointed, Jenny. I know it would mean a lot to your career to make a case study out of me—but it would be the end for me. I'd be hunted by superstitious fools wanting to kill me and pursued by scientists wanting to study me. My life would be over."

She couldn't argue with him. "When I came here, searching for the creature, I was convinced all I would find, if anything, would be an animal. An unknown species. I never for one minute thought the myths would be true—that a human being could change forms, or that a curse could be the cause. I've never believed in magic."

"And now that you've seen the living proof of it? How is that going to change your approach to this, Jenny?"

"I don't know. I have . . . I have to rethink everything." She got to her feet. "I should go." She got out of the bed, tugging the sheet around her, then bent to retrieve her clothes from the floor.

"Jenny."

She paused, not looking at him. "I won't tell anyone, Samuel. When I decide what I have to do, I'll let you know first. Before I do anything at all, I'll talk to you. I promise."

He nodded. "For some reason, I believe you." Then he came closer, slid his hands over her bare shoulders, squeezed gently. "But that's not what I was going to say."

"It isn't?"

"No."

"Then . . . what?"

He turned her to face him. "Just . . . this." He kissed her, softly, slowly, and thoroughly. When their lips slid apart, she relaxed against his chest and he held her to him. "It hasn't been this way for me in a long time. With a woman, I mean. I've . . . I've been afraid to let anyone get too close. But with you, I just—it was like I had no choice. Something else took over."

"The wolf?" she asked softly.

He tipped her chin up, looked her in the eye. "My heart, I think."

A lump formed in her throat, making it hard to breathe and impossible to speak.

"I've handed you the loaded gun, Jenny, with the silver bullet already in the chamber. I'm trusting you not to pull the trigger."

He kissed her again, then with a sigh, walked into the bathroom.

Jenny heard the shower running a few minutes later. She didn't want to see him again before she left, because she still didn't know what the hell she was going to do. She would keep her word to him, she vowed. She would tell him her decision, once it was made.

God, she felt like an assassin for even considering moving forward with her work, making a study of him, perhaps without his consent. There had to be some way she could keep his identity secret. She had to at least consider the possibility, weigh the options. How could she not?

She threw her clothes on quickly and headed back to the plantation while he was still in the shower.

CHAPTER NINE

WHAT are you working on?"

The voice, coming from so close behind her, made her jerk her pencil across the sketchbook. She drew it to her chest protectively and shot a look over her shoulder. "Dr. Hinkle. What are you doing in here?"

"I'm the project supervisor, Professor Rose. I'm supervising." He nodded at the pad. "No use hiding it. I've already seen." Then he yanked it from her and took a closer look.

"My door was locked."

"I have keys to every door in this house." He was staring at the sketchbook where she'd been drawing, from memory, the way Samuel had looked as he'd changed. She wasn't certain why she'd been drawing it. She just had to get it down, to get the image out of her head and to try to make sense of it all.

"So you saw it again last night?" Hinkle asked.

"I didn't see anything. This is just doodling." She took the pad back. "And I thought I made it clear that I didn't want you in my rooms."

"Is the drawing based on . . . anyone you know?"

"You're changing the subject. I'm going to file a complaint with the university if you don't stay out of my rooms."

"Bears a striking resemblance to the town doctor. What's his name? La Roque?"

"You're being ridiculous."

He shrugged. "You went out to dinner with him last night, according to Toby. Did you spend the night, Professor?"

"What are you talking about? I came home last night."

"Yes, after your date."

"It wasn't a date. It was research. I wanted to know if there had been any patients coming in with unexplained injuries."

"And have there?"

"No. None."

He nodded. "I never saw him drop you off."

"I felt like a walk." *God, he was catching on.* More than before, she realized Samuel was right. If she pursued this, it would be impossible to protect his identity for very long. And she wasn't sure why, but she felt an instinctive fear of Dr. Hinkle learning the truth.

"And then you left again," he said. "I checked, later on. You didn't sleep here."

"So you were sneaking around in my bedroom in the middle of the night, when you thought I'd be sound asleep? God, what were you thinking?"

"Where did you spend the night, Jenny?"

She bit back her anger—it wasn't going to dissuade him. "I

159

went back out to the woods. According to all we've got so far, this creature—if it exists at all, which I'm beginning to doubt—is nocturnal. I was hoping to spot it." She shrugged, sighed. "No sign of it, though. I say it reluctantly, Dr. Hinkle, but I'm ready to concede that you may be right. We might be just wasting our time down here."

He shrugged. "We have one more night to produce results. The moon is still full, you know."

"Yes. I know."

"If there are no results, I'm pulling the plug on this project. We'll pack up and head back to the university tomorrow."

She nodded, and tried to hide her relief. If he knew—if he had an inkling, there would be no way he would consider ending the project. Then again, why would any sane person believe a man could become a wolf? "Maybe that's for the best." She felt like crying. All her work, all her research; just when she was so close to success, she was throwing it all away. But she couldn't base her personal success on the destruction of Samuel's life. It would be unfair. Besides, as illogical as it seemed—she felt something for him. Something powerful.

"I must say, Jenny, I'm surprised. You don't usually give up so easily."

She shrugged and tried to inject her demeanor with some enthusiasm. "Who says I've given up? There's always tonight."

"Yes. There's always tonight."

There was something in his eyes when he said it, something that frightened her.

As soon as he left the room, Jenny pulled up every one of her password-protected files and deleted them. She'd made her deci-

sion. She would make her name, her career by discovering some legitimate unknown species of animal. Not by exploiting a man who
was doing his best to live his life under the heavy burden of a
curse.

She wasn't even sure she believed in curses, but she knew who
to ask. And while she'd decided not to continue her research using
Samuel as a subject, she hadn't decided to leave him alone entirely.

She thought she just might be able to help him.

Tucking her laptop into her shoulder bag, she took it with her.
She wouldn't let it out of her sight again until she'd had the hard drive
replaced and demolished the old one. Traces of her files would remain
there, even though she'd deleted them. She knew that. She headed to
the kitchen, where she found Mamma Louisa kneading bread dough.

Without even looking up, the older woman said, "Hello, *chère.*
I suppose you're lookin' for me?"

"Yes."

"He know you're talkin' to me?"

There was no point in asking who she meant. Jenny was well
aware by now that Mamma Louisa knew the identity of the loup-
garou. "No. He says there's no point in talking to you, that you've
already refused to help him."

Her head came up, eyebrows raised. "He said that?"

She nodded.

"Hmmph. Arrogant, know-it-all doctor, anyway." She made a
fist and punched the dough.

"You mean you didn't refuse?"

"I told him the truth. I can't remove the curse. Only one who
can is the one who put it on him in the first place. An' my great-
grandma Celeste is long dead by now."

"Then there's no hope for him?"

She draped a dishtowel over the ceramic bowl of bread dough and set it near a window where the sun beamed through. Then she grabbed another towel to wipe the dough and flour from her hands. "Always there is hope, *chère*. Your doctor, he stomp away from me when I tell him I can't remove the curse. He didn't ask what I *could* do. I figure he don't want my help—maybe don't deserve it."

Jenny felt hope spark in her heart. "Then there is something you can do?"

"Don't know. Not until I try. Not gonna try until he apologize, and ask me proper."

"That's certainly reasonable."

"Stubborn man don't seem to think so." She shrugged. "Even so, I don't know if I can help him."

"But you'll try?"

"He apologize, I try. It's all I can do."

"It's enough," Jenny said. "It has to be."

JENNY tried phoning Samuel three times, only to be told he was busy with patients and unable to come to the phone. She finally drove to his office, but one look at the packed waiting room was enough to deter that effort. It was crowded with sniffling kids and wheezing elders and everything in between. She was about to leave when Samuel came out, spotted her, and waved her closer.

She weaved her way through the waiting patients and wondered why it gave her such a thrill to see him again. "I can see you're busy," she said. "I don't want to interrupt."

"I can take a minute." He smiled at her. "I knew you were

here—felt you. That's why I came out." Then he turned to the receptionist. "Sally, get Mrs. Finny set up in room one and tell her I'll
be in shortly." Taking Jenny's arm, he led her into a hallway, all the
way to the end, and then into a small room where the desk was almost an afterthought to the comfy overstuffed chairs, table and
coffeemaker.

She went in before him, but didn't sit, turning to face him instead. As soon as he closed the door behind him, she said, "I deleted
all my files. I'm not going to pursue this. Not on a research level, at
least."

He frowned and studied her face. He looked a little bit wary.
"But you *are* going to pursue it."

"Not if you say no. But Samuel, I think I can help you. I spoke
to Mamma Louisa, and she—"

"Mamma Louisa won't help me. I already told you that."

She shook her head. "You asked her to cure you, not help you.
And she told you she couldn't, not that she wouldn't. There's a big
difference between what she said and what you heard."

His frown deepened. "Did she tell you something different?"

"Yes. She said that only Celeste could remove the curse, but
that she might be able to do something to help you."

"Help me in what way?"

"She didn't say. She's not even sure she can, but she's willing to
try." She shrugged. "*If* you will apologize for losing your temper
with her, and ask her nicely."

He looked angry for a moment. Jenny put a hand on his shoulder. "Samuel, she's not the one who put this curse on your family.
You can't blame her for that any more than she can blame you for
what your great-grandfather did to Alana DuVal."

His face eased slightly. "Yeah. Yeah, you're right. And I did stomp off in a huff when she said she couldn't help me. Haven't spoken to her since." He grimaced. "That was two years ago."

"It's time to let that go. Make amends, if nothing more."

"All right." He sighed. "Jenny, I've been thinking . . . about what I said before, about not wanting a cure." He turned away from her, pushing a hand through his hair. "I want to keep seeing you. I want—I want you in my life. Somehow. And if giving this thing up is what it takes to make that happen, I'll do it."

She smiled a little. "You'd do that for me?"

He shrugged. "I'd miss running wild with Mojo and howling at the moon," he said with a teasing look. "But I'd miss you more. I'd miss never knowing what could have been, what could have happened between us." He lowered his eyes. "I think you might be the one, Jenny."

The words sank into her heart like warm sunlight. Her throat tightened so much she could barely force air through, and when she did speak, her voice was tight with emotion. "I wouldn't ask you to change your life for me, Samuel. This has to be your decision. Not mine."

"But . . ."

"I think you might be the one, too. I'm not going to walk out of your life because of what you are. God, what you are is . . . is what I fell for, you know?"

He seemed relieved. "You really mean that?"

There was a tap on the office door. "Doctor, your patient is waiting."

He licked his lips. "I have to—"

"I know. Look, at least meet with Mamma Louisa. Amends

need to be made whether she can help you or not, and whether you decide to accept her help or not. At least talk with her."

He nodded. "I will."

"We'll need privacy," Jenny said quickly. "Come to that same spot where you took me last night. That grove where the Voudons danced. I'll bring Mamma Louisa. Meet us there."

"No later than eight," he said. "Before the moon rises."

"Understood. Eight it is." She started for the door, but he stopped her with an arm around her waist, pulled her close until her body was pressed to the front of his, and kissed her mouth. It was a hungry kiss; he used his tongue, probed and delved and tasted. She twined her arms around his neck and kissed him back just as eagerly.

The knock at the door came again, and reluctantly, he let her go.

JENNY went back to the plantation and battled the worst case of nerves she'd ever had in her life. She invented tasks to keep Mike and Toby busy, set Carrie to work doing more research, and tried hard to hide her jittery mood from Dr. Hinkle, though he behaved like her shadow all afternoon.

He suspected something—she was sure of it. And the way he stuck to her all day made her wonder how she would manage to slip away from him tonight.

By the time Mamma Louisa was serving them all dinner in the formal dining room, Jenny was ready to climb the walls. She hadn't even managed to let the woman know about tonight's plans. Every time she got Mamma Louisa alone and started to talk to her, Dr. Hinkle showed up like some lurking demon. She would catch a glimpse of him from the corner of her eye, or suddenly feel shivers up her spine, and turn to find him not far away.

During the meal, Jenny managed to catch Mamma Louisa's sharp eye, and she hoped to send a message, slanting her gaze toward Dr. Hinkle. A moment later, she knew the message had been received. The large woman bent to set a fresh pitcher of ice water on the table and tipped it into Hinkle's lap.

He yelped and jumped to his feet, his pants soaked through. "Damn, woman, what are you thinking?"

"I'm so sorry, mister! Eva Lynn, honey, bring towels!"

Eva Lynn raced in from the kitchen with large white towels in hand. Hinkle snatched one from her and stomped toward the stairs, with the younger woman on his heels dabbing at the back of his pant legs, even as Mamma Louisa glanced at Jenny and inclined her head.

"I'll help you until Eva Lynn gets back," Jenny said, for the benefit of the other three at the table, and then she hurried to the kitchen.

"You wanted to speak to me, yes?" Mamma Louisa said. "Without the old man listenin' in."

"Yes." She glanced back toward the closed door. "I spoke to Samuel, and he admitted he was wrong to have treated you as he did. He wants to apologize, and he'll be grateful to hear about any help you can give him with his . . . problem."

"Mmm. I'm surprised the stubborn fool gave in so easily." She searched Jenny's eyes. "You're good for him, I think. So? When do we meet him?"

The woman's instincts were amazing. "Tonight, eight o'clock, at the grove where I saw you last night."

Her eyes narrowed. "You think it's safe? To be so close to him at night, when the moon is still full?"

"He's fine until moonrise, Mamma Louisa. That won't be until after nine. Is an hour enough time for you to do . . . what you need to do? To help him?"

"If I can't help him in an hour, I can't help him at all. I will go with you, child. Now go, get back to the table before that nosy man comes snooping again. He been watching you like a hawk all the day long."

"I know."

"Don't you worry. We gave him the slip, all right. Whooeee, but how he jump when that ice water hit his man parts!" She smiled from ear to ear.

Jenny grinned, too, but wiped the smile away as she returned to her seat at the table and continued with her meal.

At 7:30, she was in her room getting ready to go, when someone tapped on her door. Fearing it was Dr. Hinkle, she almost didn't answer, then decided she had no choice. When she opened the door, she found Carrie standing there.

"Finished with all that research already?" Jenny asked.

"Um . . . no. I just . . . I wanted you to know something."

Frowning, Jenny let her in. Carrie closed the door, looking nervous. "What is it, Carrie?"

The girl cleared her throat. "When you went into the kitchen, tonight, with Mamma Louisa, Toby left the table."

"Where did he go?"

"I can't be sure," Carrie said. "But he might have gone to the kitchen, too. I started to go for another towel, to mop up the water that was still in Dr. Hinkle's chair. And it looked as if . . . as if he was listening at the door. But like I said, I can't be sure. He saw me and hurried off toward the living room, and I went back to the table."

Jenny closed her eyes. This wasn't good.

"Where is he now?"

"Downstairs, working on his computer."

"And Dr. Hinkle?"

Carrie shrugged. "He went out a few minutes ago. I didn't dare come to you until he left, the way he's been hovering over you all day."

"And now he's suddenly stopped hovering."

"That occurred to me, too," Carrie said. "I think Toby told him whatever he overheard in the kitchen. I saw them talking awhile ago, huddled in a corner, keeping their voices low. Are you in any kind of trouble, Professor Rose? Cause if I can help . . ."

Jenny glanced at her watch. "Keep the twins busy. Downstairs, for the next ten minutes. Can you do that?"

Carrie nodded hard. "Can you tell me what's going on?"

"No. I'm sorry, but it's not my secret to tell."

"Is it . . . the werewolf?"

Jenny smiled and smoothed a hand over Carrie's hair as if she were a small child. "Don't be silly, hon. There are no such things as werewolves."

Carrie looked puzzled but rushed away to do as Jenny asked. Jenny took the back stairs up to the third floor and knocked on Mamma Louisa's door.

When the woman opened it, she said, "Ready to go, then?"

"Not quite. I need to take a look in Dr. Hinkle's room before we leave. But we'll have to be fast."

"I never like that man anyway." Mamma Louisa dipped into a pocket and pulled out a jangling ring of keys. "Let's go see what secrets that man be keepin'."

CHAPTER TEN

JENNY felt as if every hair on her body were standing on end as she crept through Dr. Hinkle's suite of rooms. Mamma Louisa stood just outside the door, in the ornate hallway, keeping watch. Not that it was going to be much help, should the good doctor return. There wasn't any other way out of the rooms, just that one door. But at least she'd have some warning.

She went to the desk that was set up in a window-lined alcove, glanced through the papers that were spread over it, but found nothing. She flipped open the laptop computer and checked for the most recently opened files, but again, found only the most mundane reports on the project.

She tried the desk drawer and found it locked.

Turning toward the door, she whisper-shouted for Mamma Louisa, who poked her head into the room, eyebrows raised.

"The keys to this desk. Do you have them?"

"No, missy. The doctor, he make sure he have the only set."

That nailed it, then. If Hinkle had anything he wanted to hide, the desk had to be where it was. Mamma Louisa came the rest of the way into the room, eyes on the desk drawer, lips moving to form soundless words as she reached a hand out. She leaned over, blew on the drawer's handle, and tugged it open.

"How the hell—"

"You were mistaken, *chère*. The draw' wasn't locked at all." Turning, she hurried back to her post in the hallway.

Jenny swallowed down the rising sense of disorientation. She'd seen so many things since coming here—things her practical mind and her education told her didn't exist—*couldn't* exist. And yet, she couldn't deny her own senses. She'd *seen* Samuel's face and body twisting into something else. And she knew this drawer had been locked tight moments ago.

Now, she was staring into it, at a leather-bound volume. Beside it was the plaster cast she'd taken of that paw print in the woods. Then he *had* been the one who'd stolen it! Carefully, she took the book out and opened it, seeing pages upon pages of handwritten lines. Each page was dated. It was a journal.

Frowning, she flipped pages, reading a few lines here and there. Her own name jumped out at her, catching her eye. "Jennifer Rose is the best I've ever seen, the best I've ever worked with. But I must never let her believe I support her theories. In fact, I need to prove them wrong, discredit her, even while I use her to lead me to what I need."

She blinked. Good God, he'd practically gushed about her skill in her field. To her face he'd never done anything but criticize, belittle, and condemn her work. It was foolish, not a real science, fraudulent even.

She flipped more pages.

"I knew she would find it! Here, at last, I have the full ritual."

Below those words, she saw an outline, like a recipe, titled, "Becoming a Werewolf."

What the hell?

She read on, recognizing some of the portions from research she'd gleaned, other bits Carrie had ferreted out from various sources; still others were entirely new to her. She skimmed the lines. Third night of the full moon—that was tonight. There was a list of herbs, each one with a checkmark beside it. She knew the rite required a fire, but this list gave the precise instructions for the type of wood to burn, and the kinds of leaves to use to kindle the fire. It gave astrological requirements as well—moon in Scorpio, conjunct to Saturn. Beneath those, today's date was jotted down.

And near the bottom of the list of items needed was one that made her blood run cold.

The pelt of a werewolf.

Oh my God.

She slammed the book closed and taking it with her, turned and raced out the door and down the hall to the stairs. Mamma Louisa was right on her heels.

"What is it, child?"

"Hinkle—he thinks he can make himself into a werewolf!"

"But . . . but the only way he can do that is to be bitten by one, and then he'd have as good a chance of dying as of changing . . . unless he's found a spell. But for that he'd have to—"

"To kill Samuel, after the change," Jenny said. "He needs the pelt."

Mamma crossed herself and muttered a prayer as the two

women burst into the living room. Carrie leapt up from the couch where she'd been sitting with Mike and Toby. "My God, what's happened?"

Jenny ignored her, going straight to Toby, gripping his shoulder hard. "You followed me to the kitchen earlier tonight. You eavesdropped on my conversation with Mamma Louisa." She held up her free hand as he started to deny it. "Don't even . . . I don't have time for your lies. Just tell me, did you report what you heard to Dr. Hinkle?"

"I didn't—"

"I swear to God, if you lie to me now I'll get you thrown out of school on charges so scandalous no other university will have you, even if I have to make up every one of them. Don't think I can't do it! This is life and death, Toby. Now talk!"

He stared at her, his eyes widening. "You wouldn't—"

"You try me."

Pursing his lips, he swallowed hard. "All right. All right, I listened in. I told Dr. Hinkle what I heard. That you and Mamma Louisa were to meet someone in the grove down by the river at eight."

"He's got a head start," Jenny whispered, releasing him and turning her gaze to Mamma Louisa's. "God, he'll beat us there, and kill Samuel."

Carrie gasped. "Dr. Hinkle's going to kill someone?"

"No, *chère*," Mamma Louisa said. "He can't kill him, not until after the moon comes up. Not until after the change. To kill him before that would serve no purpose."

Jenny nodded. "Then there's still time." She ran for the door as Carrie and the twins shouted questions after her. She made it to her car, surprised when the considerably older, and much heavier woman jumped into the passenger seat only a split second after her. She was fast.

Jenny drove, and watched the sun sink below the horizon. Darkness gathered around them, and she felt as if the entire world were holding its breath, just waiting for moonrise.

THEY'D exited the car and were making their way through the woods to the grove, when Jenny heard the gunshot.

A scream ripped from her throat, and she broke into a run, with Mamma Louisa, a large drawstring bag over her shoulder, racing to keep up.

The path twisted and meandered through the thick, dense forest. She could barely see where she was going, and yet something pulled her on. Some sixth sense, tugging her the way magnetic North tugs a compass needle. She ran, barely able to see her feet hitting the ground ahead of her. She ran, heedless of the branches smacking her face and raking her arms. She ran, and then she saw him.

The wolf lay very still, so still she was nearly upon it before she realized what it was. She fell to her knees, her hands sinking into the thick, soft fur. "Samuel," she whispered. "God, no." She felt warm, thick moisture and lowered her face to the fur, hugging the animal gently. "Samuel, please?"

A soft whimper sounded in response.

Panting, Mamma Louisa caught up, fell to her knees, and tore open her bag. She took out a flashlight and pointed it at the animal.

"He's still alive," Jenny said softly.

"Mmm, but Hinkle-man got what he wanted, though. Look

there." She moved the light, revealing a strip of flesh, red and bleeding, on the wolf's side.

"My God, what did he do? What did he do to you?"

The wolf whined again, a plaintive, pain-racked sound that made her heart twist and her stomach convulse.

"We have to help him, Mamma Louisa."

She nodded, handing the light to Jenny, and taking more items from her bag. Herbs, rattles. She worked over the animal, chanting softly. As she did, Jenny used the light to find the bullet hole, high on the front shoulder. She tore a strip from her own blouse and wrapped the wound. "He'll live," she whispered. "I think it's too high to have hit the heart. I don't think there's internal bleeding." The animal's strong pulse told her as much.

"My God, what's going on out here?"

At the male voice, Jenny looked up, only to see Carrie and the twins standing on the path, staring down at the suffering animal in horror. "You followed me?" Jenny asked.

"Of course we did," Carrie said. "You said it was a matter of life and death. She stared at the animal with wide eyes."

"Is that—is that a werewolf?"

"No," Mamma Louisa answered firmly. "This is an ordinary wolf."

Jenny's hands stilled in the deep fur. She looked closer. "My God, you're right. This is Mojo!" She hugged the wolf gently, then lifted her eyes to Mamma Louisa's. "Dr. Hinkle shot the wrong wolf!"

"Dr. Hinkle shot this poor animal?" Mike asked.

"The moon hasn't yet risen," Mamma Louisa explained. "The wolf Hinkle sought is still in human form." She closed her eyes, tipped her head back, rocked slowly on her feet. "Hinkle-man, he realized that even as he tried to skin the poor creature. But the man came. The man came—only moments ago, when the gunshot rang out and the wolf pet cried. The man came, and Hinkle-man hid and waited. When the man bent over the wolf, Hinkle hit him hard, on the head. Knock him out. Took him away."

She took the light from Jenny and shone it on the ground. "Look there. One man, dragging another."

"Hinkle's taken him."

"Mm. He'll hold the man until the moon comes. Until the change comes. And then—"

"Then he'll kill him, and perform his sick ritual." Jenny turned her gaze to the three young people. "Dr. Hinkle plans to turn himself into a werewolf tonight. It's all here, in his journal. Unfortunately, he has to murder an innocent man to do it."

The twins exchanged glances. Toby took the journal from her. "I'm sorry, Professor Rose. We—we trusted him. We had no idea."

"Neither did I."

"What can we do?" Carrie asked. "How can we help?"

Jenny looked down at the suffering animal. "Can you get Mojo to the town vet?"

"Mojo?"

She nodded toward the wolf. "He's a pet. A beautiful animal. Please help him."

"We'll take care of it." The two boys knelt beside Mojo, gently picking him up, one on each end. Mamma Louisa had removed her white bandanna and torn it apart to make bandages for the animal's skinned flank. Poor creature. It whimpered as the boys carried it away, but they moved as carefully and gently as they could.

Alone with Mamma Louisa, Jenny faced her. "Where did Hinkle take Samuel?" she asked. "How can we find them?"

The older woman dug in her bag and took out a beautiful, glittering crystal suspended from a string. She let it dangle until it was still, then watched as it began to swing. The motion was barely detectable at first, but grew steadily. Finally, she gave the string a snap, caught the crystal in her hand, and said, "This way."

IT seemed to Jenny as if it took forever before she smelled the smoke. Then, gradually, she saw the faint glow, and then the dancing firelight in the distance. She picked up the pace and tried hard to move quickly but quietly at the same time. The two of them crept up to the edge of a tiny clearing and peered from the trees.

Jenny spotted Samuel. He lay on the ground, his hands and feet bound in front of him. He was barely conscious, eyes flickering open and closed, and there was blood coming from his head, glistening in the firelight as it trickled over his face.

A tripod had been erected over the fire, and a cauldron hung from it. Steam rose from the cauldron as its contents boiled, and the scents of herbs filled the air. Close by, Dr. Hinkle sat on the ground, completely naked. He was rubbing something gooey over his arms and chest. Jenny wondered if it was feline fat and felt her stomach lurch. God, how many innocent animals were going to have to suffer to satisfy Hinkle's insanity?

"What do we do?"

"He's made a circle." Mamma Louisa pointed at a ring of what looked like salt on the ground. "I can break it. Come."

She took a feather fan from her bag and used it like a broom, sweeping the air before her as they crept forward. Hinkle sat with his eyes closed, chanting the words of his spell.

As she reached the ring of salt, Mamma Louisa said, "Open!" and swept the fan in the air and then over the ground, brushing the salt away and stepping inside. Jenny followed, then froze as she saw the glowing sphere of the moon rising above them. She spun around and saw Samuel, bound there, jerking spasmodically against the ropes as growling sounds emerged from deep in his chest.

At the sound of Mamma Louisa's command, Hinkle's eyes flew wide and he sprang to his feet. "You get out of here!"

Mamma Louisa shook her head.

Beyond her, Samuel was changing. His eyes rolled and his back arched as his facial muscles contorted. The rope at his wrists snapped in two.

"In the name of Oya, in the name of Yemaya, I cast every negative force from this circle! I call in goodness. I call in white light. I call in protection!"

"No! Get out, I say!" Hinkle crouched low, reaching for something, and when he rose again he lifted a gun.

"Look out!" Jenny shouted.

But even as she said it, the wolf leapt, hitting Hinkle squarely in the chest. The gun flew from his hands, and the shot it fired went wild.

Now Hinkle was on his back, with a snarling, fiercely powerful wolf standing on his chest, growling. The two women stood there, staring, and Jenny knew full well there would be nothing either of them could do to prevent the wolf from tearing out Hinkle's throat. Not physically at least.

Swallowing hard, Jenny knew she had to try to reach the man she loved, before he made himself a killer.

"Samuel, I know you're in there," Jenny said softly. "I know you can hear me. Mojo is alive. He's at the vet, getting treatment even now. And this man will never hurt anyone again, not when I testify as to what happened here tonight."

The wolf looked toward her. Its eyes . . . they were Samuel's eyes. Mamma Louisa reached into her bag, and Jenny held up a hand to stop her. "No. No, you don't have to use magic. He won't do harm to a human being. I know it. Just wait."

The wolf growled, deep and low.

"Don't hurt him, Samuel. You're a healer, not a killer."

The animal looked back down at the man on the ground, then at her again.

"I love you, Samuel," she whispered.

The wolf focused on Hinkle's face, leaned very close, so close the man must have felt the animal's hot breath on his skin, then it let loose a series of sharp, angry barks and growls and snapped its jaws within an inch of Hinkle's face, before it turned and leapt to the ground. It didn't run off as Jenny had expected, but only moved beyond the fire's light and curled on the ground in the shadows.

Jenny ran to snatch up the pieces of fallen rope and the gun. Then she made Hinkle put on his clothes while she held the weapon on him. "What the hell were you thinking?" she demanded as he dressed. "Why would you want to do something so insane?"

He looked up at her as he buttoned his shirt. "I'm aging, Jennifer, or hadn't you noticed that? Young, sharp professors like you are coming in. Pushing me out. I miss my youth, my vitality. I've

read the accounts. With the wolf inside me, I'd be young again, strong as a man half my age."

"Wonder how fast you'll age in prison. Maybe you should have considered that."

He shook his head. "You tell anyone about this, I'll reveal Samuel La Roque for what he really is."

"Then you won't end up in prison after all." She smiled softly. "It'll be a mental institution instead."

She handed Mamma Louisa the ropes. The other woman tied him up while Jenny held the gun. Then the two women led him out of the circle of salt and set him on the ground beside a tree. Mamma Louisa returned to the fire in the center of the circle, and using her shawl as a pot holder, took the iron kettle from the tripod. She carried it a few yards away and poured its smelly contents onto the ground. She left the kettle there.

When she returned to the circle, she dug into her bag and tossed handfuls of herbs from various jars onto the glowing fire. The smoke they emitted was fragrant and good.

She turned then, her eyes falling upon the wolf that lay near the circle's edge.

It rose, as if it knew what to do, and paced slowly to her.

Nodding her approval, Mamma Louisa looked to Jenny. "Go, watch over Hinkle-man and let me do my work."

Jenny nodded. "Samuel never got the chance to deliver that apology he owed you," she said.

"He saved me from that one's bullet. I say that's as good as an apology. We be even now. Go."

Jenny left the circle of firelight and stood near Hinkle, the gun still in her hand just in case. Mamma Louisa sprinkled fresh salt in

the area where she had brushed it away, completing the ring again. Then she moved to kneel in front of the wolf, her hands pressing to either side of its head as she stared into its eyes and spoke to it earnestly.

The wolf whined as it stared intently back at her, and finally, it lay down at her feet. It didn't fight when she spread her shawl over it, and it lay still there while she moved around it, gesturing and chanting, shaking her rattles, sprinkling it with herbs and salt and lifting her hands skyward to call on her gods. She moved faster, and her voice grew louder and her rattles shook faster, until the noise reached a pitch Jenny was sure could be heard all the way back at the plantation. And then suddenly, with a loud whoop, Mamma Louisa yanked the shawl from over the wolf.

Samuel lay there, naked, shivering, maybe a little disoriented. He blinked up at Louisa as she nodded in approval. Then she swept an opening in the circle with her feather fan and waved Jenny closer. Jenny hurried to Samuel. As she sank to her knees beside him, he said, "It's still in me. I can still feel the wolf in me."

"Yes," Mamma Louisa told him, handing him the shawl so he could cover himself. He sat up, knotting it around his hips. "The wolf still lives in you. But now, Samuel La Roque, you are in control. You can become the wolf, but only when you want to—or when you lose control of your emotions. It will be difficult at first, as the wolf seeks to take you, especially when the moon is full. But it will grow easier in time, as you make your will stronger and stronger. It is the best I can do for you."

He closed his eyes, drew a deep breath. "Thank you, Mamma Louisa." Then he opened his eyes and gazed steadily at her. "I'm sorry. For what my great-grandfather did to Alana."

"I'm sorry for what my great-grandmother did to avenge her." She gave him a nod, then took the gun from Jenny's hand. "I take the Hinkle-man from here, *chère*."

"Alone? But . . ."

Mamma Louisa gave her a smile and nodded at something beyond her where Hinkle sat near the tree. Jenny turned and saw the entire group of Voudons gathered in the woods nearby, awaiting their priestess's word. "My people, they know when I need them. Don't you worry." She nodded, and two strong men rushed forward, gripping Hinkle's arms and hauling him to his feet and back through the woods.

Mamma Louisa followed and the entire group vanished into the woods.

Samuel got to his feet. He looked like some kind of woodland god, with the white cotton knotted around his hip and his magnificent chest bare. He reached for her.

Jenny went into his arms, relishing the feel of his skin against her body, against her face as she laid her cheek on his shoulder.

He held her for a long time, then he said, "Did you mean what you said before? That you love me?"

She shivered all over. "Yes. I don't know how it happened so fast, Samuel, but it did. I love you."

"Even though I—I might occasionally run with Mojo, and howl at the moon?"

She trailed a hand over his face. "Mojo might have to take a few months off, while he heals. But after that, I may just join you." She stared deeply into his deep, brown eyes. "I love all you are, Samuel. All of you. I love your wolf side, your wild side, and I swear I'll always keep your secrets."

"Just as I'll keep yours. I love you, too, Jenny."

He kissed her deeply, passionately, held her tight to his body as he lowered them both to the ground. As he peeled away her clothes, and she tugged at the shawl that covered him, Jenny heard him growl. She growled right back, and nipped his lip with her teeth as he moved his body to cover hers.

Somewhere in the distance, she heard a wolf howl.

And a few minutes later, she joined in the song.

Daydream Believer

CHAPTER ONE

✒

*M*EGAN sat up in bed, a cold sweat coating her skin, her trembling hands already clutching the telephone. Sure, it was upside down, but that was sort of beyond the point. Obviously, her subconscious thought this was it. The big one. Time to do some good. Her eyes were drawn to the television on the far side of the room. She'd fallen asleep with the set still on, and at the moment it was showing a photo of the missing woman, Sarah Dresden, smiling at the camera, obviously unaware what the future held for her. Underneath the photo was a telephone number: the Pinedale Police Department's "Tipline."

Bringing the receiver closer, she dialed the number. She had never phoned the police department after one of her episodes before. Never. God knew her visions had never inspired much action up to now. Certainly nothing police-worthy.

"PPD Tipline, can you help us?"

Quaint, she thought. "I, um . . . I need to speak with the chief, please."

"May I ask who's calling?"

She didn't want to answer that. "It's about the missing woman," she said instead. "I know where she is."

"Hold on." The voice betrayed no emotion, but there had been a brief hesitation before the reply.

A second later, a male voice came on the line. "Chief Skinner speaking."

"Good," she said. "Look, I've never done anything like this before. But . . . I think I know where your missing woman is. Sarah Dresden."

"Uh-huh. And how did you come by your information, Miss . . . ?"

She swallowed hard, gathered up her courage. "I get . . . visions."

She heard his sigh and realized she'd better talk fast before he hung up on her and filed her call away with all the other cranks he must receive. "Never anything this important. Actually, I've always wished . . . but it doesn't matter. My visions are always on the money. I swear."

"Look, lady, I don't have time for—"

"Sarah is twenty-five, a pretty brunette, a runner—"

"And all of that information has been covered by the local news, ma'am."

"She had a butterfly tattoo on the back of her neck, and was wearing red sneakers with white laces."

He paused for a moment, then said, "I don't know if that's right or not. I'd have to check the reports."

"Check. I'll hold."

"All right." She heard papers shuffling. "Why don't you tell me where you think she is while I look?"

Maybe she had his attention. Maybe he was going to take her seriously now. No one in her life ever had. God, this could be a banner moment for her. If only the information she had to share were more positive. "I had a dream about her last night. She's not alive, Chief. Her body is in the river, snagged on some rocks underneath the Amstead Road Bridge."

"Uh-huh."

She swallowed hard.

"Ma'am?"

"Yes, Chief."

"It would give you considerably more credibility if you'd give us your name. Not that we can't find that out anyway with the telephone system we have here, but—"

"Megan Rose," she said. "I live here in Pinedale, out on Sycamore Street. I own the Celestial Bakery in the village, corner of Silver and Main. And I'd appreciate your discretion about this. I'm not sure how my customers would feel about my calling you like this."

"I'm not sure that will even be an issue, ma'am."

"Excuse me?"

"I found the reports on the Dresden woman. She was last seen wearing suede hiking boots, not red sneakers. And there are no unusual markings on her body, no tattoos of any kind. Sorry, ma'am. It was a nice thought, though."

She felt her jaw drop and her head swirl. What the hell . . . ? How could such a vivid dream be so wrong? God, would her so-called *gift* ever be of any use to anyone? She swallowed hard.

"You have a nice day now, Ms. Rose."

"Uh—Chief?"

"Yes, ma'am?"

She sighed heavily. "You left your headlights on when you parked your car this morning. You might want to check."

"I'll do that."

Megan hit the cutoff button and set the phone down, then leaned back against her headboard and wiped the sweat from her brow. Damn, damn, damn. She thought she had finally seen something *important*. Something more than the useless tidbits her visions provided every day of her life. Something big.

No such luck.

The damn dream had started out as the same one she'd been having since she was twelve years old—the one where she saw the handsome man's face hovering in the mists and heard a voice telling her she was going to break a curse and save his life. Then it had taken a unique turn, and the image had changed to one of the missing woman, first smiling like in the photo on TV, and then lifeless and pale, her hair tangling around her face just below the surface of the Genesee River.

Megan licked her lips. Probably her subconscious had heard the television news report talking about the missing woman. Probably her mind had woven what she heard into her dream, a bad case of wishful thinking. Not wishing the woman was dead, of course, but wishing she could help find her, and finally be believed.

She thought again of the man, the one she was supposed to save from some kind of curse, and she sighed. "Whoever you are, mister," she said softly, "my feeling is, you're doomed."

* * *

SAM Sheridan knocked twice before stepping into the chief's office. "Morning, Chief."

"Morning, Sam. How's your mother?"

"Mom sends her love and a slice of apple pie." Sam set the Tupperware container on his boss's desk. The older man had been an intimate family friend a lot longer than he'd been Sam's boss, and old habits died hard. "She says you're expected for dinner on my birthday and she won't take no for an answer."

The chief smiled, his wrinkles showing more deeply when he did. "You bet your ass I'll be there. Your old man would come back from beyond and knock me senseless if I missed it."

Sam nodded, a twinge of sadness twisting his belly, even though it had been twenty-seven years. Ed Skinner turned to move to the window, absently parting the drapes and looking out over the parking lot below.

"Listen, Sam, I wanted to talk to you about this Dresden case. There's—well, I'll be damned."

"Chief?" Frowning, Sam moved closer to the window.

"I left my headlights on," the chief said.

Sam smiled. "Old age creeping up on you, that's all. I'll flip 'em off on my way out if you want."

The chief let the drapes fall back into place, turned to face Sam again. "Where you heading?"

"Questioning some witnesses on the Sarah Dresden case. People who might have seen something in the area along the riverbank, where we found the body this morning."

The chief nodded. "Press hasn't been notified about the body yet, have they?"

"No, sir. Hell, she's barely been out of the water an hour."

"No leaks that you know of?"

"None."

The chief pursed his lips. "Sam, I've got something else I'd like you to check on for me."

Sam lifted his brows.

"Woman by the name of Megan Rose. Knows a little more about this case than she ought to."

Sam tipped his head. This was the first thing remotely like a lead they'd had in the series of rape-murders plaguing the small western New York town. "Like what?"

"Like where the body was. I just got off the phone with her."

Sam felt a little shiver go up his spine. "Did she say how she knew?"

"Yeah. Claims she's some kind of psychic."

Sam would have laughed if the topic had been a less serious one. As it was, he just shook his head. He didn't believe in that sort of garbage, despite the fact that his grandmother claimed a touch of E.S.P. herself. She'd never predicted anything beyond his own impending demise, and he wasn't about to give that any credibility.

"I'd like to find out how she really knew—and what else she might know," the chief said.

Sam nodded. "You want me to question her?"

"I'm thinking we might want a more subtle approach; we don't want to scare her off. Let me do a little checking on her first. Stay available. I'll let you know how I want you to proceed."

Sam nodded. "Whatever you say, Chief."

CHAPTER TWO

MEGAN glanced into the rearview mirror when she heard the
siren, and cussed to herself when she saw the lights. And
now she understood her premonition that she would arrive at the
bank three minutes after it closed, and that as a result, a check
would bounce tomorrow. She'd left early to circumvent fate, and
she'd driven fast to further ensure her success.

Only now she realized that if she'd never had the damned vision, she never would have been driving several miles an hour above
the speed limit, and never would have been pulled over, and maybe,
never would have been late. Was there such a thing as a self-
fulfilling prophecy?

Not only was her gift of little practical use, it was often down-
right cruel.

She pulled off onto the shoulder and sat there, drumming her
fingers and looking at her watch while the officer took his sweet

time about doing whatever it was they did in their cars while the speeders sweat it out and everyone they knew drove past and saw them. She took her wallet out of her purse, slid her license out of her wallet. Might as well save whatever time she could. She took the registration from the glove compartment and rolled down her window. Then she drummed her fingers some more as the seconds ticked away.

Finally, a cop came walking up alongside her car, uniform, sunglasses, jack boots. He glanced inside, quickly into the backseat, then leaned down.

"Li—"

"License and registration," she said, handing both to him.

He took them, peering at them through his sunglasses. "Do you know—"

"How fast I was going? Yes. Forty-three. And yes, I know this is a thirty-five-mile-per-hour zone. I won't even argue with you. I was speeding, I admit it. Trying to get to the bank before it closes, but I'm obviously not going to make it now."

"You always finish peoples' sentences for them?"

She looked up at him, noticed the line of his jaw, square chin with a little dimple in the center. Something niggled at her. The sunglasses hid his eyes. "Always."

"A little boy's dog was hit here last week. Kid cried for three days straight."

She closed her eyes, nodding. "Point taken. Speed limits are posted for a reason."

He nodded. "I'll go run this. It'll take a minute."

She looked at her watch. "It's too late to make the bank now anyway. Tomorrow a check is going to bounce."

"You know which one?"

She glanced at him, frowning. "Yeah. Why?"

"Call whoever has it tonight, ask them to wait until noon to deposit it, and then go to the bank in the morning."

She tipped her head to one side. His solution was so simple she could not for the life of her figure out why she had bothered racing for the bank in the first place.

He tapped her license against his fingertips. "Be right back."

Something was off here. Why had her so-called gift bothered to warn her about making the bank on time in the first place? Nothing all that earth-shattering was going to happen and she could even avoid the bounced check.

She smiled to herself, shook her head at her own efforts to force her premonitions to be useful, helpful, and how those efforts always backfired. "I suck," she muttered.

Then she closed her eyes, leaned back on her seat, and waited for the handsome cop to come back. Just once, she thought, she would like to find a missing child, or identify a murderer, or solve a bank robbery. Other psychics got to do dramatic, wonderful things like that. Meanwhile, she foresaw a "closed" sign in the bank window, and failed to see the speed trap until Officer Studly back there sprang it on her.

She smiled again, almost laughed at her own silliness. At least she'd gotten to meet the good-looking cop. She wondered if he was married.

He tapped her car door. She turned to see him holding her license and registration out to her. No gloves. No wedding ring either.

"You'll be glad to know you're not wanted for anything."

"Hey, I resent that remark."

The cop, stone-faced till now, smiled slowly as he got her joke. "I meant by the law."

"So did I," she told him.

His smile flashed then, full force and almost blinding, and again something niggled at her. Something powerful. "I'm gonna let you off with a warning this time."

"Really?"

He nodded.

"Thanks, Officer. I appreciate that." She reached up to take the license and registration from his hand, but when her fingers brushed over his, she froze as a flash of light and sensation hit her all at once. She knew her hand closed powerfully around his and that her head slammed back against the seat and her eyes rolled. And then she was gone, down, down through a dark tunnel, until she emerged on the other side into the pouring rain and driving wind. Small green pup tents whipped, tore, stakes popping, cords snapping. Teenage boys huddled together, a canvas wrapped around their shoulders and mini rivulets running past their feet. A large tree. A creaking limb.

"Hey. Hey, come on, are you okay?"

His voice drew her back into the tunnel, back into her body, where she landed with the same thudding, jolting impact she always did. She felt warm pavement underneath her back, and a warmer hand cupping her nape. Her eyes popped open.

Her cop was leaning over her, a hand supporting her head, his face close to hers. He'd apparently pulled her out of the car when the vision hit. And no wonder. They'd never hit her so hard before, with such a physical impact.

She blinked her eyes clear and stared up at him. The sunglasses were gone, and she could see his eyes. They were deep brown, with thick, dark lashes. And they were painfully familiar.

He was the man she'd been dreaming about from the age of twelve. She realized it suddenly and with a shock that nearly made her gasp out loud. God, she knew his face like she knew her own.

"There you are," he said softly. "Don't worry. You're going to be fine."

"I know I am." What on earth was happening here? Something . . . this was no accidental meeting. She blinked a couple of times, pressed a hand to her head. The rush was gone. She felt normal again—physically, at least. She sat up, but her cop pressed his hands to her shoulders, telling her to stay down. "I'm fine," she said. "Really. You didn't go calling for backup over this, did you?"

"I radioed for an ambulance when you passed out," he told her. She blinked at him. "Cancel it, will you?"

"Are you sure?"

She nodded. "It's not the first time this has happened to me." It was the first time it had knocked her senseless, however. "And I didn't pass out."

"You didn't?"

She shook her head. "Can I sit up now?"

He nodded, extended a hand, and helped her into a sitting position. Then he tapped the microphone that was clipped to his collar, calling her attention to his corded neck, and spoke in cop jargon. She was pretty sure he was canceling the ambulance he'd ordered for her.

She was getting to her feet, and he was still holding her, helping her. He said, "So if that wasn't passing out, what was it? Some kind of seizure?"

She studied his face. Hell, she was going to have to tell him. It wasn't life and death, or even minor crime solving—but then again, who was she to say? It could be important. He was the man of her dreams, after all. And it would be cruel not to tell him. "It wasn't a seizure. It was . . . a vision."

His brows went up. "A vision. As in . . . a psychic vision?"

"I get them sometimes. I think when I touched your hand . . ." She watched his face, waiting for one of the looks she had come to expect: the blatant disbelief of her overly critical father, who would call her a compulsive liar and probably punish her for it; or the horrified fear of her zealot mother, who would call her evil, offensive to God, and would probably punish her for that.

The man's face betrayed no emotion, neither skepticism nor fear. "So you're psychic, then?"

She swallowed her fears. "Yeah. Just not usually about anything important. I do have some advice for you, though."

"Really? For me?"

She nodded, staring into his eyes. She didn't tell him about her dreams, about her having seen his face in her mind for such a long, long time. She didn't ask him if he were laboring under any sort of curse that he knew of. No sense giving him further reason to doubt her sanity.

She wanted to see this man again. And she kind of thought she needed to. So she'd start him off easy. And even then he probably wouldn't believe her. No one ever believed her.

He walked with her the few steps to her car, opened her door for her, waiting patiently for her advice.

She stood beside the open door, lost in her explorations of his face. God, he was handsome. "You're, um . . . taking a group of teenage boys camping this weekend?"

He blinked, clearly surprised that she would know that. "Yeah. Over at Letchworth. It's a departmental program, and it's my turn."

"It's a very, very bad idea."

He frowned at her. "That's what your vision was about? My camping trip?"

She nodded. "I saw torrential rains, high winds, soaked, miserable kids, and tents getting torn to shreds." She frowned. "And I got a bad feeling—something about a tree. Big pine, lots of dead branches."

"The one where the vultures roost," he muttered.

"Could be. I didn't see any vultures. Still . . . if I were you I'd change the date."

She got into her car. He stood there, holding her door open, staring in at her. "You're not kidding about this, are you?"

"Nope. If I were making it up, I'd predict something much more important. I mean, this isn't earth-shattering, but you might stay drier if you listen." She shrugged. "I may not change the world with my visions, but I'm never wrong."

"Never, huh?"

"Well. Almost never," she said, recalling that she'd made a complete fool of herself with the chief of police this morning.

"Then how come you didn't know I was sitting here clocking your speed?"

She pursed her lips, saw the twinkle of humor in his eyes, and knew he wasn't ridiculing her—he didn't believe her either, but he wasn't being mean. He wasn't calling her a liar or a sinner. "I've been asking myself the same thing, to be honest. If I hadn't had the vision of getting to the bank too late, I wouldn't have been speeding. I wouldn't have been stopped. And I wouldn't have been late. As it is . . ." She shrugged. "I don't know. Maybe we were supposed to meet." That was it. She knew it the moment she said it, with a certainty she rarely felt about anything.

"You think?"

"I do." She stuck her hand out the window. "Megan Rose."

"So it said on your driver's license," he said. But he took her hand in his, and it was warm, smooth, and firm. "Sam Sheridan."

"Good to meet you, Sam."

He lifted his dark, thick brows, maybe a little surprised she had used his first name. He shouldn't be. The man belonged on a police-hunks calendar. And besides, she'd known him forever. It wasn't her fault he had no way of knowing that. He was far more stunning, she thought, in person.

"I hope next time it'll be under more pleasant circumstances," he said.

And there would be a next time, she had to make sure of that. "Will you do me a favor, Sam?"

"What's that?"

"A favor? It's something nice you do for someone else." He smirked at her, and she smiled in return. "If you should take my advice about camping this weekend, and something important results from it, would you let me know?"

He frowned at her, obviously unsure she was being serious.

She shrugged. "You never know. One of these days this so-called gift of mine might actually do something useful. So will you call if you get the feeling it has?"

"Sure I will."

She smiled, tugged a little card from her purse, and handed it to him.

He looked at it. "Celestial Bakery?"

"You were expecting me to tell fortunes for a living, I'll bet."

He shrugged, tucking the card into his pocket. "I'll call."

"I hope you do."

She pulled her seat belt on, put the car into gear, and pulled into the nearest driveway to turn around, since it was already too late to make the bank.

I'M never wrong. Well, almost never . . .

Sam stood in the woods of Letchworth State Park, huddled with the boys currently enrolled in the Pinedale Police Department's Cop-Camp program. All of them were shivering and soaked to the skin. Their tents hadn't held up to the gale-force winds, and he doubted these trees were going to hold up against them much longer. He could have kicked himself for ignoring Megan Rose. Not that he thought her claims of psychic powers were anything. Hell, she could have figured this storm was coming from watching the Weather Channel.

· Though the local weather reports had completely missed it.

Something creaked ominously overhead, and her voice whispered through his brain, yet again, the way it had been doing for three consecutive nights now.

And I got a bad feeling—something about a tree. . . .

He looked up at the tall, haunted-looking tree the kids referred to as the Vulture Roost, as the woman's words whispered through his memory.

Big pine, lots of dead branches.

A limb creaked and groaned.

"Everyone out from under the tree!" Sam shouted. As he said it, he herded the cold, wet teenagers out of the relative shelter of the woods and into the open, and the full fury of the storm. "Move it!"

They moved it. And when they were standing in the clearing that had seemed like such a perfect campsite, he heard a loud CRACK and saw the overweight limb crash to the ground right where they'd all been standing.

The boys and his Cop-Camp cocounselor, Derrick, were all staring at him. One of the kids said, "How did you know?"

"Heard the limb cracking," he replied, making his voice loud enough to compete with the storm. "What, you telling me none of you heard it?"

The entire group of males shook their heads side to side.

"Well, I heard it. Good thing, I guess."

"Yeah. Darn good thing," Derrick said. He was searching Sam's face as if he didn't quite believe him.

Sam looked away, recalling Megan Rose's warning. She couldn't have seen that limb breaking on the Weather Channel.

Then again, it wasn't that big a leap of logic. A storm, plus a forest, equals falling limbs. It was only common sense. Still . . .

"I think maybe we need to get out of here."

"What about the gear?" Derrick asked.

"Leave it. We can't protect it anyway. We'll come back when the weather breaks and grab whatever's left. I think the faster we get out of these woods, the better."

Derrick nodded in agreement. "You heard him, boys. We're out of here."

"I heard that," one of the teens said.

As soon as he managed to get warm and dry and stop shivering, Sam promised himself he was going to tell the pretty redhead that her warning had been dead on target. He supposed he owed her that much. And he had to see her again, anyway. Chief's orders. Though he kind of thought he'd have wanted to see her again even if that hadn't been the case.

There was something about Megan Rose that had brought his senses to life in a way he'd never ever experienced before. Which was not a good thing, considering that the chief suspected she was somehow involved with a murderer.

CHAPTER THREE

S HE stood at the counter, blinking in surprise at the man who
stood on the other side.

He wasn't wearing his uniform, but that didn't interfere with
the instant recognition, nor with the tingling awareness that came
with it. He was still gorgeous. Still familiar. Still important to her,
even though it made no sense he should be.

She tipped her head to one side. "I wasn't speeding, I swear,"
she said.

He smiled at her. "That's what they all say. How do you know
I'm not here for the doughnuts?"

She let her gaze slide down the front of him. "It doesn't take a
psychic to see you're not big on doughnuts, Sam."

He shifted a little, as if self-conscious under her stare, so she
brought her eyes up to his again. There was a hint of fire there.
"Actually," he said, "I'm here to keep my promise." He shrugged.

"Well, technically, I guess the promise was to call if anything happened, but I, uh—I don't know. I just decided to come by."

Megan frowned, her attention shifting instantly from his looks to his words. "Something happened?"

"Yeah. Something happened."

"Hold on a sec." She turned toward the kitchen in the back and called, "Karen, I'm taking a break. You okay by yourself?"

"Sure thing," Karen called as she came walking out of the kitchen, wiping her hands on a towel. Megan took off her apron as she came around the counter. "We can talk over here. You want some coffee?"

"No, I'm good, thanks."

She led him to one of the small, round tables. There were only a handful. Most people came here to pick up orders and carry them home, but now and then someone liked to just get a doughnut or pastry and relax with a cup of coffee.

"This is a really nice little place," he said. "You seem to be doing well."

"Yeah, yeah, enough with the small talk. What happened? Did you go on that camping trip?"

"I did. It's a program the department has for at-risk teens. Cops volunteer, take groups on camping trips a few weekends every summer. It's a good program."

"Sounds like. So what happened?"

He pressed his palms to the tabletop. "I don't even believe in this stuff. I mean . . . I never have."

She gnawed her lip and tried not to bark at him to get to the point already.

"It was just like you said it would be. A storm hit, even though the weather service predicted it would miss us by fifty miles. We had high winds, heavy rain, tents blowing all over hell and gone. Everyone was huddled near a copse of trees for shelter."

"Please tell me no one was hurt."

He looked her dead in the eye. "No one was hurt. It was close, though. I don't know what happened. All of a sudden I heard the limb creaking, and your voice was in my head, repeating what you said the other day. I got everyone out of the way just before the limb fell." He shook his head slowly. "It was huge. Came crashing down where we'd been standing. I have to tell you, Megan, if it hadn't been for your warning, someone could have been seriously hurt. Or worse."

She sat there for a long moment, just staring at him. "You're not just messing with me, are you?"

He lifted his brows. "Why would I do that?"

She lowered her head. Her father had pretended to believe her once, just to trick her into elaborating on what she had seen, so he could punish her for even more lies. And after her vision came true, her mother had never forgiven her.

"We went back this morning," Sam was saying; she shook off her painful memories and focused on the present; ". . . to gather up the gear. Several trees had come down in our camping area. It was a real mess, Megan. Could've been a real disaster."

She let her lips pull into a smile. "I can't believe it. All my life, it seems, I've been waiting for this gift to be . . . useful. Helpful in some way."

"It's never been before?"

She shook her head. "It . . . tried to be once. But I couldn't make anyone listen."

He tipped his head, silently urging her to go on. But she shook her head firmly. "It doesn't matter. Ever since then it's been little things. I'd know when the phone was going to ring and who would be calling, or when the deliveryman was going to be late. I'd know which roads were going to be jammed with traffic and where to find a parking space. I knew Karen over there was going to get a puppy long before she ever thought about it, and I always know what people will order when they come into the shop."

"Doughnuts, right?"

She smiled at him. "Hey, you're psychic, too?"

"Well, just so you know, this time you did some good."

She sighed in relief. "You don't know what that means to me. I'm so glad you kept your promise and let me know."

He nodded. She started to get up and he said, "So what now?"

Frowning, Megan settled into her chair again. "What do you mean, what now?"

"Well, I mean . . . this can't be it. The end of it."

She tipped her head to one side.

"Look, you said yourself you couldn't understand the vision that resulted in us meeting that day. That you would have made the bank on time, if not for the vision messing with your head, so you drove too fast and ended up with me stopping you, right?"

"Well, yeah. But—"

"But what? You said it that day. Maybe we were supposed to meet. And we did, and you wound up saving a bunch of kids because of it."

She shook her head. "Not necessarily. You said you heard the limb creaking."

"Yeah, but no one else did. I'm not even sure I really heard it, or just thought I did because of what you had said."

"Okay, maybe."

He nodded. "I've been thinking about this ever since that limb fell. And the more I think about it, the more I think it would be stupid not to see where this thing might lead."

Shaking her head slowly, she said, "I don't understand. What *thing*?"

"Us. Working together."

She blinked precisely three times. "Tell me you're talking about you coming to work for me at the bakery."

"I'm talking about you, working with me on crimes. One crime, in particular."

She closed her eyes. "Jeez, Sam, I'm nowhere near good enough for something that important."

"I think you are."

"Well, you think wrong. One time I get a decent vision, and you want to turn it into . . ." She let her voice trail off, because she couldn't resist asking, "What crime in particular?"

He lowered his head, she thought to hide a look of triumph, and a suspicion whispered through her brain. "A string of sexual attacks. All connected. The department is stumped."

"And?"

"And what?"

"What are you leaving out?" she asked.

He shrugged. "I'm up for a promotion. If I can be instrumental in solving this thing, it will be in the bag."

She frowned at him for a long moment, feeling deflated. She'd liked him, at first. Thought he was genuine. Maybe, being psychic, she should have picked up on the fact that he was looking to get ahead, willing to use her to do it. It hurt that the first person to believe in her gift had to be so small-minded.

Pushing back her chair, she got to her feet.

He reached out and clasped her hand.

The flash hit her hard, snapping her head back with its impact, and sucking her out of her waking state, and into a vision that burned her brain with its brightness. Girls. No. Women. Two beautiful women, laughing and talking both at once, and him, Sam, right in the midst of them. And then there was something else. The dead woman, Sarah Dresden, the tattoo and the river.

The vision released her as if dropping her from a great height. She hit the earth so hard it jarred her teeth.

"Jesus, are you okay? Megan?"

She opened her eyes, found herself sitting back in the chair where she'd started out. He wasn't. He was kneeling close beside her, and across the room Karen was looking over the counter at her.

"Who are they?" Megan asked. "The women, the two women?"

He shook his head.

"All S names. Sabrina and She—Shelly?"

"Shelby. They're my sisters." He was looking at her as if she'd sprouted horns. "What did you see? Is something going to happen to them? Are they in trouble?"

She shook her head slowly. "They're fine. Who is your mother, anyway, Cleopatra?"

He frowned even harder. "I don't know what you—"

"You all look like you belong in the movies. Your sisters are as gorgeous as you—uh—as you probably already know." God, she hated the slightly stupid state in which that powerful vision had left her.

He was crouching there on the floor, looking up at her, the concern in his eyes slowly being replaced by amusement. "You're not too hard on the eyes yourself, Meg. You okay? Better now?" He gently pushed her hair behind her ear, and she was surprised at how intimate the small gesture seemed, how right it felt, and how hard she had to fight not to lift her hand to cover his, and press it to her cheek.

"I'm okay," she said. "You lied to me, though."

"I did not. I really am up for a promotion."

"But that's not why you want to catch this guy. It's not about the job at all. It's about your sisters. They're local, I take it?"

"Local, single. Walk to their cars alone sometimes. Jog in the park. Used to, anyway."

"They even have S names. Just like Sarah Dresden."

He nodded.

"Did all the victims?"

"No. It's coincidence. But it still drove it home for me. How it could just as easily happen to one of them," he said. He averted his eyes. "The thought of that bastard going after one of my sisters—"

She nodded. "You want to protect them. And you feel for the victims because you see them as someone's sisters, too. You have a real empathy for them."

He frowned. "I'm not sure how much I'm going to like hanging out with a woman who can see through me that easily."

"Shouldn't be a problem, unless you have something to hide. Which you don't. Not anymore, at least."

"And what is that supposed to mean?"

She pursed her lips. "I heard on the news that Sarah Dresden's body was found."

"So?"

"But they didn't say where."

He didn't look at her. "We like to keep some information private, Megan."

"But you already know that I know where she was found. You know I phoned your chief and told him where that body was located, and that she had a tattoo, and I'd lay odds she was wearing red sneakers, too."

He licked his lips as he moved back to his seat. "I'm not allowed to tell you any of that."

"You don't have to tell me. What I don't know is why your chief denied everything I told him that day. Or why you're really here with me now. Is it because you really believe I can help you with this case, or do you suspect me of something?"

He lifted his head, met her eyes. "You were right about the body, the tattoo, the sneakers. The thing is she was found a couple of hours prior to your call. The chief isn't convinced there wasn't a leak."

"I see."

"Obviously I don't suspect you of anything, Megan. I like you."

She searched his eyes, looking for the lie, and found sincerity there instead.

"To be honest, I'm not entirely convinced you can help me on this case, but I'm willing to give it a try. If you are."

She lowered her head. "I don't know how much help I'm going to be. But yeah, I'll give it a try. I guess. Let me make some arrangements here. I can call some of my part-timers, see if they can take on full-time for a week. Will that be enough? A week?"

"We can work around your schedule. When you have time, I'll take you to some of the crime scenes, see if you can pick up on anything from them."

"Okay. All right. And maybe I could talk to some of the victims."

"He . . . hasn't left any of his victims alive, Meg."

She closed her eyes. "How many have there been?"

"You haven't been following the case on the news?"

She shook her head. "Not until this last one. Something about her . . ." She let her voice trail off with the thought.

"Thirteen so far," he told her.

She shook her head sadly. A little voice asked her if this wasn't exactly what she had always wanted. A big case, a chance to do some good. To prove herself.

No, she thought. Not like this.

But she knew she had to try. "So when do we begin?"

"Tonight."

"So soon?"

He smiled gently. "Tonight, I'm taking you out to dinner. To thank you for saving those kids, and maybe me along with them."

She held his gaze and wondered if maybe she had fulfilled that part of her premonition—that of saving him. She also wondered if he thought he was going to have to romance her a little in order to ensure her continued cooperation.

She kind of hoped so.

CHAPTER FOUR

S o you're seeing her tonight?" the chief asked.

"Yes, taking her to dinner as ordered, but like I said, I think you're off base on this one." Sam sipped his beer and reached for a handful of pretzels. They were off duty, having a beer after work at the Cock and Bull Tavern. It wasn't an unusual occurrence.

"Come on, Sam. You heard the tape of her call to the tipline."

"I heard it. I just don't think it's all that incriminating, considering . . ."

"Considering what? Her so-called abilities aren't for real, Sam. She warned you about a storm she could have heard about on the Weather Channel. You said so yourself. She's no psychic. If she knows something about our boy, it's personal knowledge, not some crap she's getting from a crystal ball."

Sam lowered his head, shook it. "She's a nice person, Ed."

"Yeah. Prisons are full of nice people."

Sam didn't like what he was being asked to do, but he didn't have a choice. It was his job as a detective with the small city's police department. Pulling over speeders wasn't. He'd been in that borrowed uniform and cruiser for three days before Megan Rose had finally fallen into his phony speed trap. And he would have pulled her over whether she'd been speeding or not, which blew her theory, about her "vision" causing their chance meeting, right out of the water. No, he didn't believe she was some kind of psychic. He wasn't beyond crediting her with a sharper than average intuition, though.

"I don't want your opinion on this, Sam. I just want you to do your job."

"How did this end up being my job, anyway?" he asked the chief. "Was I chosen for my skill, my instincts, my record?"

Ed slapped his shoulder. "Your record—with women, that is. The ladies love you, Sam. God only knows why." He winked good-naturedly. "One-Night Sam, right? Once I found out she was in your age range and unmarried, I knew you were our best chance of tripping her up, getting her to tell us how she really knew the things she did." He tipped his head to one side.

"That's about what I figured." He sighed.

"Come on, Sam. It's in the line of duty. How bad can it be?"

Sam shrugged, thinking it wouldn't be *bad* at all. Just kind of cruel. But there wasn't much he wouldn't do for Ed Skinner, and he thought Ed knew it. That was probably a big part of the reason Ed had chosen him for this job. "How far do you expect me to take this thing, anyway?"

"As far as you have to, Sam. Date her, bed her, wed her if you have to, just get the information."

Sam rolled his eyes. Ed was being sarcastic. About the "wed her" part, at least. "All right. I'll stay on it. But you jot it down somewhere that I did so under protest, and that I'm convinced she's harmless and completely innocent. I know I'm right about this."

"You're psychic, too, huh?"

Sam made a face.

Ed shrugged. "Well, hell, maybe she is innocent. If that's the case, then you'll just get her to tell you who the killer is by using her *powers*."

SHE changed clothes three times while waiting for Sam to arrive to pick her up. The first choice, a slinky red dress, was too sexy. The second, an off-the-shoulder peasant blouse with jeans, was too casual. She finally settled on the standby little black dress, added an ivory lace shawl, and stood in front of the mirror wondering if she should put her hair up or leave it down.

The doorbell rang.

She swore and glanced at the clock. "Hell." He'd said six; it was only ten of.

Oh, well, she would just have to do. She went to the door, opened it wide.

He frowned at her. "Don't you think you ought to ask who's there before opening your door? Given the situation, I mean?"

She frowned right back at him, stepped back, and closed the door.

He chuckled softly, but he played along, and promptly rang the doorbell again.

"Who is it?" she called.

"It's Sam. Your date for the evening."

"How do I know it's really you?"

"You're psychic, remember?"

"Oh, yeah." She opened the door again. "Now perhaps you'd like to try again with your uh . . . greeting?"

He blinked, then he got it. He stepped back and looked slowly down her, all the way to her toes, and back up again to her eyes. "Wow," he said. "You look incredible."

"That's more like it."

"I mean it."

She smiled. "So where are you taking me?"

"That's a surprise. Got everything?"

"Um-hm."

He crooked an elbow, and she took it, pulled the door closed behind her, and double-checked the lock. He led her to his car, a hot-looking black Mustang, and opened the door for her. "Buckle up, now," he said when she got in.

"Buckle up, hell. I want to drive."

He smiled at her. "I've seen you drive."

She rolled her eyes at his little joke, then said, "You need to get the oil changed. It's past due."

He frowned and glanced down at his odometer. "Hey, you're right."

She shrugged. He closed her door and went around to his own side to get behind the wheel. And then he drove her to the best restaurant in town, fed her a meal that was so sumptuous it should have been illegal, and insisted on ordering a single dessert they could share.

As she spooned bites of luscious brownie sundae into her mouth, he watched her from the other side of the table. He picked up the white cloth napkin and dabbed something from the corner of her mouth, and said, "I think pulling you over that day was one of the best moves I've ever made."

She averted her eyes and felt her face color. "You're not getting any tonight, Sam. You can stop shoveling it on."

"I'm not expecting any tonight. And I'm not shoveling anything but the truth. I like you, Megan."

"Well, what's not to like?"

"Nothing I can find."

She put her spoon down and pushed the fishbowl-sized dessert away. "I can't hold any more of that."

"Me neither. I think we'd both do well to walk some of this meal off, don't you?" As he spoke, he waved at the waiter, who immediately appeared to take his credit card.

"You want to go walking?"

"Sure. The town park is just a block from here. It's a beautiful night."

"God, I haven't gone walking in the park since . . . since all this started."

"The attacks, you mean."

She nodded. Then smiled at him. "I'll be safe enough with my own cop in tow."

"Damn straight you will. How are you set for footwear?"

"Pumps," she said with a frown.

"You *must* like me, if you broke out the heels."

"You do have sisters, don't you?"

He nodded.

"Well, I only went for the two-inch ones. It is a first date, after all."

He grinned at her, flashing the dimple that made her stomach flip-flop. "Maybe next time you'll wear the stilettos?"

"You play your cards right, cowboy, I might even wear the open toes."

He sucked air through his teeth and pressed a hand to his chest. She laughed out loud.

"My sister Shelby left a pair of flip-flops in my car," he said. "One size fits most."

"You're ready for anything, aren't you?"

The waiter returned with the credit card and the check. Sam added a tip, signed the bottom, and put the card in his wallet. Then he got up. "Ready to try on the new shoes, Cinderella?"

"Ready."

He cradled her elbow in one hand as he guided her around tables and waiters to the exit. The car was waiting out front, but he only opened the back door and fished out the flip-flops. She kicked off her pumps, realized she was wearing stockings, and got into the back of the car.

"What's wrong? Change your mind?"

"Stockings," she said. "They have to go. Flip-flops have that toe thing."

"Ahh." He stood there in the doorway, and she thought about telling him to turn around or close the door, but decided to play instead.

She slid her skirt up to the top of the stockings, and pushed them down her legs, one at a time.

He was mesmerized. She couldn't remember when a man had looked at her the way he was looking at her. And it wasn't all that revealing; the stockings only went to midthigh. She noticed he only took his eyes off her once, and that was to make sure no one else had the view he was so obviously enjoying. He blocked the doorway with his body. And he whispered, "You're killing me, you know that?"

"You'd see more than this if I wore shorts."

"Then next time, wear them." She left the stockings on the seat and slid the flip-flops on. He took her arm and tugged her out of the car, and this time, he held her hand as they walked down the block, around the corner, to the sprawling, grassy Pinedale Town Park. It was minuscule in comparison to the sprawling state park nearby, but perfect for an after-dinner walk with a handsome man.

They entered one of the walking trails and followed its meandering course through the woods, until they reached the park's centerpiece, a perfect little pond, currently home to several wood ducks and a pair of swans who were permanent residents. The moon had risen; it hung low in the sky, huge and lopsided, nearly full.

They moved to the benches near the pond, and Sam took off his jacket and slipped it around her shoulders.

She turned to face him. "This is nice. You're good at this dating thing."

"So I've been told." Did he look a little guilty when he said that? "You want to sit awhile?"

"No. I want to know if you're as good at first kisses as you are at first dates."

He held her eyes, slipped one arm around her waist, and cradled the back of her head with the other hand. It made her feel delicate and cherished. He pulled her to him, bent his head, and brushed his lips across hers lightly, softly, repeatedly, before finally parting them and covering her mouth for a kiss that took her breath away.

The flash hit just as she was starting to reconsider her earlier promise that he wasn't getting any tonight. It hit bright, hard, and fast. She went stiff in his arms. And by the time he lifted his head away, it was gone.

"What is it?" he asked.

"Two things. Most importantly—the killer. He's in the park—here, now. I saw you chasing him, wearing just what you're wearing tonight. So it has to be—"

Before she finished the sentence, the night was split by a woman's scream.

"Stay close to me," he told her, and gripping her hand, he took off running.

SAM tugged her along behind him, and she surprised him by keeping up without any trouble, despite the flip-flops, the dress, and the darkness. It lifted her a notch higher in his estimation that she didn't stumble or complain or ask to stop. Though after that kiss, it would have been tough to lift her much higher.

He spotted the struggling couple in the wooded area off the trail: a larger form straddling a small one. The small one lay on her back, and the bigger one had her pinned and was pounding her face.

"Police! Get off her, you sonofabitch!" Sam veered off the trail and went crashing through the brush toward the pair. He pulled his gun, but the attacker was already on the run. The perp had rolled off his victim at Sam's first shout, sprung to his feet, and was racing through the underbrush.

Sam glanced back at Megan. She was already crouching beside the battered victim, her face stricken. She looked his way, as if feeling his eyes on her. Hers were intense, damp, powerful, and furi-ous. God, she was something else.

"Stay here, stay with her," he said.

She nodded. "Go get that bastard," she said. "But be care-ful, Sam."

He didn't believe in her powers, he reminded himself. So why did that warning send a chill right up his spine?

CHAPTER FIVE

MEGAN knelt there, half afraid to touch the young woman, but knowing she had to. The victim was frightened, traumatized, probably in shock. She needed to know someone was there, that she was safe, and Megan didn't think words alone could do the job.

She put a gentle hand on the trembling shoulder. "It's okay. The police are chasing him. He's not coming back. You're safe."

Her eyes—one wide with fear, the other split at the corner, swollen, and bloody—fixed on Megan. She couldn't have been more than twenty-five, probably younger. "H-h-he h-hurt me."

"I know. An ambulance is coming. You're going to be okay."

A twig snapped, and the woman's hand shot to Megan's like a cobra striking, and squeezed tight.

"It's just a bird. You're safe," Megan began, but then the

flashes came, rapid-fire, blinding, far more vivid and potent than anything she'd ever felt before.

She was running, her feet hitting the path, a satisfying burn in her muscles, and the rush of chilled air in and out of her lungs.

An arm like a steel band snapped around her neck from behind . . .

Can't breathe!

. . . yanked her off balance, slammed her into the ground.

Something hit her face—her cheekbone exploded in pain.

What's he hitting me with? God, is it a hammer?

But it was only his fist, again and again, while he fell atop her, knees on either side, groin grinding against hers, his free hand tearing at her spandex running pants, his white sneakers bright in the darkness.

Rapist! No. Fight, fight him. Don't let him—

She used her hands, pounding at her invisible attacker, clawing at his eyes, and kicking her feet, though they hit nothing. It was as if he couldn't feel any impact, and with a few more of his blows to her face, she was fighting just to remain conscious.

Megan felt it all. The panic, the fear, the pain of every blow, the hot blood oozing into her left eye and burning there, the weight of him, the smell of his breath. She screamed.

"Hey, hey, come on, talk to me now!"

She opened her eyes, found she was lying on her back a few feet from where the victim lay. Paramedics surrounded the wounded girl. One was leaning over Megan, looking at her as if he thought she might be another victim. Beyond him lights flashed red and white in the darkness, painting everything in alternating strokes of color. She drew a breath and pushed herself up into a sitting position. "I'm okay. I was helping her, and I—I thought I heard him. I just panicked and, uh . . . fell."

The medic frowned, but then Sam was there, moving the man aside, crouching down and clasping her shoulders, looking at her with worry in his eyes. "What happened?"

"The usual," she said, holding his upper arms for support. He pulled her to her feet, but she didn't let go when she got her balance. If anything, she wanted more contact. To be wrapped up in him completely would be a good start.

"Did you get the guy?" she asked.

"No, he took off in what looked like an SUV. It was too damn far away and too dark for me to get a description, much less a plate number." He shook his head, leading her aside, away from the others. As he did, he slipped an arm around her shoulders and held her close to his side.

Better, she thought.

"You got another flash?"

"Man, did I. That poor woman is hurting. I think her cheekbone is broken, maybe her jaw, too, by the way it felt when he hit me. Hit *her,* I mean."

He stopped walking, frowned down at her. "You . . . felt it?"

She nodded. "As if it were happening to me. God, I've never felt that kind of fear in my life." She watched the medics lift the gurney and carry the woman to the clearing where the ambulance waited. "At least he didn't rape her."

"He didn't? You're sure?"

She nodded. Other cops were arriving now, securing the scene, stringing yellow tape. One carried a camera and began flashing photos.

Sam gripped her upper arm, suddenly animated. "Meg, I don't suppose you . . ." He bit his lip.

"What?"

"Well, did you see him? In the flash, did you get a look at him?"

She thought back. "I was too scared to try. It was happening so fast, you know? I was being pummeled, trying to avoid the blows, trying to cover my face and hit back." She narrowed her eyes, remembering the experience. "I think there were times when I could have glimpsed his face. I just wasn't thinking clearly enough to try. And I think he might have been wearing a mask of some sort."

He sighed. "That's all right."

"We have to get her address, Sam."

He looked at her, frowning as if confused.

She shrugged. "You know me. The most useful piece of information I got from touching that poor woman is that there's no one to go to her house and feed her cat. She was thinking that, as she lay there. 'If he kills me, how long before someone knows I'm dead and goes to my apartment to take care of Roderick? Will he starve to death in the meantime?' "

"I'll see to it the cat is taken care of," Sam told her.

She smiled a little. "I doubt he'd starve. He's pretty overweight anyway."

Sam stared at her. "Don't tell me—you can describe the cat?"

She lowered her eyes. "Maybe it's because I have a cat of my own. Slender little gray tabby. Hers is big, long-haired, buff-colored, with one green eye and one blue eye."

"You're incredible," he said softly.

"Just not very helpful," she replied.

He swallowed hard. "You saved that girl's life."

"You did that."

"You knew the rapist was in the park."

"So did you, the second you heard her scream."

He shrugged. "So we were both instrumental. The fact is, we have a survivor now. If she got a look at him, we might finally have a description of our boy."

"I don't think she did, though. But . . . I hope you're right."

"Look, I have to go to the hospital." He clasped her shoulders, studying her face, really searching her eyes. He looked at her more deeply, more thoroughly than anyone had ever bothered looking before. "Are you sure you're okay?"

"I'm okay. You have a job to do. I'm fine."

"I'll take you home on the way to the hospital, all right?"

She shook her head left then right. "Sure . . . but . . . it's just, I thought you wanted my help on this case."

"I do, but—"

"Then why not take me to the hospital with you?"

Sam seemed to consider that, then shook his head with real regret in his eyes. "The chief would never get it. He still thinks . . . not tonight, okay? I'll take you sometime when the place isn't crawling with cops."

By now they were nearing the restaurant and his waiting car. He flicked a button on the key ring, and the locks opened. Then he opened her door for her. She got in, then he did, and he started the engine, then paused.

"What was the second thing?" he asked.

"What?"

"When I was kissing you in the park—"

She smiled just a little, the warmth of that memory chasing away the chill that had settled over her.

"—you got that flash, and I asked you what it was. You said, two things, the killer being the most important one. What was the other?"

She lifted her brows as the warmth left her in a rush. "Oh. That." She looked him dead in the eye. "It was the clear message that you're still keeping things from me. Important things." She shrugged. "Go figure."

OF course he denied it all the way back to her house, tried to cover it, but she knew. She'd felt it clearly when he kissed her. It was lingering, lurking beneath the real passion, the heat that rose between them—there was a *reason* he was kissing her. A *reason* he was even with her at that moment, and that reason was *not* the one he was trying to make her believe.

He didn't want to date her, and he didn't believe in her visions.

She sighed, disappointed. It didn't matter. She had to stick with him, see this thing through, because she, too, had reasons for being with him.

The dreams.

Besides, there was something about him. Something she liked. Not the lying, though. She didn't like that at all. At least he didn't seem like any sort of a threat to her. He'd even given her a card with his cell phone number on it, in case she needed him. As if he were feeling . . . protective of her.

Megan dropped her coat on the back of the sofa and kicked off her shoes—belatedly realizing she still wore the borrowed flip-flops. Her pumps were in the back of Sam's car. She sank into her favorite chair, and Percy jumped into her lap, nuzzled her chin. She petted her cat, thinking of the other woman, and her own pet at home alone as she stroked soft fur. "What do you suppose that fellow's keeping from me, Percy?" she asked.

Percy purred and arched his back to her hand for more affection.

"Lot of help you are. Hell, I suppose being the psychic, I ought to know. Then again . . ." She glanced across the room to where her computer sat collecting dust. "I suppose I could do a little research, couldn't I?"

She set Percy aside, ignored his mewling protests, and crossed the room to flip on the PC. A few mouse clicks later she was online, running a search on Samuel Sheridan. She was surprised at the number of hits that came up, news articles, mostly. Old ones.

Samuel Sheridan, Killed in Line of Duty.

Officer Shot Down in Robbery Attempt.

Hero Cop Gives All.

She clicked on the first link, which took her to a newspaper's Web site, but not to the article. So she went back to the search results and tried again, finding the same outcome every time. Frowning, she looked more closely at the links, each of which gave just a line or two of the accompanying story, and realized the links were more than a decade old.

Of the three newspaper sites, only one had a "Search the Archives" button, and she used it, relieved when the article actually showed up.

Whispering a silent thank-you to whoever had come up with

the idea to put the last twenty-plus years of articles online, she read through the piece, and realized Sam's father had been a cop, too, and that he'd died in the line of duty just a few days after his thirty-fifth birthday. This article was about him, not her Sam.

"Samuel Sheridan Jr. was shot at point-blank range when he attempted to foil a liquor store robbery in progress last night. Both suspects were also killed."

The article shocked her, but not so much as the line that brought her to a grinding halt.

> It is a painful irony that Samuel Sheridan's father, also a police officer, was likewise killed in the line of duty at the age of thirty-five. In the elder Sheridan's case, death came by way of a high-speed pursuit that ended in a fiery wreck, in the fall of 1950.

She blinked slowly. Both Sam's father and his grandfather had been police officers, and they'd both died in the line of duty at the age of thirty-five? God, how awful. Sam couldn't have been more than a child when his father died. The story was published in 1977. How old could he have been then? He'd mentioned at dinner that he had a birthday coming up.

A low growl made her turn her head sharply. Percival stood on the back of the sofa, staring toward the front door, his back arched and the hair on the scruff of his neck bristling. His tail switched back and forth.

"Percy, what's wrong?" She looked toward the door, too, suppressing a shiver.

Percy jumped to the floor and darted across the room, ducking through the slightly open bedroom door and out of sight.

As a guard dog, he left a lot to be desired.

Megan saved the article to her hard drive, then quickly clicked the disconnect button, got up, and walked to the front door. She hadn't locked it behind her when she'd come in, she thought. After what she'd witnessed tonight, that should have been the first thing she thought to do. She turned the locks now, even while peering through the glass panes, but they were more decorative than functional. Beveled and pebbled. Pretty, but useless.

She backed up enough to flip on the outdoor light, then moved to the nearest window to push the curtains aside and peek out.

She saw no one. Nothing. She thought she would have felt better if she had. A local dog trotting by or a neighbor out for a walk. Her cat had sensed something out there. But what?

A car passed by, and its lights fell on a solitary figure, standing across the street. A man. Just standing there, staring . . . at her house.

Megan jerked away from the window, swallowed hard, then forced herself to lean closer again, to take another look.

White sneakers.

The attacker in the park had been wearing white sneakers. It was the one thing she'd noticed, the way they stood out so prominently in contrast to the darkness of the night, and to his jeans.

Jeans. White sneakers and blue jeans. Okay, at least she had something to tell Sam.

What the hell was the killer doing outside her house? If it even was him. Hell, there were probably lots of men running around in white sneakers and jeans.

Not standing outside your house, kid. There's only one of those.

She reached into her pocket, pulled out the little card Sam had given her. Then she dialed his cell phone and prayed he would answer.

CHAPTER SIX

S AM was leaving the victim's hospital room when his cell phone
bleated. He answered it, then said "Hold on" while a scowling
nurse told him to turn it off or take it outside.

"Sorry." He headed toward the elevators, noting the signs that
told him not to use a cell phone inside the hospital, something he'd
already known and just hadn't thought about as he'd rushed in
here. When the doors slid closed on him, he brought the phone up
to his ear again. "Yeah?"

"Sam. It's Megan. There's, um . . . there's someone outside my
house."

He blinked twice, his brain quickly processing her words,
weighing the fear in her voice, and spitting out an interpretation he
didn't much like, and a rush of panic so overblown it bore further
analysis. But later. "Where?"

"He's standing across the street. Just standing there . . . looking toward my house."

The elevator stopped and Sam stepped out of it, striding rapidly toward the exit doors and through them into the parking lot as he spoke. "Are your doors locked, Megan?"

"Yeah."

"You double-checked, all of them?"

"Yes, I did that. Windows, too."

"Good girl." He hit the lock release button on his car, got in, and started the engine. "I don't suppose you're getting any flashes? As to who this guy is or what he's doing out there?"

"No flashes. Just a gut feeling. It's him, Sam. It's the killer. I know it is."

He pressed the accelerator to the floor, speeding out of the parking lot. "I'm on my way, hon. Five minutes, tops. I'm gonna click over and call nine-one-one, but I'll come right back on with you. All right?"

"I . . . guess so."

"Just for a second, I promise."

"I'm scared, Sam."

"I know. Jesus, I know. I'm coming for you."

He ran a red light while he manipulated the phone, hitting the flash key, getting a fresh dial tone and dialing 911. He hit the flash key again to bring Megan back into the call as he took a corner so fast the car rocked to one side. "I'm back, Meg."

The dispatcher's line was ringing, and in a moment he heard, "Nine-one-one, what's your emergency?"

"Hold on," he said. "Megan? Are you still there?"

No answer.

"Shit. Dispatcher, this is Detective Sam Sheridan with the Pinedale P.D., badge number seven eighty-five. I have a prowler—possible murder suspect—possible witness in danger—five-one-three Sycamore Street and I need immediate assistance."

"I'll send cars right out, Detective. Can you stay on the line?"

"No, I need the line open."

"All right then. I have officers en route."

She disconnected, but the line remained open. His call to Megan was still connected. "Meg?" Still no answer. His throat burned, and so did his eyes. He told himself he would be just as worried no matter who had been on the other end of that phone call, but he knew damn well it wasn't true.

There was something about Megan Rose. It felt as if she had sunk roots into his flesh, roots that had burrowed deep and twined themselves around his bones. He didn't *get* this way about women. In fact, he'd made a conscious decision not to. Not ever. It wasn't part of his emotional makeup and never would be. So then what the hell was this?

"Megan, for the love of God, answer me," he whispered.

Then there was the distinct sound of her phone hanging up. It shattered the silence on that line like a gunshot, and Sam's last ounce of composure with it. He slammed the accelerator to the floor, his heart pounding in his throat. God, he'd had no idea how much that redhead had gotten under his skin until this very moment. It made no sense for One-Night Sam to feel this way about a woman he barely knew. And yet, he did. And there wasn't much point in fighting it.

* * *

MEGAN dropped the telephone when she heard rattling at her back door, then the sound of breaking glass. She was already racing for her front door when the heavy footfalls came from her kitchen toward her. Her hands shaking, she flipped locks, yanked the door open, and bolted outside into the night. She ran, damp grass and then cold pavement hitting her bare feet, cold air filling her lungs.

A car came speeding toward her, its lights blinding her, tires squealing as it skidded to a stop. There was one moment of sheer panic before she stepped out of the headlights' glare, blinked, and recognized the vehicle as Sam's Mustang. And by then he was out of it, running toward her. His arms came around her powerfully and instantly. He held her hard against him, his grip ferocious, his heart pounding wildly beneath her head, one hand in her hair. "What happened? Are you all right?"

She nodded against his chest, amazed at the power of his fear for her. Amazed at how odd it felt to have someone care this much, and at the way her own arms locked around his waist in return. As if there were something between them—as if they were important to each other. As if they had been for a very long time.

"He's in the house, Sam." She didn't want to say it. She would rather have just stayed there in his arms until everything was all right again.

Gently, he pried her arms from around him, turned to face the house, and lifted the gun he had in his hand. God, she hadn't even seen it there. "Get in my car," he told her. "Lock the doors. Pull it off the road."

"Sam, I—"

"Do it now, Meg." He softened the harshness of the command

with a tender look, a quick touch, his hand cupping her head briefly as his eyes compelled her to obey.

She drew a shaky breath, nodded, and got into his car, then sat there watching in panic as Sam moved toward her house, the gun leading him. This wasn't right. She was supposed to save this man, according to her recurring dreams. Not send him walking into what might be his death.

Sam went inside, and she swore part of her went with him. Belatedly, she put his car into gear and pulled it off the road. But she had no intention of staying safe inside it while he risked his life. Swallowing her fear, she opened the car door, got out, took a few tentative steps along the sidewalk toward her home. "Sam?"

No reply. She moved closer, turning now up the walk to her front door. Behind her, sirens wailed and lights flashed as police cars came screaming up her road. Doors slammed, but she kept moving forward, shaking. "Sam?"

A hand fell on her shoulder, stopping her. "Ms. Rose? You all right?"

She nodded. "Sam—Officer Sheridan, he's in the house. There was someone in there."

The cop turned, waving to others who were apparently awaiting his orders. He pointed to two and swung his hand in an arc, pointing toward the back of her house, then he pointed to another and nodded to the front door. "Sheridan's inside. Possible intruder as well," he said, his voice low but firm as the men moved past him to carry out their orders.

Before they got far, though, Sam was coming out the front door, his gun holstered once more. When she saw him, Megan's breath rushed out of her, and her muscles went soft.

"Forget it," he said. "Whoever he was, he's long gone." His eyes found Megan's, held them as he came to her. She barely restrained herself from wrapping her arms around him, she was so relieved to see him safe. It wouldn't look good, not in front of the other cops; she knew that. But Sam did embrace her, when he joined her there. He touched her with his eyes, with his serious but reassuring smile, with how close he stood, and his hand on her shoulder telling her it would all be okay.

"Chief," he said, nodding to the older man.

"What's the story, Sam?"

"Chief Skinner, this is Megan Rose. She was a witness to the assault in the park tonight. An hour later she called in to say there was a prowler outside her house. Apparently, he broke in before we got here."

The police chief glanced at Megan, and she at him, now that she could tear her eyes from her own front door, and from Sam's. The chief was an attractive man, perhaps fifty-something, lean, strong, with neatly cropped black hair that was graying at the temples, and friendly brown eyes. She knew that he knew who she was—the crackpot psychic he suspected of God only knew what.

"You were inside at the time?" the chief asked her. His concern seemed genuine.

She nodded.

"That must have been terrifying for you."

"It was. I heard someone trying to get in the back door. Glass breaking. Footsteps. I ran out the front."

He nodded, looking again at Sam.

Sam said, "Glass was busted out of the back door. Looks like he reached through and unlocked it, walked right in. We'll want to dust it for prints."

"Terry, get that scene secured," the chief said, sending one of the officers scurrying to obey. "I'm sorry you've been through so much today, ma'am," he went on, focusing again on Megan. "Did you get a look at the man when you saw him outside your house?"

"No. It was too dark. He was just a shape. White sneakers, jeans." She shook her head, belatedly skimming ground level, noting all the shiny black shoes running this way and that way.

"And what about the one in the park? Could you identify him?"

She shook her head slowly. "No, I didn't get a look at him. But apparently, he got a pretty good look at me."

"You have reason to believe it was the same man?"

Megan lifted her eyes, shifting her gaze to Sam's, then back to the chief's. "I don't have a reason to believe it," she said slowly. "But I believe it anyway."

The chief frowned. "Why? Is there something you're not telling me?"

She lowered her head, trying to come up with an answer that would sound logical.

Then he nodded knowingly. "It's that ESP thing again, huh?" His face bore that same look of blatant disbelief she'd seen so often as a child, in her father's eyes. Though his words were kind, and his expression tried to be, she knew that deep down he believed she was a fraud.

He did remember her name, though. She almost wished he didn't. She wished she had never made that phone call the other night. "It's nothing psychic," she said. "It's just a gut feeling. That's all."

The chief nodded as if he understood. "Is there somewhere else you can stay tonight, Ms. Rose?"

"Sure. I can go to a hotel for the night."

"You do that, then. You'll be safer, more comfortable, and besides, we'll need access to the house for the next couple of hours. Sam, why don't you take her inside to pack up a few things?"

"I can manage—" she began. But she didn't want to. She didn't want to get more than two feet from Sam's side right now, and frankly, the thought of spending the night alone in a strange, impersonal hotel room didn't appeal in the least.

Sam shook his head and slipped an arm around her shoulders. "I'll go with you. We don't want you accidentally tromping on evidence, after all."

She let him guide her toward the front door of her house, belatedly turning back to the chief. "It was nice meeting you, Chief Skinner," she said, holding out a hand.

He had a notepad in one hand and a cell phone in the other, but he gave her a nod, attempted a sympathetic smile, then moved toward his officers.

"Come on, Meg." Sam led her into the house, straight to her bedroom. He stood just inside the bedroom door, looking around. "Do you think he came in here at all?"

"I don't think he had time," she said. "Nothing's out of place. He was coming through the kitchen, maybe made it almost into the living room by the time I got out and ran. And then you were there. I imagine he went right back out when he heard your car."

"Thank God the hospital's only five minutes away."

"The hospital is fifteen minutes away, Sam." She tipped her head up to look at him.

"Yeah, well . . . I'm trained in high-speed techniques."

"You were worried about me."

"I was freaking petrified."

She smiled just a little. "Thanks for that."

He shrugged, averting his eyes. She decided to let it go for now, but God, it did her good to know he felt the power of this . . . *thing* between them as clearly as she did. She tugged an overnight bag from a shelf in her closet, tossed it onto the bed, then went to her dresser to open drawers. She pulled things out almost at random, her attention not on the job as she tucked items into the bag. In the end she didn't even know what she'd packed. She was too busy analyzing what was happening between her and Sam, wondering what her dreams had been telling her all this time, speculating on the killer's reasons for coming after her tonight.

"You need anything from the bathroom? Toothbrush, makeup?"

She nodded vaguely, realizing she had gone still with her hands buried in her top drawer. She shook herself, then went into the bathroom off her bedroom and gathered more items. "What do you think he wanted?" she asked.

Sam stood in the bedroom, beyond her range of vision. "We don't even know for sure it was him."

"Of course we do. Your Chief Skinner does, too. At least, he didn't disagree."

She heard Sam sigh.

"He seems nice, Chief Skinner. Even if he doesn't believe I'm for real."

"He's a decent guy. Taught me everything I know about being a cop."

She frowned, coming out of the bathroom with her hands full of things from her counter. Hairbrush, makeup, deodorant, toothbrush. She stood in the doorway, where she could see him. "I would have thought your dad would have done that."

He looked at her sharply. "You know about my father?"

She shrugged, moving to the bed to drop her collection into her overnight case. "I got curious. Did a little Internet research on you tonight."

"Why?"

"I told you earlier, I got the feeling you were being less than honest with me about something. I thought maybe I could find a clue what."

He sighed. "And I told you I've got nothing to hide from you, Megan. My father was killed in the line of duty. I was only a kid at the time."

She nodded slowly, bent over her bag to zip it up. "What happened to him?"

"Liquor store robbery. He and his partner showed up before the perps got out of the store. One took the back door, one the front. Bad guys decided to shoot their way out the back. Dad chose the wrong door."

She felt the heartache in his words, the loss. It still hurt. "I'm sorry."

"Skinner opened fire, got them both. Too late, though. Dad was already down."

"Skinner? The chief was your father's partner?"

He nodded. "It hit him as hard as it did the rest of us, I think. He took us under his wing after that. I think he felt like it should have been him, instead of Dad. He didn't have a wife or kids."

"Survivor's guilt," she said.

"Yeah, I guess so. He was there for us after that. Kind of stepped in, took care of things my father would have. My grandmother resented it, I think, him stepping into her son's place. But the rest of us were awfully glad to have him around."

"God, it must have been awful for your mother. How many kids did she have?"

"Three. My two sisters and me. And my grandmother, to boot." He moved to the bed, picked up her bag. "You ready?"

"I can't find Percy."

He frowned.

"My cat." She looked in all Percy's usual hiding places—under the bed, in the bathtub, in the closet—all the while wondering if she wanted to pry further than she had into Sam's personal history, and decided she might as well. "Your grandfather died in the line of duty, too, the paper said."

He frowned at her. "You really have been snooping, haven't you?"

"The article mentioned it."

"Yeah, he died on duty, too. Car wreck. Anything else you want to know, Megan?"

"Quite a lot, actually."

He watched her face, waiting, his own seeming clouded or angry or something.

"But not now." Did he seem a bit relieved by that? Hard to be sure. "The Windsor's right in town, ten minutes from here. I can get a room there. I'm sure they aren't booked up this time of year." She looked around, but there was still no sign of Percy. "There's plenty of food and water here. I guess he'll be all right."

"I'm sure he'll be fine. But you're not going to the Windsor."

"I'm not?"

"No. I want you someplace safe, someplace this guy wouldn't think to look for you, just in case your hunch is right."

She blinked. "And what place would that be?" she asked.

He sighed. "Mine. I'm taking you home with me, Megan. And I don't want to hear any arguments, okay?"

"I'm not going to give you any." He looked at her, brows raised. "Arguments, I mean." Hell, that didn't come out right either. "You know what I mean."

"I know." He actually smiled a little, and it lightened the somber mood brought on by what had happened tonight, and by her morbid, probing questions. "And I'm going to pry into your past to pay you back for prying into mine. Come on."

CHAPTER SEVEN

*D*ID you get to see the girl from the park at the hospital to-night?" Megan asked, probably to change the subject.

He glanced at her as he drove, decided to let the matter of her snooping go, for now. Hell, he had all night. "Yeah. Her name's Linda Keller. I didn't get much out of her, though. She didn't get a look at the guy, and was still too shaken up to give me anything helpful."

She swallowed hard. "Maybe . . . I could see her."

He blinked, looking at her face, her eyes. Still worried about trying to help, even after all she'd been through tonight. "I don't know if you noticed, Megan, but being involved in this might very well have put you at risk."

"If I could talk to her, touch her hand again, I might be able to get something."

"You did that once. All it got you was knocked on your ass and feeling her pain. Not to mention a visit from the suspect."

"Maybe."

He didn't have much doubt himself. "Why are you so determined to help?"

She shook her head, shaking off his question. "I wasn't expecting the vision to hit so hard last time. This time I'd be ready. I could look more carefully, see things I missed before. She might have seen things she doesn't realize she saw, or is too traumatized to remember."

His lips thinned. "All right. I'll take you to the hospital in the morning."

She nodded.

"If you tell me why you are so damned determined to do this."

She shrugged. "What makes you think there's a reason? Why can't it be something I just want to do?"

"Come on, Megan, I know it's more than that."

She closed her eyes. "You don't know anything about me."

"I know a lot about you, Meg. Way more than I ought to. I want to know more." He smiled at her. "Besides, I told you I was going to repay your prying with some prying of my own."

She drew a breath, sighed. "I haven't had a vision about anything this important since I foresaw my father's death."

He swung his head toward her, stunned by her words and the pain he sensed behind them.

"I saw it all. He'd been drinking, left the bar, got behind the wheel, went off a bridge on the way home. The car exploded. He was gone. I tried to warn him. He didn't believe me. Called me a liar just the way he always did when I claimed I had a vision. I got the back of his hand for this particular lie, and was sent to my room. Then my mother came in and made me kneel and pray with her rosary for nine hours straight. She believed visions like mine could only come from the devil."

"I had no idea. Meg, I'm sorry."

She shrugged. "When the vision came true, just the way I said it would, she was even more certain I was evil. Said I had caused it. She barely spoke to me after that, and eventually sent me to live with her aging aunt, where I basically became a caregiver. My mother died a few years later. For years after that, the visions just didn't come—except for this one recurring dream I could never understand."

She averted her eyes when she said that.

"What was the dream?"

"It doesn't matter, Sam."

"Okay," he said. "Okay, I won't push on that. But what about the visions? Why did they stop?"

She shrugged. "I don't know. Maybe I suppressed them. Maybe on some level I believed I was to blame for my father's death. I don't know. But when they did come back, they came almost tentatively. Minor things, nothing big, nothing I had to prevent or change. This is the first time I've had a vision about something this important. And I guess I'm afraid if I don't do what I'm supposed to do, they'll go away again and maybe never return."

He nodded slowly. "You think you stopped having visions because you failed to save your father. And you'll stop again if you fail again."

She shrugged. "Maybe. Maybe saving this girl is part of my penance." She was silent for a moment. Then looked at him quickly. "If the killer is going after witnesses, Sam—"

"She's safe. We've got a guard on her hospital room door, and her house is under surveillance."

"And . . . what about her cat?"

Damn. He'd forgotten about the cat. "Tell you what," he said. "You and I will go by her place and feed her cat ourselves, all right?"

"That would make me feel a whole lot better," she told him.

He shook his head slowly. "All you've been through and your chief concern is still a damn cat."

She shrugged. "I like cats."

"Yeah. I kind of figured that out."

Sam wasn't 100 percent convinced they were going to find any cat at all, much less a buff-colored, overweight one with one green eye and one blue. But he phoned the hospital as he drove and asked a nurse to put him through to Linda Keller's room, but only if she was still awake.

She picked up the phone, and Sam had her put the cop who stood outside her door on the phone to verify who he was, just to put her mind at ease before speaking to her. When she came back on the line, he said, "I wanted to check in, see if there was anything you needed taken care of at your house while you're in the hospital."

"Is there any—have you caught him yet?"

"Not yet. But we will, I promise you that." He hated that he couldn't bring her better news, tell her the bastard was in custody and wouldn't be hurting anyone ever again. He hated it. "When we talked earlier, you said you didn't have any family or friends in town, being new here. I thought I should check in, see if there's anything you need taken care of at home."

"I'm . . . thank you. That's so thoughtful of you."

"It's the least I can do, believe me."

"There is something you could do for me, if it's not too much trouble. There's really no one else I can ask. . . ."

"That's why I called. And it's no trouble at all, really."

"I have a cat at home. I was out of cat food this morning, so he missed his breakfast, and if he doesn't have anything tonight he'll be just miserable."

Sam caught Megan's eyes, saw the knowing look in them. "I'll pick up some cat food and feed him for you. Is your house locked?"

"Yes, but there's one of those hide-a-key rocks near the front walk. Um . . . he likes Frisky Cat, the tuna flavor."

"Got it. Is there anything else I can do?"

"Yes, actually. That woman, the one who helped me in the park . . . is she all right?"

"Fine. She's with me now. Actually, this call was her idea."

"Thank her for me, will you?"

He glanced at Megan, a thought crossing his mind. "What does your cat look like?"

She seemed taken aback by the question, but answered after a brief pause. "Yellow gold. I guess you'd call him buff. And terribly overweight. He's got two different colored eyes, which makes him sort of bizarre looking, but I think that's what drew me to him in the first place. Why do you ask?"

A funny little wave of something washed through his stomach and head.

"I, uh—just curious. Listen, if you like, you can thank that woman yourself. She'd like to come by and see you tomorrow, if you're up to it."

"I'd like that," she said. "Yes, I'd like that very much."

"All right then. I'll see you in the morning."

"Thank you, Detective Sheridan. For everything."

"You're welcome."

He flicked off the phone, glancing sideways at Megan. "You nailed the cat. To a tee."

"You sound surprised." She tipped her head to one side. "You *are* surprised, aren't you?"

He shrugged. "I just—I'm not used to seeing this kind of thing in action."

"I thought you believed me about the visions, Sam."

"I do."

"No," she said. "I'm not so sure you do. I don't think you're sure you do."

She sounded almost heartbroken. Hell, he didn't want to hurt her. He cared about the woman way more than he ought to, and to be honest, while he'd never believed in this kind of psychic bullshit—had actively refused to believe in it—she had him wondering. Her childhood tale was goddamned heart-wrenching.

Unlike his chief, he didn't believe she had any real knowledge of or connection to the killer. He was on her side in that. And while technically, he was working here, getting close to her to get the truth out of her, the truth was, he was with her because he wanted to be. And he was starting to believe in her abilities.

"This kind of thing takes getting used to, Megan," he said, aware she was still waiting for him to reply. "It's never been a part of my experience. That's all."

He turned the car into the parking lot in front of a twenty-four-hour convenience store, and they went inside for the cat food.

Frisky Cat, tuna flavor. Then they drove to Linda Keller's address, and he easily located the key in the fake rock. Too easily.

He picked it up, took the key from the compartment in the bottom, then held the rock out to Megan. "This is way too obvious," he said. "She might as well leave the key in the door."

"Oh? Where do you suggest people leave a spare key?"

"In their pocket." He put the key into the lock and opened the door.

Megan came in behind him, carrying the cat food. The biggest cat he'd ever seen came bounding toward them with a plaintive meow, and proceeded to rub itself against Sam's leg. Megan located the cat's dishes and promptly filled them. The cat pounced on the food as if starved, though Sam estimated he could probably live several weeks without a bite. She filled the water dish, too.

Sam saw the collar, heard the jingle of the tags that hung from it, and out of curiosity, crouched down to take a look. He read the tag with the cat's name, Roderick, engraved on it. "Well, I'll be damned," he muttered.

"Got the name right, too, didn't I?"

He glanced up at her.

"Wish I could get the name of our killer that easily."

"So do I." The voice of reason, and force of habit, told him it wasn't proof of anything. Hell, now that he thought about it, the victim could have told her about the cat back in the park, while he was chasing after the perp.

But he didn't really think so. "So are we set here?" he asked.

"Yeah." She squatted down beside him and stroked the cat. "You'll be okay for the night, won't you, boy?"

A throaty purr that did not interrupt the feeding frenzy was the beast's reply. She rose again, and Sam did, too, walking to the door, pocketing the key. "Tomorrow we'll take this to her at the hospital. Leaving it where it was is just asking for trouble."

"You're the expert."

They walked out to his car, and he drove the rest of the way to his home, a small, functional shoebox in a residential neighborhood. He wasn't that surprised to see all the lights on and three cars lined up along the roadside out front. "The troops have arrived," he said softly.

"I thought you lived alone."

Was that a hint of disappointment he heard in her voice? He searched her eyes to see for sure, but there was too much going on in them for him to pick out or identify any one emotion.

"I try to live alone," he said, offering a smile to lighten things up. "With my family, it's not always easy. At least they left me a parking spot this time." He pulled into the driveway, which was only big enough for one car, and shut off the engine. Before they even got to the front door, it was opening and people were spilling out. Sam waved to them and tried to look happy to see them.

"Megan Rose, let me introduce my family. This is my mother, Evelyn, and these are my sisters, Sabrina and Shelby."

Evelyn smiled and nodded hello to Megan. "I'm sorry if we've interrupted a date, dear."

"Please, Mom," Sabrina said. "It would have been over in a couple of hours anyway. They don't call him One-Night Sam for nothing, you know."

He felt Megan flinch, realized he still had a hand on her arm, and promptly released her.

"It's not a date," Megan said quickly. "It's . . . business."

"Megan's a witness to a crime. Now do you mind parting the waters and letting us in?"

The women exchanged curious glances, but moved aside. Sam and Megan went in, and he saw that his grandmother was there as well, sitting in his favorite chair, watching a football game on his big-screen TV.

"Told you he was all right," she said, barely looking up. "Hello, grandson."

"Hello, Lily."

"These hens heard over the scanner that you were chasing after a murder suspect and got worried. I told them tonight wasn't the night."

"I'm fine, as you can all see." He frowned, sniffing the air, turning toward his mother again. "You cooked, didn't you?"

"Oh, just a little, dear," his mother said. "As long as we were here, you know, we thought it wouldn't hurt to toss a few potatoes into the oven."

"Smells like chicken," he said.

"Well, the oven was already hot. No sense wasting gas, you know."

"And cake?"

"I hate to leave an oven rack empty."

"Mm-hm. Nothing like a full blown meal at 11 P.M."

She smiled. "I'll just go set an extra place for your guest."

He closed his eyes slowly, then turned to Megan. "They're staying for a post-dinner dinner."

"I got that."

"You, girl!" his grandmother called. Megan turned her head

sharply, and the old woman waggled a finger at her. "Come on over here and sit with me. It's halftime anyway. You may as well be polite."

Megan blinked in shock, sending a look at Sam. "Sorry," he whispered.

She smiled, an amused, indulgent smile, and went to obey his grandmother's summons.

CHAPTER EIGHT

MEGAN sat alone with Sam's grandmother, while his mother and sisters coerced him into the kitchen, obviously wanting to talk to him in private. The old woman had a face like aged leather and twinkling blue eyes. She had short curly permed hair, and wore a pair of faded jeans and a sweatshirt that was two sizes too big. It had a fat cartoon cat on the front, with the caption *Cats Rule. Dogs Drool.*

"I'm Lily," she said. "You're my grandson's flavor of the week?"

"I'm Megan." She offered her hand and the old woman took it, then paused, frowning, squeezing tight, and looking more closely at Megan's face.

"Megan," she repeated and released her hand. "They come and go so fast, I don't bother learning their names. Yours though, maybe I will. You have any pull with Sam, girl?"

"Pull?"

"Influence. Does he listen to you?"

"I really haven't known him that long, Mrs.—"

"Lily. Just Lily."

"Lily." Megan wasn't sure where this conversation was going, but the woman had her curious. "Why? What is it you would want me to . . . influence him to do?"

"Quit his job."

Megan blinked. "Quit the police department?"

"That's what I just said. And soon, girl. His birthday's next week, you know."

"I'm afraid I don't under—"

"His *thirty-fifth* birthday," she said, as if that were significant somehow.

"I didn't know. But I still don't see why—"

Lily leaned forward in her chair and gripped Megan's forearm, her clasp powerful. "His father—my own son—was a policeman, you know."

"I know. I'm so sorry for the way you lost him."

She shook her head. "We all lost him. That wife of his keeps his den like a shrine. Won't even let anyone in there. Hasn't changed a thing since he died." She sighed deeply. "Shot down in his prime, he was. The week of his thirty-fifth birthday. Just like my husband."

And suddenly the light dawned. Megan met the old woman's piercing blue eyes. "And you believe Sam will be killed as well?"

She nodded slowly. "I know he will. It's . . . it's some kind of curse," she said.

The word "curse" seemed to echo endlessly in Megan's mind. It made her knees go weak, and she sank into a chair near the older woman.

"If he doesn't quit that damnable job in time, I'm afraid we'll lose him, too." Her lips thinned. "I'm a tough old bird, but I think it would kill his poor mother. And those sisters of his. It's not right they should suffer like that just because he's too stubborn to listen."

Megan licked her lips, understanding now why Sam's family tended to panic every time they heard what seemed like a dangerous situation on the scanner. "Have you talked to Sam about this? Maybe if you told him—"

"Talked myself blue, girl. He says he doesn't believe in curses, doesn't believe in any of that sort of hoo-ha. Much less my intuitions."

"You have . . . intuitions?" Megan asked, lifting her brows.

Lily nodded slowly. "I knew something bad was coming before my husband went to work that day. I had that same bad feeling the day Sam Jr. died, and I think he did, too, the odd way he'd been acting all week." She tipped her head to one side. "You get feelings, too, don't you, girl."

It wasn't a question. "Sometimes. I . . . see things."

"You have the sight," she whispered. "I knew it. Felt it when I took your hand." She bit her lip, shaking her head slowly. "You're with my grandson for a reason, girl. God didn't send you to this family by coincidence, and I think you know it."

Megan drew a breath. Her gift had changed since she'd met Sam. The visions had grown stronger, more important, more frequent. And never before had they hit her with such crippling impact.

"You're the one who can break this curse and end this family's grieving once and for all. You can do it. You can save Sam."

Break the curse. Save his life.

Megan took Lily's papery-soft hand. "I'll try my best."

Maggie Shayne

"That's all I can ask."

"What's all you can ask, Lily?" Sam said, coming in from the kitchen.

"I've just promised her my favorite recipe," Megan said, seeing the note of panic in the older woman's eyes and knowing, as Lily apparently did, that Sam would be furious if he knew what they'd really been discussing.

"You cook, too?" he asked with a smile. "You're just full of hidden talents, aren't you, Meg?"

"She's a keeper, this one," Lily said. "And if this wasn't a date, then you're a damn fool. Now, are you people gonna put some food on the table before I starve to death or what?"

Sam shook his head slowly. "Dinner—or rather, an all-out Sheridan-family midnight snack—is served," he said.

THE meal was pleasant, which surprised Megan. She ate only enough to be polite, since she and Sam had already enjoyed one luscious meal tonight. Sam's mother, Evelyn, seemed naturally friendly, and the sisters dropped their attitude at a single, swift, meaning-laden glance from Lily. The old woman had apparently decided to view Megan as her ally.

When the meal was over and the dishes were done, they didn't linger. Just said their good nights, and left.

Sam stood in the doorway, waving and smiling until they were all out of sight, then he closed the door, turned, leaned back against it, and heaved an exaggerated sigh.

"Oh, come on," Megan said. "They're not so bad."

"They're not bad at all. Just a little . . . exhausting." He

256

straightened from the door, looked at her, then beyond her, to where her overnight bag sat beside his sofa. "Hell, you didn't even get to settle in."

"From the sounds of things, none of your dates ever do."

He scowled at her. "I meant for the night."

"So they usually spend the night, then?"

"Megan."

"The way your sisters talked, I got the idea you hustled them out of here before the sweat began to dry."

"Oh, that's lovely imagery."

She shrugged. "You're the one they call One-Night Sam."

"This is pretty irrelevant."

"I don't think so. After all, I'm not *just* a witness to a crime you're trying to solve. You did kiss me in the park tonight. Or was that . . . part of whatever game it is you've been playing with me, Sam?"

He narrowed his eyes on her. "I kissed you because I wanted to kiss you, Meg. That wasn't part of anything, not the case, not your abilities. Nothing. I'm sorry if things my well-intentioned sisters said are making you have doubts about that, because I'd really like to kiss you again."

"Oh, I'd like that, too," she said. "But I'd kind of like to know what to expect afterward."

He came to her, slid his arms around her waist, and tugged her close. "Haven't you ever heard of living in the moment?"

"Heard of it. Never practiced it much."

"No time like the present." He leaned closer, and she tipped her head up. He kissed her, slowly and softly. It was wonderful. It was also revealing. And this time the knowledge didn't come to her as a vision, and it didn't knock her off her feet or snap her head back. It just slipped gently from his mind to hers.

When he lifted his head away, she blinked up at him. "You don't get involved because you don't want to leave someone behind, the way your mother was left behind. And your grandmother."

He frowned down at her.

"The way you were left behind."

He shook his head. "Grams has been talking again."

"She believes there's a curse on the Sheridan men."

"It's silly superstition."

"But, Sam, what if it's not? Don't you think you should . . . take some precautions, just in case?"

He released her, turned, and paced across the room. "She convinced you to try to get me to quit the force, didn't she?"

"Before your birthday, if possible." She smiled. "It's only because she loves you, Sam."

"Hell, I know that." He turned and sank onto the sofa. "Look, I don't even believe in curses. I'm certainly not going to start letting one dictate the way I live my life."

She nodded and crossed the room to sit on the sofa beside him. "You don't believe in psychism or precognition either, do you?" He opened his mouth to argue, but she held up a hand. "It's okay. I get it. It's tough to believe in one without believing in the other, and if you let yourself believe in the curse, you're faced with a terrible choice. Your life or your life's work. So you refuse to believe in either."

"Megan, it's not that I don't believe you—"

"No, I know it's not. Because you do. Deep down, you do. And you believe in the curse, too."

Daydream Believer

He looked at her as if she were speaking a foreign language. "And how did you make that leap of logic?"

"Because you already are letting it dictate your life. One-Night Sam." She got to her feet, picked up her bag, and slung it over her shoulder. "So where's my room?"

"Top of the stairs, second door on the left."

"Night, Sam."

"You're wrong, you know."

She walked up the stairs, shaking her head. "No, I'm not. And you know it. And just for the record, that dream I've been having since I was twelve? It was about you, Sam."

She was wrong. Dammit, she was dead wrong. He didn't believe in the curse. He lived his life exactly the way he wanted to. Did exactly what he wanted to do, every single day. Lived every day as if it were . . .

"My last," he whispered, finishing the thought aloud.

Hell, what was it with Megan Rose, anyway? One date, and she'd turned him inside out, read his mind, met his family, and was spending the night. One date. Two kisses. Most women barely remembered his last name, after considerably more than a couple of kisses. Most didn't know or care what made him tick.

Most didn't touch him the way she did, either. He was so wrapped up in her he barely knew which end was up. Thinking about her every waking moment. Dreaming about her at night ever since the speed trap.

She claimed she had been dreaming about him for years. And hell, he was inclined to believe her. God knew there was something powerful between them.

She seemed able to look right inside his head—not only that, but she managed to see what was going on inside him . . . even more clearly than he did himself.

He closed his eyes slowly. Okay, so maybe she was right. Maybe he did believe in the curse on some level. That didn't mean he was going to surrender to it. It didn't change a damn thing.

So why was he having so much trouble sleeping tonight?

He'd done some paperwork, checked his e-mail, taken a shower. It was 2 A.M. and he still couldn't shut off his mind. He rolled over, punched the pillow, lay on it a moment longer, and then finally gave up. He might as well get up. He wasn't going to sleep. He sat up in the bed, swung his legs around to the floor. Some of that leftover chicken might take his mind off things.

Damn Megan. He'd been perfectly content to keep this looming death sentence buried in his subconscious mind. Now it was right there on the surface. Three days. Three days left until he turned thirty-five.

A soft tap on his bedroom door made him turn his head sharply.

"Sam?"

Frowning, he said, "Right here, Meg."

She opened the door, stepped into his darkened bedroom, and then stopped. She was silhouetted by the light from the hall, which she must have turned on to find her way to him. Backlit that way, her white nightgown was virtually transparent, though he didn't suppose she would have any way of knowing that.

"I can't sleep in there."

He lifted his brows, saw her peering at him through the darkness. He sat there with nothing over him but a sheet, and he could tell her eyes were adjusting by the way she stared.

"I keep drifting off, but as soon as I do, I hear that glass breaking, the door opening, that man coming after me, and I wake up with my heart racing."

"Come on in, Meg. Stay in here with me. Maybe we'll both feel better, huh?"

She swallowed hard. "Maybe." She came in the rest of the way and closed the door behind her. He lost the luscious view, but could still see her form as she padded across the room toward the bed. She didn't go to the opposite side, though. She came to his side, instead. "How long until your birthday?" she asked softly.

"Three days. Why?"

She shrugged. He saw her shoulders move with it. "Because I don't do one-night stands," she said softly. And then she peeled the nightgown over her head and stood there, in the dark, waiting.

Sam stood up, took a single step closer, and put his hands on her shoulders. They were small and soft, her skin warm to the touch. She pressed closer, breasts to his chest, belly to his belly, hips to his hips. Her arms twisted around his neck, and she tipped her face up. Sam kissed her, letting his hands slide lower, tracing the gentle slope of her spine, the curve at the small of her back, and then lower over her rounded buttocks and lower still until he could cup them and hold her harder against him. He was hard, wanting her in a way that was new to him. Unfamiliar. Usually, at this point, the thing he felt himself wanting, yearning for, was sex. Release. Pleasure.

This time was different. This time the thing he wanted,

craved . . . was her. Megan. He felt her mouth open beneath his, a silent invitation, and he slid his tongue inside, tasting her. He moved a hand lower, between her thighs from behind, and touched the wetness there. She moved against his hand, rubbing herself over his fingers, and when he slid one inside her she sighed into his mouth.

Turning her gently, he eased her onto the bed, never taking his body from hers. He slid his mouth over her jaw, down to her neck, over her collarbone, and lower until he captured a breast and sucked at the nipple. Her hands clutched his head as he worked her there. He slid around to the front of her, between them, touching her, finding the spot that made her squirm and pant. And then he felt her hand, closing around him, squeezing and rubbing.

She spread her thighs to him, guided him to her center. He moved his mouth to capture hers again, and pressed himself inside her. Soft, wet heat surrounded him, enveloped him, welcomed him. He moved slowly, carefully, until she wrapped her thighs around him and pulled him into her swiftly and completely.

Sam buried his face in her neck, overwhelmed with more than just passion. So much more. "God, Megan," he whispered.

She moved with him, taking him in a way no woman had ever done. And the wonder he felt in this was rapidly overwhelmed by the tidal wave of passion that swept them both away in a frenzy of clutching, writhing, straining. He felt her nails digging into his back and heard her cry his name as spasms of release racked her body, squeezing around him until he, too, found release. He came inside her, and it felt as if he were filling her with his soul as well as his seed. He held her there to take all of it, all of him, as he drove to the hilt and stayed there, pulsing inside her.

Slowly, her body unclenched, relaxed. Slowly, his did, too. He started to roll off her. She held him where he was, and when he looked into her eyes, wide and sparkling in the darkness, she whispered, "No." And she began to move again. "I need more of you than that, Sam. Much more."

He gave her what she asked for.

CHAPTER NINE

MEGAN woke in Sam's arms, rolled over, and found him staring at her. His eyes, roaming her face as if seeing it for the first time and trying to memorize every feature. When he realized her eyes were open, he smiled, and the solemn expression faded.

"Sweat's dry," he said, stroking a finger down her cheek. "I didn't throw you out."

"Good thing. I'd have been really pissed."

"Hungry this morning?"

"Starved."

"Take the first shower then," he said. "I'll make us some breakfast."

She shook her head slowly. "Shower with me. And we'll go out for breakfast."

"I like the way you think." He sprang from the bed without

warning, came around to her side, and scooped her up in his arms to carry her to the bathroom. As he held her, he asked softly, "Will you tell me, Meg? About your dream?"

"There's really not much to tell. It's short, simple. I see your face." She lifted a hand, palm to his cheek. "Your wonderful face. I hear a voice. 'Break the curse. Save his life.' That's all."

"That's all?"

She shrugged. "Except that seeing that face of yours always does something to my insides. It's like every cell in my body recognized you as someone—important to me."

He lowered his eyes.

"You are, Sam. You are so important to me. I know it doesn't make any sense, but—"

He stopped her speech by kissing her deeply. She was utterly engulfed by him, held in his arms, possessed by his mouth, her head supported only by his strong, large shoulder. It was intoxicating. When he broke the kiss, she was breathless.

"I'll be damned if I'm going to let you get yourself hurt or killed trying to break some fictional curse, much less save my life. I'm a cop, Megan."

"Then maybe you shouldn't be."

He met her eyes, shook his head firmly. "Don't. Don't do that. Don't ruin this by making it about my job, Megan. It's not what I do. It's who I am."

She nodded gently. Getting him to give up his career was not the right approach, she decided. Especially not if it broke the spell between them. "I won't suggest it again," she promised.

"Good." He smiled, letting it go, set her on her feet, and reached past her to turn on the shower.

* * *

By midmorning, Megan was in Sam's car again, munching on a cheese Danish and sipping coffee from a Styrofoam cup, actively resisting the urge to talk more about what was going on between them. Where it could be going. She knew he didn't want to. She knew that her uncertainty about their future together—or lack thereof—was nothing compared to his uncertainty about his own future. He wasn't even sure he would be around next week, much less whether he would still want her by then. Besides, she wasn't naive enough to think that one night with her would alter his One-Night Sam persona. Though she liked to think it had. He'd silenced her with a kiss when she had brought it up before, and while she loved his methods, she wondered about his motives.

He stopped at a traffic light and looked at her. "What are you thinking about?"

"About Linda Keller," she lied. "I'm not sure what to say to someone who's been through what she has. Why, what were you thinking about?"

"I was thinking about whether you were going to come home with me again tonight."

She smiled at him, just a little. "Would that make me your first two-night stand?"

He looked at her steadily for a long moment, as if considering his reply. Finally, he said, "You're more than that to me, Megan. Whatever happens, I want to make sure you know that."

His words set her heart racing, both in delight that he seemed to be telling her she meant something to him—and in fear that he was expecting the worst. "Nothing's going to happen to you, Sam."

A horn blew. The light had turned green. He didn't reply, just put the car back into motion.

When they arrived at the hospital, Megan's earlier lie became true. She honestly didn't know what to say to the young woman. But as it turned out, she didn't have to know. When Megan walked into the hospital room, she was at first stunned by the bruises on Linda's pretty face. They hadn't been so colorful last night. Now they were vivid—deep purple, dark blue, nearly black in places. Her shock quickly turned to relief, though, when Linda smiled at her. She was sitting up, the bed in an upright position, one eye still swollen shut, but the other clear and brighter than before. She held out a hand to Megan.

"I'm so glad you came," she said.

Megan's tension faded instantly, and she went to the girl, took her hand, felt only genuine warmth. "I wanted to make sure you were all right."

"I am. I'm going to be fine." She looked down at her hands. "I've only just begun to realize how lucky I am. If this is the same man who killed all those others—" Then she shook herself and snapped her head up again. "But what about you? Are you all right?"

"Of course I am. I'm not the one who was attacked." Megan sat down in the chair beside the bed.

"No. But . . . *something* happened to you out there. When I took your hand, I felt it. Like a jolt zapping from my hand to yours. I know you felt it, too. It knocked you flat on your back."

Megan glanced at Sam, who stood near the door. He gave her a nod, silently encouraging her to go on, to tell the girl the truth as she had planned to do. She took strength from his presence, and the look in his eyes—a look that could almost have been described as loving, though she told herself to stop thinking things like that. Then she told herself it was too late.

Megan said, "Linda, sometimes I get . . . well, visions."

"You're psychic?"

She nodded. "Yeah."

"So . . . when I took your hand, in the park, you had a vision?" Meg nodded, and Linda went on. "Wow. That's what knocked you flat? What did you see?"

"I saw what happened to you. Felt it, all of it, as if it were happening to me. Even down to you worrying about your cat."

The girl frowned at her, studying her seriously.

"It was so fast and so unexpected . . . I didn't see anything that could help us identify the man."

"If you were only seeing what I saw, then that makes sense," Linda said. "I didn't either."

"But it was the same for you, sudden, unexpected. And you were terrified."

Linda nodded, averting her face, failing to suppress a shiver.

"We don't have to talk about this now if you don't want to," Megan said.

The girl licked her lips, lifted her eyes again. "It sounds as if you think . . . there's something more you can do."

"There might be. I was thinking if I could hold your hand, and you could try to remember what happened, this time seeing it from a safe place, where you know he can't touch you, well, between the two of us, maybe there is something we can learn. To help the police catch him."

"Before he does this to someone else. Someone who might not be lucky enough to have you two close by to save her."

Megan nodded. "Yes. Yes, exactly that. I know it won't be easy, and that you'd probably rather not think about it at all, but—"

"I can't stop thinking about it. At least this way I can put those thoughts to good use, huh?"

"Maybe."

She nodded again. "What do I have to do?"

Megan got up onto the edge of the girl's bed, clasped both her hands between both of hers. "We need to go back there, together. In your mind. You talk me through it, everything that happened, and remember it as you do. I'll do the rest."

The girl closed her eyes as if searching inwardly for strength. "All right. All right." She took a breath and began, her voice shaky, but determined. "I was running. . . ."

And then Megan was there. Side by side, she and Linda Keller were running along one of the winding paths through the town park. Megan felt the night breeze on her face, the cool air in her lungs, the heat of her body, her own steady footfalls and the other girl's hand in her own.

"Remember, we're safe. This is over, in the past. Nothing can happen to us."

"I know. It's still so scary." The girl's steps slowed, and she came to a stop. "It's up there, right around that bend. He must be hiding behind that tree, there."

Megan strained her eyes, but couldn't see any sign of anyone.

The girl squeezed her hand. "Okay, here we go." And she began running again. They approached the bend, and her grip grew tighter. They started around it, and then Megan felt the powerful arm snap around her neck, jerk her backward to the ground.

"It's not real," she said, though her voice was strained. She was on her back now, and the man was straddling her. His weight on her made it almost impossible to breathe. Beyond the hulking form she saw Linda standing there, a petrified onlooker, still clutching Megan's hand. When the rain of blows fell, Megan's head snapped with every one and pain shot through her, and she heard the girl begin to cry.

"Megan, stop, it's enough!"

That was Sam's voice, and it was rough with emotion.

"It's all right. It's okay," she managed. "Slow it down, Linda. Remember it as if in slow motion."

"I'll try."

And the scene playing out slowed. Megan was able to look up at the dark shape that loomed over her. To see every blow coming at her before feeling its impact. He was bigger than Sam, heavier. She couldn't see his face, only the black ski cap that covered it. The blows came slowly, but she still felt the pain of them. She fought to stay as calm and as cold as ice, even when she felt his hands tearing at her clothes.

She was seeing through only one eye now, as he jammed a hand down her pants, and she gripped his wrist with one hand, just as Linda had, to stop him, touching not the glove he wore, but the skin above it.

Then Sam was there, shouting, and the man tore himself off her and ran.

* * *

SAM was on the floor beside Megan, and so was Linda Keller. They'd started out on the bed. Linda had been describing everything that had happened, while holding Meg's hand, but Megan seemed to be the one living it. When Linda got to the point where the man grabbed her from behind, Meg had come off the bed as if jerked from behind herself, hitting the floor back-first. Linda came off the bed with her, grappling to grab hold of her hand again, and Sam rushed to Meg's side, terrified of what he was seeing. Meg jerked her arms up over her face as if warding off blows, and then one hand shot down to clutch at something—at nothing. Just air.

"Megan, honey, come on, it's enough. You're killing yourself with this." He gripped her shoulders, shook them gently. "Meg, I mean it. It's enough, come back!"

Her eyes opened slowly. Sam was shocked to see a trickle of blood coming from her nostril. "Jesus, what the hell?"

She touched the blood, looked at it on her fingertips. "Your body believes what your mind tells it," she whispered. She took a few breaths, seemed to try to shake off the vision. "Mine thinks it just took a beating. This is a little more realism than I expected, but . . ."

He helped her sit up, realized he was shaking as badly as she was. It was as if he'd just witnessed an assault on her by some invisible force. And he realized she was hurting as if that were exactly what had happened. She held a hand to her jaw as he lifted her to her feet, then helped her to the chair. She sank into it.

The girl handed him a box of tissues, then got back up onto her bed. "Megan, did it work? Did you see him?"

Megan lifted her head, clutching a tissue to her nose, while Sam leaned over her, stroking her hair and back and shoulders. It tore him apart to see her going through all of this. He hated it.

"No," Megan said. "But I felt him. You touched him, grabbed his wrist to stop him from groping you. And so I did, too. And I felt him."

Linda frowned, looking at Sam. "I don't understand."

"Neither do I," Sam said. "There was no skin under her nails, Meg." He looked at Meg, but she said nothing. "I'm sorry we put you through all that, Linda," he said, without taking his eyes from Megan. "I really think I should get her home."

"Me, too," Linda said.

"Will you be okay?" Sam asked, forcing himself to look at the girl.

She nodded. "They're letting me go home today."

Meg came out of her thoughts and smiled a little. "Roderick will be so glad to see you."

"I know. I miss him." Linda shifted her eyes to Sam's again. "Will I be safe there?"

He nodded. "We'll have a car watching the place, and set you up with a panic button. You hit it, and officers will be there within seconds."

She nodded. "Thank you again." Then she looked at Meg. "I can't believe you put yourself through that once, much less twice. Will she be okay, Detective Sheridan?"

"I'll make sure of it." Sam bent to scoop Megan up, but she shook her head. "I can walk. You go carrying me, they're going to want to check me in."

"Are you sure?"

She nodded, so he held her close, supporting her as they walked slowly out of the room. And then Meg said, "She called you Detective Sheridan. I thought it was 'Officer.'"

He closed his eyes. "It's Detective."

"I didn't think detectives routinely worked traffic," she said.

"They don't." He sighed, wishing this had come at a better time. "Meg, I'm not going to lie to you. The speed trap was a setup. No one believed you knew the things you knew about that last victim through ESP. I was assigned to get to know you, try to find out what was really going on."

She looked as hurt by that revelation as she had been by the attack she'd just experienced. God, she was barely holding her own weight. He felt like the meanest bastard in the world as she stared up at him, her eyes as betrayed as if she were a puppy who'd just been drop-kicked by her beloved master.

"That's what you were keeping from me."

"It doesn't matter, Meg. I believe you now. I do."

"Do you? Or is that just another part of your cover story?" She sighed, her eyes flooding. "And last night? Was that part of your investigation, too?"

"Meg—"

"Oh, God," she whispered, backing away from him as her tears spilled over. "I thought it was real."

"Sam, I need a word." Chief Skinner was in the hospital corridor, waiting for Sam when they came out of Linda Keller's hospital room, demanding his attention.

Sam gave Megan's hand a squeeze. It *was* real, he thought, and he hoped to God she could see his message in his eyes, even though he couldn't say it out loud, not with the chief standing right at his shoulder now. He willed her to see the truth in his eyes. But she only kept backing away, shaking her head from side to side. And then she turned and ran for the elevators.

CHAPTER TEN

*H*E was surprised she made it to the elevator without collaps-
ing, and only the chief's firm grip on his shoulder kept him
from racing after her.

"Jesus," the chief muttered. "What happened to her?"

Not sure how to answer without losing credibility with the man
whose respect he valued above all others, he said, "She took a little
fall, that's all. I need to go after her, Chief."

The chief nodded. "Yeah, I know you do. Thirty seconds, okay?"

Sam sent a worried look toward the now closed elevator doors.

"So, are you getting anything out of her?"

"No." He took a step toward the elevator.

The chief put himself right in Sam's path, blocking it. "Then
she hasn't come up with anything on the killer?"

"No, nothing yet." It was all he could do not to shove the
man aside.

"We didn't find any prints at her house," Ed Skinner said, shaking his head with regret. "Are you sure he was even there, Sam? Hell, she's the only one who saw him. For all we know she could have smashed that window in herself, just as an excuse to make you come running."

Sam frowned deeply, finally focusing on the chief. "She's not the kind of woman who'd do something like that. You don't know her, Chief."

"You don't know her either, Sam. You only met her a few days ago. She probably doesn't seem like the kind of woman who'd hang around with a serial killer either. But she must be, or she wouldn't know what she knows."

Sam licked his lips. "Chief—Ed, I know this is gonna sound crazy, but what if she really does have some kind of . . . ability? What if she's telling the truth about how she knew where that last body was found?"

"I don't buy it," he said.

"Apparently, the killer does. I think that's who was at her house last night. I really do."

"What makes you think so?"

Sam shook his head. "Instinct. And I know she hasn't come up with anything solid yet, Chief, but I think she's close. I think she might just come up with what we need to break this case."

"How? She know what the guy looks like?"

"No. She said she knows what he feels like, though."

"Feels like? I don't get it."

Just then, the elevator doors opened, and Megan came through them and walked up to stand beside Sam. "I was going to wait in the car, but . . . I forgot the keys," she said.

She didn't look good, worse than she had a moment ago, if that were possible. She was pale and trembling. He reached into his pocket for the keys even as it occurred to him that wasn't why she'd come back. She'd come back because she was hurting bad, and because she needed him. She sagged a little and reached out a hand to steady herself on the chief's shoulder.

"Hell, Meg, come here." Sam slid his arms around her waist, pulling her against him. "I gotta get her out of here, Chief."

"Yeah. Yeah, you go on," he said. "Feel better, Ms. Rose."

She lifted her head slowly, her eyes finding the chief's, just before Sam helped her back into the elevator. As soon as the doors closed, she slumped in Sam's arms and passed out cold.

He scooped her up, swearing, thought he ought to take her right back in and hand her over to the nearest nurse. But she wasn't suffering from anything physical, he knew that. Not really. She wanted to get out of there, and he was compelled to give her what she wanted. He knew she would be all right in a few minutes. So he ignored his practical mind and heeded his instincts, carrying her out of the elevator when it stopped on the ground level, and then out to his car. He lowered her onto the passenger seat, then knelt in the open doorway, pressing his hands to her face.

"Megan? Honey, come on, are you okay?"

She blinked her eyes slowly at him. "No. Far from it." She suddenly looked back toward the hospital, as if frightened, and he followed her gaze, only to see his boss, the chief, leaving through the same doors they'd just exited, heading for his car in some other part of the lot.

"Get me out of here, Sam," she whispered.

"Okay. All right." God, they had to talk. He had to explain

himself to her, but he'd like her at least coherent when he did. And he wasn't even entirely sure just what it was he was going to say. "Do you want to go back to my place, or to yours?"

She stared into his eyes. "I need to see your grandmother."

Sam was tempted to check her for a fever, or ask how many fingers as he held a couple up in front of her. "I'm not following."

"Neither am I."

"You know something. Or you think you do. What is it, Megan?"

She swallowed hard, nodded slowly. "Chief Skinner—" she began. And as if saying his name invoked him somehow, the chief's car passed by on its way out of the parking lot, and Sam saw him staring at the two of them.

"What about him?" Sam asked as he waved at his trusted friend.

"He's the rapist. He's the killer."

Sam's hand froze in midair. He felt his face change with the shock of her words, and quickly shot her a look of sheer disbelief. "Don't be ridiculous—hell, Megan, did you hit your head or something back there?"

"It's him. I touched him, and I saw it, felt it. It's him, Sam."

He swung his head toward the chief's car as the man drove away, and caught him looking back, his face troubled.

"No. No way, you're wrong. You're dead wrong about this, Meg."

"I know I'm right. And there's more, but I . . . I have to see Lily before I can be sure."

He shook his head. "He's been my mother's best friend since my father . . . I'm sorry, Meg, but I can't let you go making all kinds of crazy accusations to my family. He's practically a *part* of my family, for God's sake." Then he looked at her again. "It's Lily who put this crazy notion into your head, isn't it? She's never liked him. And now you want to go making some wild accusations that will convince her she's been right all along."

"Maybe Lily never liked him because she's slightly psychic herself. She calls it intuition. Whatever it is, somehow she knows he's rotten inside. Evil." She pressed a hand to Sam's face when he looked away from her. "Sam, look at me. You know I wouldn't repeat any of this to your family. And no, it isn't coming from Lily and I'm not going to make any accusations to her or to anyone else. Only you, Sam. I can't not tell you this. Not this. Because . . . because all of a sudden, I understand what it means."

"You're three steps ahead of me, then. What does it mean?"

She held his face between her palms. "There's no curse. There never was."

He was having trouble trying to follow her as her train of thought seemed to jump the tracks. And focusing on her words was damn near impossible when she was touching him, when her mouth was so close to his and her eyes were sparkling the way they were. "No curse?"

She smiled softly. "No curse." Then her smile died as she looked past him, and her eyes widened. "He's coming back."

Sam turned to see the chief's car rolling back into the parking lot.

"Sam, we have to get out of here!"

She was terrified, clearly, of his boss and mentor and friend. And it made no sense at all, but something wouldn't let him brush it off. He didn't believe any of it, but for Megan, he would give her the benefit of the doubt. Act as if there were some remote chance she could be right. Because he believed in her. "We're going," he promised. "Buckle up, Meg."

He closed her door, went around to his side, got in, and got going.

On their way out they passed the chief in his car. He watched them closely, didn't return Sam's friendly wave or his forced smile. Something was off, something was wrong.

"Sam, we have to keep him away from Linda Keller."

"He already knows Linda didn't see anything. Even if he was our boy—and I gotta tell you, Meg, there's no way in hell he is— but even if he was, Linda would pose no threat to him." He glanced back to watch the chief's car, in spite of himself. "And even if she did, he wouldn't do anything at the hospital. Not when she lives alone, and is being released today."

And yet he watched. The chief's car only circled the lot and left it again. "Look, he's not even stopping."

Megan was watching, too. "He only came back to see what we were doing. He's checking up on us, Sam. He may realize we're on to him."

"We're not on to him."

"You're not. I am. And I think your father was, too."

"My . . ." He couldn't talk for a second. It was as if her words stole his breath. He managed to catch it and tried again. "You think my father believed this? Jesus, Megan, he was a cop. If he thought his own partner was a violent criminal he'd have turned him in, no matter how close they were."

"Yeah. Exactly. So Skinner would have made sure he never got the chance."

"No. No, no way was Ed involved in my father's death. They were like brothers, Megan."

"Lily said your father had been acting oddly for a week prior to his death. Don't you want to know why?"

He stared at her, and something icy cold seemed to solidify over his chest as he finally considered how easy it would have been. His father and Ed Skinner had been the only two cops on the scene of that liquor store robbery. And Ed Skinner had been the only survivor left to tell the story.

He tried to shake off the chilling feeling. "There could have been a hundred reasons for him to have been acting off-kilter that week."

"You're right. There could have been." She covered his hand with hers. "Lily told me your mother hasn't changed a thing in your father's den since he died. That it's like a shrine to him in there."

Sam nodded as he drove. "It was always off-limits to the rest of the family, that den. Mom still doesn't let anyone in there. Guards it like a lioness. She's the only one who can go inside. Says she feels closer to Dad when she spends time in the den."

"Has she ever let Skinner inside?"

He shook his head. "Never."

"Has he ever asked?"

Sam blinked, recalling how determined Ed had been to get into his father's private den right around the time of the funeral. Hell, it had been a source of added worry to his mother and had infuriated Lily. He slanted a look at Megan. "Actually, he did. Right after Dad's death. Something about some missing files that pertained to a case they'd been working on."

"And did your mother let him go in?"

"No. As I remember it, she told him she had gone through the room from top to bottom and had boxed up everything that had to do with work. She gave that box of files to Ed." He tried to swallow but the memories seemed to be drying out his throat. "It was odd. He asked her if she'd read through them. He seemed almost—scared. When she said she had been a policeman's wife long enough to know better than to snoop through private files, he seemed satisfied, took the box, and as far as I know, he never asked again."

Megan nodded slowly. "I wonder if he found the evidence your father had on him in those files."

"Megan, this is all speculation on your part."

She held his eyes, and he thought maybe she could see that he was trying to convince himself as much as her. She didn't even waver. "We need to convince your mother to let us go through that room, Sam. I don't know how I know it, but I do. If there's anything to find, your father left it in there for us."

"She'll never agree to that," he said.

Megan lowered her eyes.

Sam drew a breath. Everything in him was telling him to trust her. To believe her. And he was damned if he had it in him to do otherwise. "All right, Meg. If you feel this strongly, we'll do it."

She looked up at him, an emotion he couldn't name shining from her eyes. "You believe me?"

"I trust you like I've never trusted anyone. If you say we need to check it out, we need to check it out, Megan." He saw the tears gathering, and then it hit him why she was reacting so strongly to him believing the unbelievable at nothing more than her word. "I'm not your father, Megan."

She smiled. It was shaky, unsteady, and wet. "No, you're not even close."

There was so much more to say, so much to explain. But she didn't give him the chance. "How are we going to get in if your mother won't agree to let us?"

He glanced at the clock on the radio dial. "She'll be out all morning. Volunteers at the Ladies' Auxiliary till noon. If we're lucky, Lily is with her. She often goes along."

He drove her to his mother's house, the house where he had grown up. And while he was at it, he phoned the hospital and spoke to the guard on Linda Keller's room, told him not to let anyone, including police officers, even the chief himself, be alone with her and to delay her release from the hospital until further notice.

Then he pulled his car into the familiar driveway. The house was a big old Victorian, and his parents had lived in it for as long as he could remember. It had changed very little over the years.

Meg seemed to have recovered physically during the course of the drive. Still, he held her arm as he led her up the walk to the front door. *She* might be feeling better, but he wasn't sure *he* was after seeing her take a phantom beating and pass out like that, much less hearing the things she had to say afterward.

"Lily's not home, either," he said, deducing as much from the fact that the door was locked. "She refuses to live behind locked doors. If she were here, it would have been open."

Megan nodded, and he led the way into the house. He looked around first, making utterly sure they were alone, before leading the way down a hall to a closed door. Then he paused, hesitated.

"It's not easy, is it?"

He turned to face Megan, saw her looking into his eyes. "Mom would consider it a betrayal, my bringing you here. Invading Dad's space."

"I wouldn't ask if I didn't feel it was vital, Sam."

He nodded. "I know that. And I wouldn't bring any other

woman in here. Dad . . . Dad would be rolling over in his grave if I did. But somehow—I just don't think he'd mind so much with you."

"There's something in there he wants us to find. Maybe even needs us to find."

Sighing, Sam nodded and turned to face the door again. His hands felt clammy and his heart heavy as he inserted the key into the lock.

CHAPTER ELEVEN

SAM opened the door to his father's den and was immediately transported backward in time. He was seven years old again, tapping on the door of his father's inner sanctum, waiting without drawing a breath until that deep, powerful voice, laced with just a hint of laughter, called, "Hmm, if it's important enough to interrupt my quiet time, it must be pretty important. Come on in, then."

He looked at Megan, saw her watching him, feeling what he felt. "Dad usually stole a half hour a day in his den," he told her. "It was off-limits to us kids, to everyone except Mom. He didn't even bring his friends in here."

She nodded as if she understood. "It's okay, Sam. Take your time."

Stepping farther into the room surrounded Sam in the very essence of his father. He could smell old cigar smoke, and expensive leather, and aging books. So much his dad, those smells. "God, no wonder Mom likes to come in here sometimes, just to sit alone."

"It's bringing back a lot of memories for you, isn't it?" Megan put a hand on his arm as she asked the question.

"It's like he never left. Like he could just walk in here like he used to, pick up where he left off."

"You loved him a lot."

He nodded. "Still do."

"He'd be proud of you, Sam. He is. I feel it."

He met Megan's eyes. Could she know what her saying that meant to him? Yeah, he thought. She knew. He'd never been with a woman who knew him the way Megan did.

"Sam, if he had kept anything related to work, private files or cases he was working on . . ."

"Mom found everything he had here, gave it to Ed."

She tipped her head. "Probably. But there's a chance she could have missed something. She must have, because I feel very strongly there's something here. So where would he have kept them?"

Sam shrugged and looked around the room. The big oak desk took up most of one wall, face out, a chair behind it, so his father could sit there and work and still see the TV set. It held an oversized IBM Selectric typewriter with the cover securely in place, a leather blotter, an earthenware mug full of pens and pencils, a stack of blank sheets of paper, a paperweight—clear acrylic with a forever-frozen spider inside, a Father's Day gift from Sam—and a couple of framed photos of the family, as they had been many years ago.

"I don't know. The desk I suppose." He moved behind his father's desk and opened its drawers. None were locked, but then there was no reason why they should be. He didn't find anything like what they were looking for in any of them, but the small center drawer's contents brought him up short.

It held his father's badge.

"I know this is hard for you, Sam. I'm sorry. God, I'm so sorry to put you through this."

"I know you are." He took the badge out and held it in his hands as he moved from the desk to the file cabinet, which was nearly empty. The badge was in a folder the size of a wallet, with his father's photo ID card on one side and his badge on the other. He couldn't stop looking at it as he searched the room. Within a few minutes, he realized Meg wasn't joining him in the search. Instead she was standing patiently aside, while he checked all the obvious places. She seemed engrossed in the family photos on the desk.

She felt his eyes on her and looked up, meeting them; she offered him a sad smile. "Your father was a handsome man. You look like him."

"Think so?"

"Mm-hmm."

"You can help me look, Meg."

"It feels like a sacrilege," she said softly. But she joined him in the search, even crouched down to look under the sofa and chair, while Sam checked beneath the cushions. He felt the backing and upholstery for unusual lumps or bulges. Nothing.

It was while he was performing that last little function that he dropped his father's badge on the floor. Meg was on her hands and knees peering under the chair, and it fell right beside her hand. Naturally, she stopped what she was doing and picked it up, looking at it, her eyes somber as she rose to her feet.

And then her head snapped backward so hard Sam thought she might have wrenched her neck. Her eyes widened and rolled back, and she staggered backward until her body slammed into the bookcase.

"Jesus, Megan." Sam went to her, reached out to her, but she spun away from him, her arms flailing and knocking books to the floor.

"Easy, Megan, easy."

"No, no, no!"

She wasn't seeing him, wasn't hearing him, he realized. She was seeing something else. Some vision brought on by the touch of his father's badge.

God, he was almost afraid to speculate. . . .

Meg backed into a corner and sank to the floor, curling her legs up to her chest, hugging them and rocking. Sam knelt beside her, touching her. "Megan," he said. "It's okay, baby, it's okay. I'm right here." He stroked her hair away from her face. But she didn't seem to feel him, didn't see him, was beyond his reach, and clutching his father's badge in a death grip.

He could do nothing but leave her alone until it passed. She seemed to need space to recover. So he backed off, turning to return the books to the shelf and minimize his mother's outrage at his invasion of what was, to her, sacred space. But when he lifted the first several volumes to the shelf, he stopped and just stood there, blinking.

In the space left by the fallen books, there appeared to be a false bottom on the bookshelf. He could see the fissures on either side of a short expanse of the wood. And when he gripped it and tugged, it came away, revealing a shoebox-sized compartment underneath. Inside that compartment was a manila envelope, folded in half, lengthwise, and tucked out of sight.

He gently pulled the envelope free, swallowing hard as he turned it over. But before he could examine the contents, Megan's blood-chilling scream split the silence.

MEGAN shook off the debilitating impact of the vision and shot to her feet when she saw Chief Skinner walk through the door into the room. She tried to form words to warn Sam, but couldn't seem to make her lips form anything coherent, and finally poured every ounce of energy she had into warning him in any way she could, clenching her fists, opening her mouth, forcing sound to come. The result was a scream.

Sam spun around, wide-eyed, an envelope in his hands, but it was too late. Skinner had already drawn his weapon and was pointing it at Sam. "I'll take that file, Sam."

"Ed, what the hell is going on here?" Sam asked.

The chief looked momentarily confused, then angry. "Trying to pretend you haven't already figured it out isn't going to help."

"No, it didn't help his father after all. Did it, Chief?" Megan asked from behind him. She'd found her voice. It was weak, shaky, far softer than normal, but at least she could put words together now.

The chief turned his head slightly. "Get over there next to him." He directed her with his gun.

She stayed where she was, lowering her gaze to the badge she held in her hand. "I know what you did that night at the liquor store. I saw it, all of it."

"You don't know a damn thing, Ms. Rose."

She looked past him, met Sam's eyes. "They got the call. Armed robbery in progress, and they went over there. To the liquor store. It was called Joe's Wine and Spirits. There were tubes of red neon in the shape of a giant wine bottle in the front window. I don't think it's there anymore."

"No. They closed it after . . ."

"Your father went around the back. Skinner went in through the front. The place was empty except for those two kids and the clerk, who was lying on the floor, unconscious, bleeding, maybe already dead. It was the perfect opportunity, wasn't it, Chief?"

"What did you do?" Sam asked.

"Pulled his gun and shot both of the suspects," Megan said softly. "Never shouted a warning. They didn't even know he'd come inside. Your father heard the shots, came in to help. He saw that his friend had it under control, and he lowered his weapon." She narrowed her eyes on Skinner. "That's when you took the gun from one of the boys you'd killed, pointed it right at your best friend, saw the shock and horror in his eyes, and shot him down. Pumped three bullets into his head."

"Stop it!" Skinner cried.

"Jesus, Ed," Sam whispered. "Why? My God, why?"

Skinner faced him again. "Because of that file you have in your hands. All this time, it never surfaced. I figured it never would. Your mother gave me everything that was in this room. When I didn't find the evidence there, I thought maybe I'd been wrong. Maybe he really didn't have anything on me after all. Maybe I killed him for nothing."

His eyes turned distant, pain-filled.

"And that's why you took care of us, stepped into Dad's shoes the way you did," Sam said. "It was guilt." He shook his head.

"And you're gonna make the same mistake now that you thought you'd made then, Ed. Because I don't even know what's in this file, and neither does Megan."

He lifted his brows. "You really don't know?"

Megan could see Sam trying to inch his hand toward his gun. But he couldn't do it with the other man's eyes on him.

"Oh, come on, Sam," she said. "You can guess, can't you?" The chief turned his attention her way. "Skinner is the man who's been raping and murdering girls in town. And I suspect he was doing it long before the police realized they had a serial killer on their hands." She added, "He knew someone was on to him when I phoned the police with that tip on where the next body would be found."

"I still don't believe you have any so-called psychic powers. But I had to find out for sure," Skinner said.

"So you assigned Sam to get close to me, try to find out how much I really did know and how I knew it. That way you could keep an eye on both of us."

"None of this is relevant," Skinner said. He swung his gaze back to Sam's, held out his free hand. "Give me the file, Sam."

Sam held it out. Skinner reached for it and seemed to realize at that moment that Sam's gun was no longer in its holster. "Don't, Sam!"

Skinner lifted his own gun higher, even as Sam brought his around from behind his back. It all seemed to happen in slow motion, barrels pointing, fingers squeezing, shots exploding, muzzles flashing.

Megan launched herself, hitting Skinner in the side just as his gun went off, so that he stumbled and fell. Rolling onto his back, he turned his weapon on her.

"No!" Sam shouted.

Skinner's gun bucked in his hand. The shot exploded in a deafening roar, and Megan felt the blaze of red hot metal slice through her midsection; she doubled over at the impact long before she felt the pain. She lifted her head, shocked, stunned. Skinner was taking aim, would have shot her again if not for the shot Sam fired that made the chief's head snap backward, leaving a neat hole between his eyes. His body went lax, his arm and gun dropping to the floor, and then he was still.

"For the love of God, what's going on?" someone cried. Megan heard feet crashing through the house, female voices crowding around her. But Sam was her only focus. He knelt beside her, his face stricken.

"Megan, hold on." Without looking away from her he told his mother, grandmother, whoever was within earshot, to call 911. "Tell them there's an officer down," he said. "It's the truth, and it'll get them here faster." He added that last with a meaningful look at Skinner.

Then he was leaning over her again, holding a hand to her belly, where she felt warmth and pulsing wetness. "Don't leave me, Megan. Hold on."

She smiled softly, staring up at him. "Guess I was another one-night stand after all, huh?"

"No. Not by a long shot." He held her desperately. "Jesus, Megan, you have to know I wasn't pretending. Not from the first second I set eyes on you. This is real, this thing between us."

Her hand closed around his. "I know that, Sam."

"The curse is lifted," Lily said in her raspy voice, from somewhere nearby. "The girl broke it, exposed it, took it upon herself."

"There was never any curse, Grams. Skinner killed Dad."

"And would have killed you, too, if not for this woman and her gift." She knelt on Megan's other side. "Bless you, child."

Meg smiled, shifting her gaze from the old woman's back to Sam's again. "Finally did something important with my abilities. Finally got someone to believe me."

"Yeah. And I will never, ever doubt you or your visions, Meg. I promise." He leaned closer and pressed his lips to hers, and she kissed him back until the darkness swallowed her up.

EPILOGUE

MEGAN was in the darkness, and it occurred to her that she might be dead. Oddly, she felt no terrible grief or resistance to that idea. She had reached one of the most important goals of her life—she'd understood, at last, why she had been given these powers. What earthly use they could be to anyone. They had been useful. Vital. They had saved an entire family, broken a curse, of sorts, solved a string of murders, prevented who knew how many other women from being victimized by Ed Skinner. And maybe kept Sam Sheridan from an early death. God, that was worth anything, wasn't it?

He'd believed in her, in her gift. So had his grandmother. And so had she.

That was all she had ever wanted. Validation. Respect. And the chance to use her gift for something good.

"I love you, Megan."

No, not love. She'd never asked for that. Just to be believed, just to be useful, just—

"Do you hear me? I love you. I've never said that to a woman before, and I'm not about to lose the only one. I want you back. I want you to stay with me. Always."

Sensation seemed to return by degrees. She became aware of a warm, strong hand holding hers. And she opened her eyes and stared up into a pair of familiar, loving ones.

"There you are," Sam whispered. "You gonna stick around, then?"

"I think so."

He squeezed her hand, and a vision flashed, making her suck in a breath and close her eyes, just briefly.

He frowned at her, his face filled with worry. "What is it, honey? What are you seeing?"

She drew her brows together, wondering if she should tell him what she had seen. The two of them in a photo a lot like the ones on his father's desk, with two little angels standing in front of them, golden ringlets and strawberry curls. A boy and a girl. She smiled and knew she still had a whole lot left to do in this lifetime.

"Meg? You gonna tell me what you saw?"

She blinked and met his eyes, saw the love in them, knew it was going to last. "You parked in a terrible spot. You're going to get a ding in the Mustang."

Sam smiled slowly. "That's my Megan."

"Yours?"

"Oh, yeah. And I'm not leaving this room, even if someone's going to total the Mustang."

"No?"

"No. And as long as you're still having visions, I'd like you to try one on for size. Will you do that for me?"

"I . . . guess I could try."

He nodded, taking both her hands in his. "Look into the future, honey. See if you can make out a long and happy one—one you'll be spending with me."

"I don't need any psychic skills at all to see that, Sam. If we want it, we can make it happen."

"I want it, Megan. Do you?"

"With all my heart."

He leaned closer and pressed his lips to hers. "Then that's the way it's going to be."